Kiss my Book

Kiss My Book

Jamie Michaels

DELACORTE PRESS

Published by Delacorte Press
an imprint of Random House Children's Books
a division of Random House, Inc.
New York

Delacorte Press and colophon are registered trademarks
of Random House, Inc.

www.randomhouse.com/teens

Educators and librarians, for a variety of teaching tools,
visit us at www.randomhouse.com/teachers

Library of Congress Cataloging-in-Publication Data
Michaels, Jamie.
Kiss my book / Jamie Michaels.—1st ed.
p. cm.
Summary: Fifteen-year-old Ruby is on top of the world after
having a novel published, but accusations of plagiarism send her
into hiding at her eccentric aunt's home in upstate New York, where
she gets involved in an old mystery and finds her true self again.
ISBN 978-0-385-73499-8 (trade pbk.)—ISBN 978-0-385-90493-3 (Gibraltar
lib. bdg.) [1. Books and reading—Fiction.   2. Authorship—Fiction.
3. Self-actualization (Psychology)—Fiction.   4. Interpersonal relations—
Fiction.   5. Plagiarism—Fiction.   6. New York (State)—Fiction.]   I. Title.
PZ7.M5813258Kis   2007
[Fic]—dc22   2006034542

The text of this book is set in 11.5-point Minion.

Book design by Angela Carlino

Printed in the United States of America

10 9 8 7 6 5 4 3 2 1

First Edition

For Jane and Miriam

For Michael

. . . who make "DGLM"

the best letters of the alphabet

I Am Famous

My English teacher asked me for an autograph.

It was June 12, exactly two weeks before the end of the school year. The sixth-period bell had just rung and I was reaching into my bag for a notebook and a pen when a shadow fell across my corner of the grimy cafeteria table. Startled, I looked up. Then I blinked. Twice. Old Mrs. Gallagher was standing over me, stylishly dressed in one of her usual calf-length checkered dresses buttoned tightly at the neck. And she was *smiling*.

"Ruby, would you do me the honor?" she asked in a shockingly sugary tone.

I glanced down and saw that both of her arms were outstretched; her left hand held a black ballpoint pen, and in her right was a hardcover copy of my first novel, *The Heart Stealer*. It was a sobering sight, because the book had landed in stores only a few days earlier. I didn't think anyone aside from the members of my immediate family had bought it. Yet. There had been a few ads in magazines and a mention of the book on one of the early-morning talk shows, but I wasn't expecting instant recognition.

"Oh," I replied. I think I even gasped. "I . . . uh . . . of course. Yes. Sure."

"Take your time with the inscription," she said gently. "I'm sure no one will mind if you get to your next class a little late today."

I reached out and took the pen. I laid the book—*my* book, complete with a glossy cover and *my* name in bright block letters across the top—down on the table. I felt my cheeks blush. All around me, the cafeteria went silent. Students who would have otherwise bolted for the double doors were suddenly witnessing what had to be the freakiest incident in the history of Frasier High School: an *English teacher* asking a *student* for an *autograph*.

And not just *any* English teacher.

Mabel Marie Johnson-Gallagher was a cold, disapproving, PhD-from-Yale-toting literary snob. An elitist in every sense of the word, she preferred metaphors to music, poetry to perfume, and probably sentences to sex. She had a cat named Brontë. She wore her black hair in one of those smooth, oily, Emily Dickinson–style buns. She even scolded us in Shakespearean tongue.

Dost thou not remember / thine homework from yester eve? You gall me with hell!

In short, Mrs. Gallagher wasn't a favorite among students because she had a tendency to make us feel brainless. I supposed it was just her style of teaching, though I had never forgiven her for writing *'Tis drivel and poop!* across the bottom of one of my best essays in comparative literature. And I never expected her to care about a commercial novel written by the sixteen-year-old who rarely spoke up in her classroom and would never swear in iambic pentameter.

I should have been flattered, but getting singled out by Mrs. Gallagher was a lot like winning a bowling tournament: all you had to show for it was a geeky grin and a bad pair of shoes.

Now she was staring at me with wide, expectant eyes.

I was frozen. An autograph? It wasn't as easy as just scribbling my name across the page. People want more than that—especially when they've invested twenty-five bucks in a hardcover. And what kind of inscription was she expecting? She hadn't exactly been nice to me for the past ten months. *To Mrs. Gallagher,* I thought, imagining my hand gliding across the page. *Does this mean my writing isn't drivel and poop?* No, that wouldn't work. Too edgy. Not even remotely Shakespearean. She still hadn't submitted my final grade for the year, and I wasn't taking any chances.

"I read that wonderful article on you in *TeenGirl* magazine," she gushed. "There you were—right on page twenty-six! Oh, Ruby, I had no idea what tremendous news this book of yours is! And the fact that you'll be making an

3

appearance tonight at the American Literature Club—it's just astounding."

Her voice boomed across the cafeteria. My cheeks felt hotter. The article in *TeenGirl* wasn't one of my favorites, because the picture of me had been taken before I'd lost those pesky eighteen pounds. As for the Literature Club . . . it *was* pretty astounding. The event I'd be attending in just a few hours was big and by invitation only. I'd be rubbing bookends with some of the greatest writers on the planet. A new inscription suddenly popped into my head: *To Mrs. Gallagher, Read—don't speak. Love, Ruby Crane.*

"Was the article correct?" she continued. "Is *The Heart Stealer* going to be adapted into a *movie* next year?"

I felt the cafeteria crowds thickening behind me. It wasn't really news to anyone—the whole school had known about my book's being published since September—but now that it was so in their faces, I felt strange. Or maybe just a little pressured. Or completely strange and nervous and pressured. How about that? Strange. Nervous. Pressured. Yeah, that works. I hoped my insecurities weren't showing. *To Mrs. Gallagher, Have you ever been slammed in the head with a hardcover? Love, Ruby Crane.* I held on to my smile and gave her a meek nod.

"Oh! How wonderful!" She did a little jump, as if a jolt of electricity had shot up from the carpet and zapped her in the butt. The bun on the back of her head bounced. "And just to think how young you are!" she continued. "You have a brilliant literary career ahead of you, Ruby. And . . . and who knows? Maybe even an *acting* career! Will they let you star in the *movie*?"

I held the smile in place. *To Mrs. Gallagher, Hast thou gone totally freaking berserk?*

"Oh, you would be so wonderful in the movie!" she said, clapping her hands.

Someone two tables away let out a chuckle. It was likely one of the mean, golden-haired cheerleaders who hated me for becoming famous, for burning through the dark web of sophomore-year obscurity like a forest fire.

I had experienced a lot of that in the past few months—snickers, sneers, eyes rolling whenever someone mentioned my book. I'd entered Frasier High School a nameless freshman, then risen through the socially envied crowd at breakneck speed. There were a lot of people—girls, mostly—who didn't like it, who viewed me as an unworthy shadow intruding on their world. It took me a while to understand why they felt that way.

Popularity is a full-time job. If you're popular because of your good looks, you have to work around the clock to make sure your skin stays clear and your waist stays small. If you're popular because of your athletic abilities or your fearless confidence, you have to pound the pavement to stay on top and in the know. You have to sit with the right girls, flirt with the right guys, heartlessly ignore the friends you had in junior high. It takes effort and skill. I bypassed all of that by landing a book deal with a major publisher, having my face plastered in magazines, and taking a spring break trip to Hollywood to meet the producers who were adapting *The Heart Stealer* into a motion picture.

My popularity was inevitable; it also transcended the everyday boundaries of high school life. People didn't want to be my friend because of my new hot looks or the clothes I wore. No, people wanted to be my friend because I was a celebrity in the making, and there had never been a celebrity student in the history of Frasier High School.

Oh, you're a gorgeous cheerleader and you're dating the hottest guy on earth? That's nice. I'm going to the Oscars next year and I just spent three thousand dollars on a new Prada gown.

See what I'm saying? No guy is hotter than Oscar.

I threw a glance over my shoulder and caught Bethany Jacobs rolling her eyes at me. Senior. Swim team captain. Popular her whole life. And, if the rumors were true, her initials explained exactly why she was the object of every guy's affection. It was eating her up inside that a lowly sophomore like me had achieved spotlight status.

Bethany sighed, visibly irritated. "Like, aren't *all* little girls pretty enough to star in movies?" she remarked to one of her blond and equally perfect friends.

Even worse than Bethany's cruel comment was that, to a certain extent, it rang true. I still had that prepubescent look—definitely more girl than young woman. I had hoped that with the onset of literary fame, I'd develop bigger boobs and fuller lips. It totally didn't happen. Under normal circumstances, I would have sunk deeper into my chair and allowed her words to intimidate me. That was the formula, after all: Nobody Sophomore shrinks in the shadow of Popular Senior.

But sitting at that grimy cafeteria table, I suddenly realized that I had waited a long time for a day like this—a day when I *wouldn't* have to sink into my chair or feel invisible in the presence of someone prettier and gutsier than me. So I wasn't about to let Bethany Jacobs knock the books from my newfound shelf of self-esteem.

I glanced up at Mrs. Gallagher. Maybe her embarrassing display of admiration served a purpose after all. "Actually, I *might* have a part in the movie," I lied, using a nauseatingly cheerful tone. "I'll be speaking to my agent about it tonight. Then I'll probably speak to my publicist, who'll speak to the people who are coordinating my *fifteen-city author tour.*" I paused for effect. The room was so quiet, I could've heard a fly fart. "When I'm in Los Angeles next week, it'll likely be discussed. So, the bottom line, Mrs. Gallagher, is that *anything* is possible."

I shot another glance over my shoulder. B.J. was scowling.

Top that, Princess Perfect.

As I moved the pen into position and flipped open the cover of my book, I felt every eye in the cafeteria zoom in. A few of my classmates were genuinely happy for me. A slightly larger number didn't comprehend what was happening to me. But most of them were unabashedly jealous of me.

And at that very moment, I couldn't blame them.

To my teacher, Mrs. Gallagher, I wrote. *You've inspired me more than you'll ever know. With love, Ruby Crane.*

I signed my name slowly, giving the *R* a long, dramatic lower swirl. Just like the enigmatic title character of my favorite novel, *Rebecca.*

Then it was time for the well-rehearsed Author Dance Move.

Drop the pen with my right hand. Close the front cover of the book with my left. Lift my head and smile as I hand it back to the waiting fan.

Mrs. Gallagher read the inscription and nearly swooned. "I can't *wait* to start it, Ruby," she said, cradling the book against her chest as if it were a sleeping baby. "I'll be sure to let you know how much I loved it."

"Thank you." I kept my smile in place as Mrs. Gallagher shuffled out of the cafeteria. There was no point in facing the mean girls again, so I stood up and grabbed my Louis Vuitton messenger bag from the chair beside me. After that little power flaunt, I wanted to make a quiet exit. No cold stares. No triumphant smirks. Just a slow, cool walk past the envious crowd.

It was what any celebrity would have done.

I had spent my whole life dreaming about it. Not fame or the fun that comes with being the center of attention, but the thrill of seeing my name in print. Of knowing that someone could walk into a bookstore and find me on a shelf and start reading the novel I'd written. I'd never had a fantasy bigger than that.

It might sound a little strange, especially when you consider that most girls my age dream of becoming actors, models, rock stars, fashion designers, or professional cheerleaders. My problem? I've never been a fan of soap operas, and the thrill of prancing around a football field in a miniskirt and waving pom-poms totally eludes me. Don't get me wrong; being showered with positive attention is flat-out awesome, but the spotlight takes a lot of getting used to. On the downside, you're constantly under a microscope, so you always have to be on guard: no quick nose-picking or snorts of laughter, no coffee stains on your starched white shirt. The upside is fairly obvious, wouldn't you say? People want to be around you, people are eager to hear you speak, and people like you even though they hate you. The spotlight had made my life pretty damn spectacular . . . especially because bookworms like me weren't supposed to find happiness in their freshman or sophomore year of high school. The debate team? The yearbook club? The squash squad? Those were the circles someone of my caliber should have been relegated to.

Picture a little girl sitting cross-legged on her bedroom floor, surrounded by an array of cool toys: neatly dressed dolls, an accompanying dollhouse, a flashing red train that went *choo choo* when touched, several colored building blocks . . . and a tattered picture book purchased from the local drugstore. Guess which of the items caught my eye. The book, of course. I used to sit there for hours and flip through the pages, amazed by the pictures but entranced by the big printed words. I learned to read early on, and it pretty much became my childhood obsession. And some obsessions are with you for life.

My first conscious memory is of books. Two specifically: *Goodnight Moon* and *Where the Wild Things Are.* I remember sitting on my mother's lap and listening as she read to me. Who needed television or movies? It was way better to imagine how the night sky looked or what was around the next shadowy bend in the forest.

Stories. Characters. Dialogue. Entire worlds created on the page. Worlds that could sweep you away or frighten you, make you laugh or cry. Worlds that allowed you to escape to another country or time. Worlds built piece by piece of ink and punctuation. That was where power had always lived for me: in books.

And now the power was mine. It didn't matter where I was or what I was doing; everybody looked at me and saw a bright little star.

Okay, maybe the spotlight hadn't taken *that* long to get used to.

My slow walk out of the cafeteria had cost me a good fifteen seconds, so I had to rush through the crowded halls. I hated being late for chemistry. Mr. Snow was a nice guy, but he didn't tolerate tardiness. The problem was that I couldn't just dash up the stairs to the fourth-floor science labs because there were too many people I had to acknowledge. Mostly strangers who had developed a habit of waving and smiling at me as if I were an old friend. Ignoring them was an option, but I didn't want to be labeled a snob so early in my career. So I waved to the short red-haired girl from my gym class, the two boys with the big noses from global studies, and the new music teacher with the sweat stains under his arms. I was out of breath by the time I made it to the classroom.

Fortunately, Mr. Snow was absent. And the sub hadn't arrived yet.

I was about to run back into the hall and to the bathroom when someone called my name.

"Ruby!"

I knew his voice like I knew the words of my favorite song. My eyes found him the moment I turned around. And my heart started melting right there on the spot.

Jordan Lush was tall and gorgeous and built like a gladiator. He had dark wavy hair, blue eyes, and a smile that could have brightened Dante's ninth circle. One of the school's most ambitious athletes, he also played violin and wasn't ashamed to tell people that his parents were both librarians. He was a junior and—best of all—totally into me.

"Hey," I said, instantly forgetting the mean girls, the cafeteria, the world as I knew it.

"Hey yourself." He swaggered over to me, his backpack hanging on his right shoulder. He hooked his hands around my waist. He pulled me to him. Then he planted a hot, delicious, I-want-everybody-to-see-this kiss on my lips.

I held it for as long as I could. And I thought, *I'm totally becoming a romance novelist when I grow up.*

"So," he said, finally pulling away from me, "how's my favorite famous writer doing?"

"Stop it," I told him sheepishly. "I'm not a famous writer. I'm just like any other girl in this school."

"No, you're not. You're a *heart stealer.*" He smirked. "You're totally different and much more amazing than any other girl in this school."

Duh. Tell me something I don't know. I smiled again and stared into his eyes. I had never been the type of girl who gets all fluttery and wobbly at the thought of falling in love. That was probably because I had never been the object of anyone's affection, but a lot had changed in the past few months.

Jordan Lush was every girl's dream. The first time I saw him walking out of the gym all sweaty and breathless, I nearly tripped over my shoes. But he was off-limits. Completely out of reach. To put it figuratively: I was the basement; he was the penthouse. So, like every other girl in school, I resigned myself to fantasizing about him; these were normal, fairly innocent fantasies of the crush variety—what Jordan looked like naked, if Jordan read books while he was naked . . . that sort of thing. Then, in April, I got invited to Amber Lamorna's sweet sixteen party—for A-list students only—at this swanky restaurant in Greenwich Village, and I was standing there at the edge of the dance floor when Jordan came up to me and said, "Hey, you're Ruby Crane, right?"

He knew who I was. He told me he had read about my book deal in one of his mother's literary magazines. We sat and talked for almost two hours, shouting over the blare of music and sneaking sips from a beer bottle he'd stolen from behind the bar. It turned out we had a few things in common. We were both native New Yorkers. We both hated math and science. We even shared a secret childhood dream of running away from home to hide out in the Metropolitan Museum of Art, like the characters in one of my favorite children's books, *From the Mixed-Up Files of Mrs. Basil E. Frankweiler.* Mostly, I liked Jordan because he didn't roll his eyes or make dumb comments when I talked about how much I loved *Jane Eyre, Wuthering Heights, Little Women, A Moveable Feast,* and *The Scarlet Letter.* He didn't laugh when I admitted that I could recite the first twenty lines of Poe's "The Raven" by heart.

At one time, those facts had made me an Official Nerd; now they granted me an air of intellectual coolness. Amazing what a little publicity can do.

Snapping me back to reality, Jordan swung his backpack off his shoulder and unzipped it. He pulled out a tattered copy of the *New York Post.* He flipped through the pages quickly, smiling when his eyes found what they were looking for. "Check *this* out!" he said loudly.

The newspaper landed on the nearest desk with a thud.

A crowd of students appeared, pressing around us like hungry wolves. There were little gasps and smatters of "Oh, wow!" and "How cool!"

My eyes widened as I took in the small grainy picture hovering beside the headline: TEEN LITERARY SENSATION HEADED FOR BESTSELLER LIST. The blurb was practically glowing. And, thank God, the author photo actually looked good: in it, I was wearing a tight black shirt, and my hair had been styled in that sexy/trendy windblown way.

I stepped out of the circle and surveyed it from a distance. It was too surreal. I couldn't get used to the fact that *I* was a newsworthy person.

"Ruby," someone said, "what's the book about?"

"Ruby, who's gonna star in the movie?"

"Hey, Ruby, you're rich now, right?"

I blinked. I nodded. I shook my head. Then I blinked some more. Was this what celebrities went through on a daily basis? No wonder they had attitudes.

"Ruby," Jordan said, "this is, like, the beginning of something *huge*!"

I didn't know it then, but his words were an omen.

The Last Chapter of
My First Life

I spent the rest of the day getting ready for the night. I cut my last two classes, caught a cab to the East Side, and then crawled through the gridlock of midtown Manhattan until I reached my apartment building at Sixty-third and First. My parents were still at work. Grateful for the silence, I went into my bedroom and tore off my clothes. Then I yanked open my closet doors and started rummaging through my wardrobe; it had changed a lot since the book deal.

Everything had changed a lot since the book deal.

I was reminded of that when I caught a glimpse of

myself in the mirror. My strawberry blond hair hung past my shoulders in shiny tendrils. My waist, once the size of a hula hoop, was now bikini ready. The hundreds of dollars I'd been advised to spend on facial products and makeup had done the trick—glowing skin, not a single zit. I liked the image staring back at me. Everyone liked the image, maybe because it was so radically different from the one they used to know. No more big baggy jeans. No more oversized sweaters. My old wire-rimmed glasses had been replaced with contact lenses. By all accounts, Ruby Crane had gone from nondescript to totally hip.

As I dressed—black Vera Wang miniskirt, matching Armani blazer—I stared at the framed book cover on my bedroom wall. *The Heart Stealer.* A story about an introverted and insecure but very smart high school freshman who manages to seduce the hottest guy in school with her brains, not her body. A rarity in this boob-and-booty-obsessed world. I had never known a girl who'd accomplished such a feat. But when I'd written the book the summer after graduating from junior high, I couldn't have imagined it would end up being nearly autobiographical.

That was the first question my literary agent had asked me: *Are you the main character in this book, Ruby?* I told her I wasn't. Then, a few weeks later, sitting in the executive offices of Hart & Dobson Publishers, I told my editor the same thing—that the book was a total figment of my imagination, that I was smart and introverted but not the type of girl who snagged hot guys. I was also not the type of girl who cared about popularity, romance, or having crowds of friends. *That,* I said, would never be me. I wasn't impressed with status or recognition or the perks of being cool. When I signed those thick, wordy contracts, I did so offhandedly, almost defiantly. *Sure, I guess a few hundred thousand dollars for my book is okay.* I didn't want anyone thinking I was eager to change the drabness of my life. Deep down, of course, that was what I had always yearned for. I can admit that now. But back then, when I'd been a proud nerd, I'd railed against any insinuation that my bland identity could use a little spicing up.

And yet on the night of June 12, there I was walking out of my apartment building and into a waiting limousine, designer clothes on my body, three-hundred-dollar sunglasses shielding my eyes. If there'd been a catwalk in sight, I would have shuffled down it like a caffeine-cranked model. I smiled at the chauffeur and stared out the window as the city sped by in bright, dizzying flashes. I glimpsed the crowds on Second Avenue, the gridlock on Third, the hordes of pedestrians crossing east and west. The pulse excited me. My city. A writer's city. The greatest city in the world. And I was anything but a faceless New Yorker. I kept picturing my parents dancing around our apartment the way they had in the days following the announcement of the book deal: Mom crossing into the living room with a little two-step, Dad singing that one line from Sinatra's "New York, New York" whenever I walked into the room. *If I can make it there, I'll make it anywhere . . .*

So pathetically corny. But so undeniably true.

As the limo turned onto Houston Street, I opened my

purse and pulled out the folded sheets of paper that my publicist had faxed me a few weeks before; they detailed the longest and busiest itinerary I'd ever seen. After tonight's event, I was scheduled to do four local book signings in the next three days. Then I'd be on a fifteen-city tour, crisscrossing the country like a jumbo jet, meeting fans from Miami and Michigan to Seattle and South Dakota. It made me nervous. I had never traveled that extensively, and I found myself worrying about the smallest inane details. Would my hotel rooms be equipped with hair dryers? Would there be a major department store within two miles in the event of a fashion emergency? I couldn't imagine a Neiman Marcus in the middle of an Iowa cornfield, or a Barneys floating around the Great Lakes. Photographers would be snapping my pic from every angle and I didn't want to look like Mary Shelley's undiscovered female character, Frankenstein-ette.

The American Literature Club was located on a tree-lined street in Greenwich Village. The turn-of-the-century brownstone boasted a wall of thick, trailing ivy and a gold placard beside the wide front doors. Literary luminaries had been chilling there for more than a century. I could practically smell ink and old pages as I made my way up the front staircase and into the gilded Great Hall. I imagined Edith Wharton sitting at a table in a far corner, James Baldwin flicking a cigarette as he walked by. I was *so* in my element.

The air buzzed with conversation. A three-piece orchestra played Bach while waiters served glasses of champagne and white wine. Within the first minute, I spotted three living legends and almost turned into the screaming, celebrity-obsessed kind of girl I despise. Fortunately, I managed to hold on to my composure until someone recognized me.

"Ruby!"

I turned and saw my literary agent, Cassie Kritch, waving from the opposite side of the huge room. Relief flooded me. Tall and thin and naturally beautiful, Cassie looked way younger than her forty-three years. I viewed her as something of an angel. It was she, after all, who had plucked *The Heart Stealer* from obscurity and sold it to my publisher. She was the one who had changed my life.

I walked over to her and entered the circle she was standing in. It was one of those poofy-foofy circles where everything was intellectual, where people talked about Shakespeare as if he were an old friend, and where you automatically assumed an English accent. *Good day,* I wanted to say. *Will you be joining me in the library for tea and biscuits in a quarter of an hour? We can sit on our bums and talk 'bout blokes till the queen retches.* Don't worry—I didn't say it.

Cassie put an arm around my shoulder and made the introductions. Standing two feet from me were some of my favorite writers: novelists Aidan Billings and Joanna Moloni, *New York Times* journalist Sue Ellen Black, poet Rita Lanei. My eyes widened and my heart nearly exploded. How many people can say they met their idols? In that moment, I was proud of my nerdy past. Get crazy and excited about screeching rock stars or actors addicted to Botox? No, thank you. I'd rather worship the writers who can play words like musical notes. Who happily spend more time in the universe of their own imaginations than in the real world. That was what amazed me, even as a kid, about writers—their ability to imagine people and places with perfect clarity and then make those people and places totally real on the page. To shape whole books from a single first sentence. Where does it come from? And how do you keep it coming time after time, story after story? Thinking about it can intimidate you. It can completely blow your mind. I mean, how does what's *invisible* become *legible*—even *tangible*?

". . . because Ruby really is very modest," Cassie was saying in her breathy, confident voice. "The day I called her and told her that virtually *every* publisher in New York was fighting for her book, she said, 'Oh, I'm so flattered they actually like me that much.'" A dramatic laugh shot past her lips. *Ahhhhh-hahahahaha.*

I plastered a smile on my face.

"It was a five-day auction," Cassie continued. "And when I finally called Ruby and told her Hart and Dobson had won out, and that it was a *major* deal, I told her to take a little while to think about it. And she said, 'Think about it? Call them back right now and tell them yes before they change their minds!'" *Ahhhhh-hahahahaha.*

Which was followed, of course, by a resounding stream of haughty laughter.

Ahhhhh-hahahahaha.

A waiter suddenly appeared at my side and handed me a glass of what looked like champagne. It was, in fact, sparkling apple cider. Total bummer. Getting a little drunk would've helped me relax. I sipped the cider as I accepted compliments, answered questions, and accepted more compliments. Aidan Billings asked me how old I was when I started writing. Joanna Moloni asked me where I got my inspiration. It went on like that for about ten minutes—questions, compliments, musings about all the phenomenal power my future held. I didn't shy away from any of it. For the second time in one day, the crowds around me were thickening.

My editor, Liza Smith, found me in the middle of the whirlwind. Small, thin, and also naturally beautiful—what was it with these women and their looks, anyway?—she had worked with me for several months and helped shape the original manuscript of *The Heart Stealer* into a book. We had developed a close relationship over the past year. After my mom, she was the woman I respected most. Liza had gone to Harvard, majored in English literature, and even spent a year studying at Oxford. She was only in her thirties but had already worked with several bestselling authors.

"You look beautiful!" she said, wrapping her arms around me.

I struck a little pose, modeling my outfit.

"Come with me," she said. She led the way out of the main hall and into another big sprawling room just behind it, where dozens of people were mingling. "I want you to meet Anna Clayton, the senior editor of *Chapters* magazine; she's interested in interviewing you for an upcoming issue. And I want you to meet Peter Wantrell; he's one of our up-and-coming novelists, and he's eager to speak with you. Oh, and there are a bunch of other press people you should meet. . . ."

My head was spinning with excitement. When Liza wasn't looking, I spotted a passing waiter and quickly switched my glass of apple cider for a long, lean champagne flute. I shot half of it down in a single gulp, then fought to control the burp clawing its way up my throat.

Suddenly, Liza pointed at something across the room. "Check *that* out," she said.

I checked it. And nearly jumped out of my skin.

Mounted on a wall, beside the American Literature Club's glistening gold crest, was a poster-sized copy of *The Heart Stealer*'s cover. Five guests—three famous writers, two well-known Broadway actresses—were studying it and chatting. *Oh, blessed champagne,* I thought, *please work faster and grant me a buzz.*

But before I could recover from the awesome shock, my publicist found me.

Aaron Keen was the epitome of . . . well . . . publicity. He also attracted it the way the captain of the football team attracts sluts. He was muscular and totally hot—good looks, by the way, are an unspoken prerequisite to being successful in media-related jobs—and his flamboyant character made him all the more charming. His charcoal suit and the blue scarf around his neck had to have cost more than a month's tuition at a private prep school on the Upper East Side. He always approached me as if we were already in the middle of a conversation.

"So I spoke to the people who are coordinating this event," he began, giving my arm a tap. "You're going to take the stage with two other writers in about fifteen minutes and there'll be a brief question-and-answer period. Don't mention money. Don't mention too much about the movie deal for *The Heart Stealer* either. You can talk about meeting the producers, but try to steer your answers toward your upcoming tour and how much you're looking forward to meeting your fans. Got it? Good. People might ask you about what it's like being a famous writer who also happens to still be a high school sophomore; again, steer your answers toward the book, and how you're a serious writer regardless of your age. Got it? Good. You'll be fine."

I nodded. What else could I do? Aaron was like a bomb two seconds from exploding, and if you're standing near a bomb, the last thing you want is for it to explode. I brought the champagne flute to my lips and sipped again. I had inadvertently made it to the center of the room when I spotted someone staring at me.

A *big, important* someone.

Samantha Golding was one of the best television news reporters on the planet. She was also a popular personality with ties to Hollywood. She covered the Oscars, the Emmys, the MTV Video Music Awards, and all the hot stories related to pregnant celebrities. Maybe that was because she herself looked like one—a celebrity, not a *pregnant* celebrity. She was small and skinny, and she had big boobs and thick black hair flowing past her shoulders. That she had decided to cover this small event—small compared to the Oscars, I mean—was astonishing.

I met her hard, probing stare but then looked away quickly. I couldn't believe it.

Samantha Golding. Here. To interview *me?*

I mean, Virginia Woolf would've been impressed.

Out of the corner of my eye, I watched as Samantha Golding whispered something to the nearby cameraman while giving her hair a perfunctory fluff. She held out her hand and took a microphone from him.

I chugged some more of the champagne. Was she going to approach me soon? *Ho. Ly. Shit.* My heart was dancing in my chest.

"Look who's here," Cassie whispered in my ear. She gestured toward Samantha Golding.

"I can't believe it," I whispered back. "Did you know she was coming?"

"Absolutely not. No one knew. But the important thing is that she's here." Cassie smoothed a hand down the front of her blazer, checking to make sure she would look good on camera.

A moment later, Liza and Aaron appeared at my side. Liza was smiling, insinuating the obvious. And Aaron, for once, wasn't talking.

I took a deep breath. I squared my shoulders. I tossed my head back.

Samantha Golding turned and started walking directly toward me, cameraman already filming.

Stay calm. Don't stutter. Pray that everyone in school watches the news tonight.

A hush slowly fell over the room, and all eyes landed on me.

"Ruby," Samantha said, coming closer. She didn't smile. She didn't so much as squint. She simply held the microphone up and out. "How do you respond to charges that nearly thirty percent of your first novel, *The Heart Stealer,* was plagiarized?"

Cassie gasped. Liza stared at me. Aaron looked as if a pit bull had bitten him between the legs.

And, needless to say, I dropped the champagne flute.

I Am Infamous

Imagine the most embarrassing moment of your life—and then magnify it a million times. Put it under a high-powered microscope and look at every unwanted, minuscule molecule up close. Now scan it, download it, and double-click the image so that it's so big it makes your eyes bleed.

Maybe you were walking through a crowded cafeteria at school holding a tray full of food when, suddenly, you lost your footing and went flying through the air . . . only to land in front of the popular crowd's table face-first with your skirt around your ankles and your Hello Kitty underwear in full view of the world.

Mortifying, right? Magnify it a million times.

Maybe you were on a first date with a guy you'd wanted to kiss, eating pizza and laughing out loud and snuggling closer to him, when, suddenly, a stream of bubbly soda spurted out of your nose like a gunshot.

Mortifying, right? Well, magnify it a million times.

Maybe you were standing at the podium in the gym making your bid for student council president, talking up a storm, when, suddenly, you took a deep breath and a burp boomed past your lips . . . only to be met by stunned silence.

Magnify it, baby. A million freakin' times.

If someone grabbed me by the shoulders and yanked me out of the room, I don't remember it. That was exactly what someone did, of course, but my memories of how everything played out immediately afterward are fuzzy at best.

Following Samantha Golding's question, there was a brief period of stillness, of hold-your-breath shock. In a room full of writers, editors, and journalists, that single horrifying word—*plagiarism*—has the impact of an earthquake. Whispers rose on the air a few seconds later, and the din of voices got louder and louder and my heart beat faster and faster and my vision tunneled until I saw strange shadowy shapes that resembled . . . shoes.

My shoes.

In that first moment of lucidity, I found myself sitting in the back of the limousine again, hunched over as if in pain, staring straight down at my beautiful black heels. I didn't understand what was happening. I didn't understand why I had been whisked away so quickly. Why hadn't I been given the chance to answer Samantha Golding's claim? Why was I trembling uncontrollably? And why the hell was the damn limo flying along Houston Street at breakneck speed?

I turned my head and saw my parents, Anne and Steve Crane, sitting beside me. I hadn't seen them enter the American Literature Club in the minutes before that bogus, bitchy question fired up the air.

My mother was decked out in the amazing Versace dress I'd bought for her a few months back. Her brown hair was short and styled in a pixie cut. She's never been able to conceal emotion or stress, so the wild, worried look in her eyes told me that something was terribly wrong.

My father, on the other hand, has the rare gift of composure: nothing ever excites him, and when everyone else in the world is panicking, he brings his poise up a notch. He's the kind of guy who in the middle of a burning airplane would say *Now where are those swell emergency exits?*

Judging by the state of my nerves, I thought it was a safe bet that I had my mother's neurotic genes.

She reached a hand out and smoothed it over my hair. "Honey," she said, her voice cracking, "I just can't believe what that ugly reporter did to you. Don't be upset. It'll . . . we'll . . . you'll . . . everything will be okay."

I stared at her. I tasted tears and realized I was crying. "Why didn't they let me answer her?" I blurted out. "Why did they rush me out of there so quickly? It's not fair!"

My father leaned forward in his seat. "Just listen. Your mother's right: everything will be okay. Just calm down."

"Calm down?"

"I'm sure there's a reasonable explanation, Ruby. We'll find it soon enough."

"No," I snapped. "*Soon enough* isn't good enough. This is my *life*—"

"You're still a sixteen-year-old girl," my father said. "Pulling you out of that room was the right thing to do. It's best to let professionals handle this, and I'm sure that's what your publishers are doing right now."

My book. My life. My fame. Everyone will see the news tonight. It'll all come crashing down.

The heat in the limo was oppressive. I clawed at the door and pushed the buttons until the window rolled down. What the hell was going on? How could something like this have happened? *Plagiarism?* Would I be able to face my friends in school the next day? Would anyone believe me when I got a chance to explain?

The embarrassment was too much. I could already feel it surging around me like a raging river. If it hadn't been for the expensive clothes I was wearing, I probably would've peed.

How do you respond to charges . . . ?

What charges? *Hello?*

My brain was racing. Finally, in desperation, I turned back to my parents and shot them a pleading look.

"Trust us, Ruby," my father said slowly. "We'll talk about this when we get home."

"Are you *listening* to me?" I screamed. "There's nothing

to talk about. It's all a lie. Why can't I go back there and defend myself? I don't know what Samantha Golding is talking about."

He stared at me. There might have been a flash of genuine panic in his eyes. "I think it's best for us to just go home and keep a low profile right now," he said.

I gritted my teeth. "Low profiles are for losers! It's gonna be all over the news tonight! That camera was rolling when she asked me that question!" I raked my hands across my face, wiping away mascara-laced tears. I knew that my mother wouldn't be able to answer me, so I shot a hard, demanding glare in my father's direction. "Did you talk to Cassie or Liza before I was yanked out of there? Are you gonna tell me what's really going on? I mean, *why* would someone accuse me of plagiarism?"

My father sighed and looked down. My mother bit her lower lip. They *had* spoken to Cassie, or Liza, in the minutes following Samantha Golding's question. And now the silence between us was dangerously thick.

"Why," I asked again, "would anyone accuse me of *plagiarism*?"

Strangely enough, it was my mother who spoke up. She put a hand on my shoulder and said, as gently as possible, "Ruby, that's a question only *you* can answer."

* * *

The scandal officially broke later that night. Samantha Golding appeared on the eleven o'clock news and laid the whole story out for the world to see, like a garish literary tarot.

The Heart Stealer, she said, was not an original novel, and its author, sixteen-year-old Ruby Crane, was not the writing sensation Hart & Dobson Publishers was promoting her to be. Piece by gut-wrenching piece, Samantha took the book apart, claiming that as many as forty-two passages were "unquestionably" plagiarized. She had a copy of *The Heart Stealer* in front of her on the anchor's desk, and she held it up several times as she spoke. She read from it a few of the passages that had allegedly appeared in another novel four years earlier. And then she picked up *that* novel—*My Broken Soul,* written by bestselling author Adella Morgan—and compared the passages in *her* book to the passages in *my* book.

They were nearly identical.

It went on for about fifteen minutes. My book. Adella Morgan's book. Page thirty-two of my book. Page seventy-six of Adella Morgan's book. Third paragraph to fifth paragraph. First sentence to fourth. Here, there. Language, voice.

My words.

Adella Morgan's words.

My Broken Soul, published four years earlier. *The Heart Stealer,* published just the past week.

With firm, unrelenting candor, that Golding bitch accused me of "robbing" another writer. She accused Hart & Dobson Publishers of "neglecting integrity in the mad rush to make a buck." When she stopped speaking, the screen flashed to my face, bright and hopeful, as it had been a few hours earlier at the American Literature Club, and in the next second, Samantha was holding the microphone and asking the Question.

How do you respond to charges that nearly thirty percent of your first novel, The Heart Stealer, *was plagiarized?*

Talk about a bomb dropping.

The tape captured what I couldn't remember: Aaron Keen stepping in front of me, Cassie grabbing me by the arm and hustling me through the gawking crowd. Liza's frantic voice asking "What's going on here?" before the microphone was pushed hastily away. Then the camera spun out of focus, as if someone had slapped it or knocked the cameraman off his feet.

When Samantha Golding appeared on-screen again, she said, "It is a sad occasion tonight, not only for sixteen-year-old *would-be* author Ruby Crane but for the media industry as a whole. With such glaring, irrefutable evidence, could anyone really *not* have noticed this travesty? I felt it was imperative to report this story to my viewers, because I believe plagiarism is a serious offense—and one that's not taken seriously enough. What does this say about our respect for the written word?"

I reached for the remote and flicked off the television. I was sitting in my bedroom, still dressed in the black mini and the matching jacket. My hands were clammy, my forehead slick with sweat. I was, of course, speechless. Not that I had anyone to speak to; I'd dead-bolted the door to keep my parents out. The thought of facing them was too horrible.

I lowered myself onto my bed and stared up at the ceiling, not flinching this time as a fresh wave of tears poured from my eyes. It wasn't a hiccupping, sobbing display of emotion; it was more the silent, sour cry born of shock, anger, and disbelief. I couldn't move. I couldn't even think. Every time I inhaled, I heard Samantha Golding's voice circle me like a bad song. I kept wondering how many of my classmates had watched the news, how many of them were grabbing their cell phones to mouth off about what was happening. And what about Mrs. Gallagher? Had she thrown her autographed copy of *The Heart Stealer* into a frying pan and turned the flames up high? Was she using it as kitty litter for her cat, Brontë?

How do you respond to charges that . . . your first novel . . . was plagiarized?

Plagiarism.

Freaking plagiarism.

I sat up. I started pacing the floor. Suddenly, my room seemed too small. I'd lived in it more than half my life, and suddenly it was too small.

"Ruby? Are you okay?" My mother's voice sounded strained. She jiggled the knob from the other side of the sealed door.

"Go away!" I shouted. "Just leave me alone!"

"Honey, we have to talk."

"No!"

"Dad and I are worried about you," she went on. "How about just five minutes? Please, Ruby?"

I spotted one of my running sneakers beside my bed, picked it up, and hurled it at the door. The thump was louder than I'd thought it would be. "Leave. Me. *Alone*," I screeched. I closed my eyes and listened to my mother's footsteps retreat down the corridor and into the kitchen.

Talk? No. I didn't want to talk. There was nothing to say, anyway. How do you articulate the cruelty of life—of fate? In a few short hours, my life had gone from enviable to embarrassing, from beautiful to impossible.

How do you respond to charges . . . ?

What would come next? I wondered. How far would this all go? A television interview? More magazine articles? Would I have to face the public and tell my side of the story? Well, if that was the case, I knew exactly what I'd say.

I went to the mirror behind my closet door and stared at my reflection. I pictured Samantha Golding sitting across from me in a bright studio, cameras rolling. This time, when she dropped the question, I'd be prepared.

I did not plagiarize any of Adella Morgan's books. What I wrote, I wrote by myself. My characters are original; my story is original. If there are similarities between my work and Adella Morgan's, they are simply coincidences. I am not a plagiarizer.

If I was fierce enough, adamant enough, people would believe me. Right? There was no *real* proof that I had plagiarized Adella Morgan's novel.

I am not a plagiarizer, I repeated in my head. *I am a serious writer and I have always been a serious student. I have my own imagination and I don't need to steal from other writers, thank you very much.*

Words, I thought. *They're just words.*

The breath shot from my lungs in short harsh gasps.

Just words. And commas and periods and quotation marks.

Little by little, the image staring back at me through

the mirror grew dimmer. I couldn't see my hands or legs. I couldn't see my arms.

I wrote my novel because I wanted to give teen readers like me something good to read, a book they could identify with. That's what The Heart Stealer *is—a fun romance that addresses issues every high school girl is familiar with. It's my work and no one else's.*

I kept staring at the reflection. My nose and lips disappeared. Then my eyes. But the voice resounding through my brain was too strong to ignore.

In truth, I am not a fan of Adella Morgan's books. In fact, I have never even read one of Adella Morgan's books.

Still crying, I knelt down, grabbed the tattered copies of Adella Morgan's books from under my bed, and hurled them into the garbage can beside my desk.

✳   ✳   ✳

You know what happened after that.

The front page of the *New York Times,* the front page of the *Chicago Tribune,* the constant replay of that ugly clip airing on *Good Morning America,* the *Today* show, the evening broadcasts of CNN. Over the following week, *The Heart Stealer* became the subject of countless headlines, debates, and opinionated articles. The story even made the airwaves in Europe.

My fame had grown tremendously, but my infamy was what mattered.

I didn't go back to school for the last two weeks of the year. Under the circumstances, my parents agreed that my venturing out and into the eye of the storm would only be worse. My mother had the terrible fear that I would be mobbed by reporters while I waited for the bus on the corner of First Avenue. My father, always more realistic and thoughtful, said he knew how cruel kids could be, and he didn't want me to have to deal with it. So I spent a long span of days sitting in my bedroom in front of my laptop, surfing the Internet and eating way too much ice cream. There was a part of me that thought—hoped—the scandal would come to a sudden stop and Liza or Cassie would call me and say that it was all a mistake or that it had been forgotten. But it didn't happen.

When Cassie *did* call, she spoke to my mother. After months of being treated like an adult, I was being treated like a toddler who couldn't even handle a conversation. They spent a long time talking about things, and I watched from the kitchen doorway as Mom took notes and nodded or shook her head. My presence would be required at a number of upcoming meetings, where I'd likely be questioned by attorneys and publishing executives. The words *unfortunate* and *sad* were used a lot.

The movie version of *The Heart Stealer* was scrapped. The publication of my second novel, which I had begun writing in April, was canceled. Every day brought a new and crushing development, and I found myself wondering if there was a billboard in Times Square with my picture on it and LOSER printed across it.

But then came the morning when it all hit me. I mean, when it really sank in. When the reality of what was happening jumped up and slapped me straight across the face.

It was around ten o'clock on a Saturday morning, and I was helping my mother with her usual weekend cleaning. The television played in a corner of the living room while I fluffed pillows and wiped dust off picture frames and ran a cloth over the coffee table. The air between Mom and me was tense: she didn't know what to say to me, and she knew I didn't want her saying anything. Tired of the silence, I flicked on the vacuum and started pushing and pulling it across the area rug. Strangely enough, it was the best sound I had heard in a long time. I stared down at the wheezing bag and wondered how difficult it would be to get sucked up in there with all the dust and dirt and fuzzy hair balls. Why did that smattering of day-old cookie crumbs on the floor have the luxury of simply disappearing into thin air? Why couldn't it be that easy for me?

I was about to run the vacuum over my foot when my mother screamed at me and flailed her arms from across the room. "What is it?" I snapped, flicking the vacuum off.

"Look!" She pointed to the television and dove for the remote.

The sound shot up. And so did my blood pressure.

Adella Morgan, the novelist whose book I had been accused of plagiarizing, was staring back at me from the screen. She was a pretty, dark-haired woman who lived a quiet and quintessentially literary life in Vermont. Right then, however, she was sitting in a Manhattan TV studio, talking to Katie Couric about *me*.

"Volume!" I screeched.

My mother pressed and shook the remote.

I froze, my fingers tight around the vacuum's handle.

"The entire incident is terrible, and it's been emotionally draining for me," Adella Morgan was saying. "I have a new book coming out in a few months and I just want to put this whole thing behind me."

Katie held up a copy of *The Heart Stealer* and asked Adella what she thought of me.

Adella paused for a moment, then said, "I wish Ruby Crane the best of luck and hope she never loses her passion for books."

And it was over. They both said other stuff, but my mind went completely blank. A total whiteout of the brain. I felt sick as I lowered myself onto the couch.

National news. Adella Morgan, once one of my idols, talking about me.

"Oh!" Mom said. "Oh my God! Ruby! Did you . . . did you hear that? Did you just hear—" She stopped talking the moment she looked at me.

I wish Ruby Crane the best of luck and hope she never loses her passion for books. . . .

But I *had* lost it. The very sight of a book got my stomach roiling and made all the muscles in my neck tense. I didn't want to know anything about writers or words or stories. I didn't want to pass by another bookstore for as long as I lived. I felt as though I should've been walking around with a scarlet *P* pinned to my sweater so that the whole world could just point at me and judge.

Mom tapped my arm. "Ruby? Are you okay?"

I didn't respond. Suddenly, the idea of getting sucked

into a vacuum bag seemed trivial. *Nothing* would make the storm disappear. There was no place to hide because I couldn't hide from myself.

Mom went back to her cleaning. I don't know how long I remained in that pitiful position on the couch, but it must've been a good while, because when I finally snapped back to reality, the living room was spotless.

"Mom?" I said, finally breaking the silence between us. She turned to face me.

"Do you think I'll ever write another book?" I asked her. "I mean, do you think my life will ever be normal again?"

She didn't smile or nod or try to make light of my question. She just met my stare and held it. "Maybe," she answered quietly.

But I knew better than to believe her. I knew my life was over.

* * *

Amber Lamorna, Diana Kitsin, Lisa Blackley, Kelly Marie Conner, Jessica Delgado, Nicholas Archman, and Damon Kurtz—my friends at Frasier High School. The cool crew that had accepted me into their forbidden circle. The juniors and seniors everyone wanted to hang out with. If you were a freshman, you lowered your eyes when you saw them walking down the hall.

A year earlier, after the news spread that I was a soon-to-be-published author, and that *The Heart Stealer* would be made into a movie, they had ushered me into their world.

You're Ruby Crane, right? The writer? I heard about you. So what's up?

Hey, Ruby, come on over and sit here.

From the back of the cafeteria to the very front table. From the library to the student lounge. From the loneliness of obscurity to the dizzying rush of popularity.

I couldn't help remembering that chilly Tuesday afternoon in October when I'd cut class with Jessica and Diana to go shopping at Barneys. Laughing and telling each other to be quiet, we snuck past the security guards and then made a mad dash for the closed double doors. We ran down Amsterdam Avenue to Broadway and then along Central Park West. Breathless and giddy, we caught the crosstown bus and spent hours trying on clothes and shoes, comparing bags and scarves and accessories.

I couldn't help remembering that night in December, walking into the Junior Formal Dance on Damon Kurtz's arm, pausing by the bleachers to pose for pictures that would later be in the school newspaper. And afterward: stopping by Rockefeller Center with Amber and Lisa, Kelly Marie and Nicholas, the five of us huddling together as we drank hot chocolate and stared up at the glittering tree.

This was a year before the publication of *The Heart Stealer*, but it was the beginning of my new life, a golden time. Not yet famous to the world but famous in a way I'd never dreamed possible.

Shortly after the scandal broke, I e-mailed my friends one by one. None of my e-mails were answered.

I don't remember the date or even the exact time, but I was sitting in my room pretending to reorganize my closet when the courage came to me. I had been thinking about doing it since the very beginning, since that night at the American Literature Club. Wanting to hear that strong, familiar voice. Wanting to hear soothing words from the one person I stupidly believed might still care about me.

It was dark outside. I had turned the air conditioner up high to drown out the noise of traffic, but the noise in my head was too loud to ignore. So I snatched the cell phone from my desk drawer, flipped it open, and dialed the number.

He answered on the third ring.

"Jordan?" I said.

Silence.

I cleared my throat. I lowered myself slowly onto my bed. "Jordan, it's me—it's Ruby."

"Yeah," he replied quietly. "I know."

Three simple words falling from his lips, and my heart started hammering. "Um . . . what's going on?" I asked him. "I . . . I haven't heard from you and I know you've probably been afraid to call, but I didn't—"

"I haven't been afraid to call," he cut in briskly. "I just . . ."

"You what?"

He exhaled into the phone.

"I know what you're thinking," I said. "But really, it isn't true. Everybody's got it wrong. Everybody's—"

"Everybody's what? Making it up? The whole world's got it wrong?"

I heard the edge in his voice. I felt the pangs in my stomach. "It's just being blown out of proportion," I told him. "The media, the reporters."

"It's been really rough for me these past two weeks," he said coldly. "In school, I mean. It's like everybody thinks I knew about it. Knew that you plagiarized—"

"But it's not . . . like that," I said. I was clutching the phone hard and staring around my bedroom wildly. Trying to grasp at something—anything—that would make the words sound right.

"I just don't think it's a good idea," Jordan finally said.

"What's not a good idea?"

"Me and you. Together."

There it was—what I had been fearing, and what I should have expected all along. But in those desperate moments, common sense eluded me. "But why?" I said. "Don't you want to hear my side of it? What about the past few months?"

"It's just not the same now, Ruby." He sighed into the phone again. "I just don't feel the same way about things."

"But don't you want to hear my side of it?" I asked him again.

"No." His voice was firm, adamant. "I just don't know you anymore, Ruby. I don't *trust* you. And I can't be with someone I don't trust."

Before I could say anything else, he hung up. Before I

could gather my thoughts, the tears started flowing from my eyes.

Jordan Lush, the gorgeous guy who had swept me off my feet.

Jordan Lush, the sweet-talking boyfriend who couldn't get enough of my spotlight.

Jordan freakin' Lush, the celebrity hog who threw me out like a disco CD once there wouldn't be a movie premiere to attend the next year.

I shouldn't have been shocked, but I was. And then came the harshest realization of all: Jordan hadn't liked me for anything more than who I was on a book cover. He would never even have approached me or held my hand or kissed me without the glitz and glamour. Without my being Ruby Crane the Writer. And sitting there on my bed, more alone than I'd ever been, I learned that people really can cry themselves to sleep.

*　　*　　*

A sea of days. A cloud of silence. A world I couldn't escape.

In the mirror, I looked like the Ruby Crane who had autographed a copy of her first novel for a giddy English teacher. But inside, I felt like another person entirely. I had cried as much as I possibly could and submitted to more questions than someone on trial for murder.

Yes: of course I think plagiarism is wrong.

Yes: of course I recognize the suspicious similarities between my work and the work of novelist Adella Morgan.

Yes: I am sorry for the entire scandal.

Then why did you do it, Ruby?

I had no answer. And as far as I was concerned, I would never have an adequate answer. It *was* coincidental—to me, at least.

Why, Ruby?

They could have asked the question a million times, and still I wouldn't have had an answer.

And then there came the day—a Monday? a Saturday?—when I stared at the bookshelves that lined my bedroom walls and felt nothing but pure hatred for every last book in sight. In the world. Just like that, I had lost my passion for the very thing I had always been most passionate about. My lifelong love had come to an explosive end, and I alone had sparked the fire. There would be no more late-night reading binges, no more rainy afternoons spent lazing in the aisles of whatever bookstore.

I will never read another book for as long as I live. I will never speak of books ever again and I will never write another word.

It was a solemn promise. It was the only promise I could have made to myself.

June 25: the night I escaped.

I don't want to sound totally dramatic or crazy. I don't want anyone thinking I dug a tunnel out of my bedroom and climbed out onto First Avenue through a sewer drain. When I left, I did so with a sense of resolve. Maybe it was even peace. But, looking back, I think it was probably just desperation disguised as desire.

I'd had two solid weeks of chaos. Two weeks of grappling with a very personal—and very public—disaster. The newspapers and the television screens told one story, but the story I was living both physically and emotionally never made it into headlines. The loss of my friends, the loss of my boyfriend, the cold realization that they were never my friends and he was never my boyfriend in the first place. The psychological roller coaster that resulted from being famous one day and infamous the next.

Loved, then hated.

Respected, then shamed.

And all within a few short days.

Can you begin to imagine it? I don't think so. It's not something I would wish on my worst enemy. Not even on Samantha Golding.

Okay, maybe on Samantha Golding.

The point I'm trying to make is that when you screw up in front of your family or your friends or even a few complete strangers, you still have the priceless gift of being able to start over again. You still have anonymity. The lipstick you stole from the mall, the math test you cheated on, the kiss you snatched from your best friend's boyfriend—they might seem like big scandals while they're happening, but eventually, the people closest to you forget and life resumes its dreary old pattern. Your little transgressions won't make it into history books.

I didn't have the option to start over. I had screwed up

in front of the *entire world,* and my existence had become synonymous with failure. With creative thievery. And for someone who's always wanted to be a writer, there's no worse fate. People thought I was a sham—nothing but a bad imitation.

Plagiarism. Plagiarism. Plagiarism.

Sitting there in my bedroom, I tried to think about what my life would be like in five years, or even ten. Was there any hope of my getting into a good college? What about my first job interview? Can you imagine the cheap shots? *Oh, is this your essay or did you copy it from somewhere else? Ms. Crane, is this your résumé or are half these jobs stolen from someone else?*

It's not very far-fetched. People are mean.

And speaking of people, the only ones who still liked me were the ones who shared my DNA—and I wasn't entirely sure *they* wanted me around either. The scandal had wrought havoc on my parents' lives. Whenever the phone rang, they stared at each other for a good five seconds and three rings before one of them finally picked up the receiver. They were afraid of the reporters, the attorneys, the distant relatives calling to ask why their daughter had a cat turd for a brain. I think they were afraid most of all of being branded liars, losers, or cheaters too, as if plagiarism ran in the family as a dominant trait.

And I thought, *It's too much to bear. I can't handle it.*

I thought, *I can't stay here.*

It was midnight when my parents shut their bedroom door and drifted off to sleep. In the eerie silence, I tiptoed into the bathroom, showered, and then positioned myself directly in front of the mirror. I knew what I had to do. The tears dripped from my eyes like rain as I took a pair of shearing scissors from the medicine cabinet and cut off the long, wavy strands of my hair. I pulled and snipped until I had a boy's scraggly mop.

Next was my face. I chucked my contact lenses into the toilet and reached for my worn wire-rimmed glasses. When faint blotches rose on my skin, I didn't reach for my makeup.

Back in my bedroom, I ignored the designer clothes in my closet. Instead, I pulled on battered jeans and a wrinkled T-shirt and stepped into sneakers. The bag I packed contained a toothbrush, underwear, bras, socks, sunglasses, two pairs of jeans and a few shirts, and a picture of my parents. Half an hour later, armed with my ATM card, the tears still flowing from my eyes, I walked out of the apartment and out of the building. At the corner of Second Avenue and Sixty-fourth Street, I hailed a cab. It took all of ten minutes to reach the Port Authority Bus Terminal.

The gritty terminal didn't offer much comfort. After buying a one-way bus ticket north, I spotted a seat in one of the shadowy corners and sat down. Homeless people pushed shopping carts and dragged dirty plastic bags filled with cans. The minutes ticked by slowly, painfully, but I didn't think about heading back home.

Finally, the speakers above me crackled and a mechanical voice announced the 2:00 a.m. upstate express.

This is it, I told myself. *Ruby Crane, would-be writer and accused plagiarist, no longer exists.*

I walked toward the waiting bus and climbed up the little stairs. And I didn't cry as the bright lights of the city gave way to the inky blackness of the open highway and the strange promise of a new life.

The First Chapter of My Second Life

Whispering Oaks, New York, is not the kind of town you'd label a tourist attraction. Nestled in the foothills of the Adirondack Mountains, it's about the size of Manhattan and boasts a whopping population of 724 residents, most of whom have never set foot in a big city. The town prides itself on a rich history of pumpkin pie, apple cider, flannel shirts, and good old American values. It has two traffic lights, a diner, and a general store that stocks milk and ammunition in the same aisle.

I kid you not.

If you're going to hunt deer, you may as well kick back with a cold glass of milk, right?

It was dawn by the time the bus pulled into the empty parking lot behind the town's tallest building—a squat three-story brick-and-stucco structure that served as the town hall and the mayor's office. I stepped onto solid ground with wobbly feet and immediately reached into my bag and yanked out my shades. The sun was just beginning to send rays of light from the east. That early in the morning, the streets—and I'm not sure you could actually call them that—were deserted, save for a paperboy making his rounds on a rusted bicycle. The kid swerved by me without so much as a glance, then chucked a folded newspaper onto the steps of the building.

I ran for it and picked it up. Fortunately, it was a copy of the *Whispering Oaks Gazette,* not much thicker than a pamphlet. My eyes were blurry after several hours in the dark cabin of the bus, but I managed to skim the smattering of stories spread across the pages. The big news? The general store was receiving a fresh shipment of summer produce, and the post office had finally agreed to install a new mailbox on Main Street. Yawning, I left the paper where it was and tried to steer myself in the right direction.

I hadn't set foot in Whispering Oaks in more than two years. I remembered the small stretch of Main Street and the long dirt roads but not much else. I was too wired to let that bother me, though, and as I stood there in the rising sun, gazing out at the spindly treetops and listening to the grand silence, I felt the anxiety of the past two weeks melt slowly away. My scandal had been huge news, but I doubted that the headlines had been of interest to anyone here.

I walked out of the parking lot and around to the front of the building. I looked south. I looked north. I looked for a sign of life anywhere. There were power lines and more trees, and a trash can being assaulted by a raccoon. I decided to follow the paved concrete path to the next corner, where several simple houses sat baking in the hot sun. The front porches were empty. Cars sat idle in driveways. It was ten minutes before I reached the slightly familiar sight of Main Street and its ever-popular general store. Then I knew exactly where I was.

I walked the four full blocks to the corner of Cherry Pine Road and hung a right. The dead-end street was short and wide, and five steps in, the ground changed from concrete to dirt. No cherries. No pines. But the house at the very end of the cul-de-sac was what I'd been looking for. It was a whitewashed colonial with a picket fence and a lumbering weeping willow on the lawn. Blue shutters hung neatly over the windows. The grass was overgrown, the thick rosebushes looked downright dangerous, and the golden retriever sprawled out on the steps hadn't changed a bit.

For the first time in what seemed like years, I cracked a ghost of a smile.

Sensing my presence, the dog lifted her head and barked. Then she bounded down the steps and jumped at my knees. "Hi, Waffle," I said, crouching to scratch behind her ears. "How the hell are you?"

She stared up at me and wagged her tail.

I crossed the lawn and circled around to the backyard.

I could have been anywhere in the world and recognized the smell cutting a path through the humid air. Eucalyptus and juniper incense. I followed it until I came to a clearing in the messy brush. The yard had gotten more Zen in the two years since I'd last seen it. Rocks of all shapes and sizes created a long, winding path to a man-made reflecting pool, and dozens of crystals hung from tree branches, their sharp edges catching the sun's rays. As I dropped my bag, I saw Pancake, my favorite calico cat in the world, sunning himself by the wind chimes that were not, at the moment, chiming.

It was the strangest, freakiest, and warmest house I had ever known. And it could have been created by only one person on the face of the earth.

My aunt, Finny O'Dell, has never been . . . well . . . *normal.* I know there isn't a definitive example of what normal is, but everyone who's ever met Aunt Fin has come away a little shocked. She's eccentric. She's original. She's totally whacked-out. My mother's younger sister, Fin has long, curly, bright red hair that flows down to her waist, and smooth white skin dotted with freckles. There are always "things" in her hair—butterfly clips, handmade rubber bands, black ribbons stamped with leprechauns or wolves. She's even worn tiaras for no apparent reason.

That has everything to do with her being an artist, but sometimes even her "art" goes way beyond the scope of the imaginable. When she paints, her canvases have a tendency to combine beautiful landscapes with sketches of broken bones and dead rats. When she sculpts, the sculpture usually ends up looking half human, half aardvark. In recent years, she's become a New Age goddess of sorts. She reads tarot cards, conducts séances, casts spells, and then goes to church on Sundays. The day after I snagged my book deal, she called to tell me that she'd contacted the spirit of J.R.R. Tolkien, and that he loved the movie versions of *The Lord of the Rings*. Do you get where I'm going with this? I love Aunt Fin more than anything, but she's a few pages short of a chapter, if you know what I mean.

Like my mother, Aunt Fin was born and raised in New York City, but she moved up to Whispering Oaks shortly after her twenty-third birthday. I never really knew why. I still don't understand it. Why would anyone choose dirt roads over Madison Avenue? I grew up talking to her every week and visiting her most summers. Despite the distance between us, we've always shared a special bond.

And I knew she was the only person who would understand what I was going through.

I stepped deeper into the backyard and followed the thick trail of incense. Just behind the next bush was Aunt Fin. She was sitting cross-legged on the rutted ground, her eyes closed, her hands resting palms-up on her knees. Lost in meditation, she was wearing a bright blue kimono and a purple turban. Instead of calling the fashion police, I cleared my throat and said, "Hi, there."

Her nose twitched. "Oh, yes," she whispered without opening her eyes. "I can hear you, O great spirit of the cosmos. Speak. Speak."

"Aunt Fin," I called out, a little more loudly this time.

"You may call me what you wish, O ancient lord." She threw her head back, opened her mouth, and started chirping like a bird. "Speak. I am listening."

I leaned down until I was only a few inches from her face. "Aunt Fin!" I screamed.

She screamed too. But it was okay, because she finally opened her eyes and looked up at me. It took a moment for my face to register in her—oh, what's the right word?—*cloudy* mind. And when it did, she smiled broadly and jumped up.

"Hi," I said, pulling the sunglasses off my face.

"Ruby! Oh my God—honey!" She rushed forward and threw her arms around me. She squeezed. And squeezed. And rocked me from side to side as she spouted her usual slightly babyish jargon. "My honey-bunny, my sweetie-kiwi, my bright little angel sent from heaven . . . oh, how *are* you?"

I eased myself from her embrace and stared her directly in the eyes. Her expression was one of complete happiness, but it did little to calm the angst still boiling in my stomach. I heaved a sigh. I looked down. I started crying.

"Oh," she said, reaching into her kimono and yanking a handkerchief from her bra. "Oh, no. Oh, honey. Until this moment I'd completely forgotten what's going on. The scandal. I know. It's so terrible. I wasn't trying to pretend. I'm just so happy to see you." She dragged the handkerchief across my cheeks. "I called your mother just yesterday. And nearly every day before that too. Did she tell you I've been calling? She told me you've been too upset to speak with anyone. She told me . . ." Her voice trailed off.

I held my breath. Now for the shocker.

Aunt Fin glanced over my shoulders and around the yard. Then she peered into the bushes and down at the reflecting pool. "Honey, where's your mom?"

I bit my lip.

"Ruby, sweetheart . . . where are your parents?"

I could have said anything. I could've told her they were on a second honeymoon or a wilderness trek in Yosemite. I could've told her they'd been hired as bodyguards for Mickey Mouse. Instead, I told the truth. I had come that far and wasn't about to open a new can of worms. "They're home," I whispered.

"Home?"

"Yes."

"You mean . . . you got here by yourself?"

Sniffle. Hiccup. I nodded.

Aunt Fin's eyes widened. "You hitched a ride?" she asked in a hushed tone.

Sniffle. "I took the bus."

"Do your mom and dad know you're here? That you did this?"

Sniffle. Hiccup. Phlegm-in-my-throat cough. "No."

She gasped. "Ruby! You could've gotten yourself killed!" She came at me with the handkerchief again, running it over my cheeks and my chin. "Why didn't you call me? I would have driven to New York to pick you up if I'd known you wanted to come here. Or I would have at least sent you a spirit guide for protection. Oh, this is just awful. Awful."

I shook my head and took a step back. "Does that mean I can't stay?" I asked nervously. "If you're thinking of sending me back, forget it. I can't go back to the city. I can't go anywhere people might recognize me. I just *can't*."

She put her hands on her hips and frowned. The turban on her head moved a little to the left. "Of *course* you can stay here. You can stay as long as you like. But . . . Ruby . . . what on earth happened? Your book. How on earth did it . . . ?"

I hung my head and started crying again. "I don't know." I choked on the words. "I swear, Aunt Fin, it's not true. I didn't . . . I didn't . . ."

She hugged me again. "Of course you didn't. Of course not. And there's no point thinking about it now, anyway." She ran a finger over my cheek and touched the messy, chopped ends of my hair. "I guess that's why you did this to yourself, huh? You look different from that girl on TV, I'll tell you that much."

I buried my face in my hands.

Plagiarism. Plagiarism. Plagiarism.

Shut the hell up. Shut the hell up. Shut the hell up.

Aunt Fin gave me a sad smile. "Well, Ruby, if you want to start a new life, you've come to the right place. Whispering Oaks is that kind of town." She put her arm around my shoulder. "Welcome home, kiddo."

My mother screamed at me for the better part of an hour. She rattled on about how shattered her nerves were and how, when she'd woken up and realized I was missing, she'd assumed I'd been led from my bedroom at gunpoint by an intruder. Then she'd gotten *really* twisted and started thinking about all those people in Arizona and New Mexico who disappear in the middle of the night only to reappear days later claiming to have been abducted by aliens.

As I held the phone to my ear, I kind of wished aliens would beam *her* up. Just for a few days.

My father was cool about my escape. From what he let on, that is. He was standing somewhere in the background, saying, "Let her be, Anne. She has a lot to think about. Let's be thankful she's safe."

But my mother wasn't hearing it. Between gasps and gulps, she told me that she was getting in her car and coming up to get me. She said the biggest lesson I had to learn was that sixteen-year-old girls couldn't just get up in the middle of the night and take buses toward Canada.

I was about to tell her to blow it out her ziplock bag when Aunt Fin grabbed the phone.

"Now, you listen here, O sister of mine," she snapped at my mother. "Ruby's here because she needs to restore both her sanity and her spirit. She's safe. She's sound. Now, if you want, I'll send you some Saint-John's-wort tea to ease those nerves of yours, but otherwise—"

She paused in midsentence, and I heard my mother chattering in a high-pitched voice. She went on like that for a good two minutes.

Aunt Fin looked at me and rolled her eyes as she listened. Then she raked a hand through her red hair and said forcefully, "Damn you, Anne. If you show up here like some crazed loon, I swear, I'll send phantom elves your way. They'll bite at you until you itch, and you'll have to spend the next month in an oatmeal bath. Do you hear me? *Do* you? Ruby's in good hands, and it's a good time for her to be away from home—the moon is in Pisces." She sighed. "Yes. Okay. Yes. Fine. I love you too." She slammed the phone down.

From the look on Aunt Fin's face, I knew I'd be staying. I also understood my mother's sudden change of heart: phantom elves would freak me out too.

Sighing with relief, I leaned back on the couch and stared around the living room. It was cute—in an eerie sort of way. The walls were red, the floors hardwood. Every corner was occupied and . . . well . . . *glowing:* candles to the left, twinkling white lights to the right, a life-size mermaid lamp in front of me, and what looked like a neon Ouija board just behind my shoulders. Plants hung from the ceiling. Bunches of small candy dishes—all of them filled with different charms and crystals, not candy—sat on the bamboo coffee table, on the end table, at the foot of the stairs leading to the second floor. Both Waffle and Pancake apparently knew not to dine on the trinkets; they sniffed briefly, then skirted the colorful displays and hopped up onto the couch.

I liked the house. It was a good size but not large by any means. If it had been owned by anyone other than Aunt Fin, it probably would have looked like a typical Whispering Oaks box—fading white paint, cracked shingles, weeds overgrowing the lawn. But Aunt Fin had her own style. The house was a country abode, yet it had character and even a little charm. Which, of course, made the thought of staying there for an extended period of time a little more bearable.

Upstairs, I unpacked my bag in the small guest bedroom and dropped onto the lumpy bed. The big window in the corner soaked up the morning light. The view was pretty, I guess, with tall oak trees and evergreens and the Adirondack peaks glistening in the distance. Sitting there, I kept waiting for the silence to be shattered in customary Manhattan fashion. But sirens didn't pierce the air, nor did the sounds of skidding cabs or a dozen barking dogs. Rising just above the whistle of the summer breeze was a chorus of birds. I listened as attentively as possible, all the while trying to convince myself that I would make it there, that my new life in a small town would somehow prove successful.

The only problem was that I didn't have a clue what to do. I mean, people in the country aren't exactly on the move. What went on in a place like this day after day? Would I be spending my time planting apple trees and mowing the lawn? Was I supposed to wait at the edge of the woods for Bambi to show up? My walk from the bus stop to Aunt Fin's house had been short, but other than the paperboy I hadn't seen a single soul, let alone another teenager. Were there more than six in the whole damn town? Did they know about anything other than plant fertilizer, hunting season, and hay bales? Don't get me wrong; making friends and creating a social life weren't priorities. I was just hoping to spot at least *one* person my age in town.

So, I thought, staring around the bedroom. Home. New life. A place where, hopefully, no one knew my name or what it was synonymous with. I stood up and checked my reflection in the mirror mounted above the bureau. It was true. I looked totally different from the girl in the author photo. Totally different from the girl in that video clip, the girl being slammed by Samantha Golding. I had cut my hair sloppily, and the result was, well, fairly country bumpkin. I wouldn't have a problem blending in with the townsfolk. Whether I'd have a problem blending in with the town itself remained to be seen.

I showered in the small bathroom, rubbing away at the sweat and grime of the seven-hour bus trip. I smelled like stale potato chips and coffee. Standing beneath the weak jets of hot water, I thought about my bathroom back home in the city, with its clean white tiles, fountain sink, and claw-foot tub. None of that was here. The walls were mottled shades of pink, and about six feet of space stretched between the bathroom door and the standing shower. Within two minutes of my turning on the faucets, the air had become thick and cloudy and muggy. And the organic no-frills soap Aunt Fin bought felt like a piece of leather in my hands.

Oh, joy.

When I walked back into the bedroom, swathed in a towel, I found Aunt Fin rummaging around. She was dropping potpourri into drawers and sprinkling some sort of aromatic powder over the floor. It smelled like bananas.

"This is to ward off negativity," she said without looking at me. "There's been a lot of that around you lately."

No shit.

I sat down on the bed and started running my fingers through my damp hair. Aunt Fin had changed her clothes: out with the kimono and the turban and in with bell-bottom floral-print blue jeans and a white shirt with huge ruffled cuffs. A black fedora sat on top of her head, and her hair was flowing down to her waist.

She turned around and stared at me. "Hurry up," she said. "Get dressed. I don't like to be late."

My eyes widened. "For what?"

"Work."

"Work?" I shook my head. "I don't have a job here, Aunt Fin, remember?"

"Well, you have a job now." She smiled and put her hands on her hips. "You're coming to work with me. You can't just sit around and mope and hide from the world. Life goes on."

"My life as I knew it is over," I told her. "So life does not go on. I need time to rest and settle myself. I'm still afraid people will recognize me."

"You'll be safe with me. End of discussion. Now get ready!" She clapped her hands and turned to leave.

"Wait," I yelled, standing up. "Aunt Fin, you have to remember; I'm here to try to start a new life, to forget about my old one. We have to come up with a story. People can't know I'm your niece, because they might make the connection. When the book deal happened last year, you mentioned it to people around here, didn't you?"

She bit down on her lip. "I probably did. Here and there. I was proud of you."

"That's what I mean. You have to forget about calling me Ruby. I need a new name, got it?"

She frowned. "Well, what in the goddess's name am I supposed to call you?"

I grabbed a pair of jeans and a T-shirt from my bag. "I don't know," I said. "But definitely not *Ruby*. Okay? Ruby is gone from the world. Vanished. Done. Ruby Crane no longer exists. Understand?"

I knew exactly who I *wasn't*. I just had no idea who I was about to become.

The Curious Cup

East of Main Street, on Star River Road—no stars, no river—sat the Curious Cup, Aunt Fin's coffee shop/curios store. The only establishment of its kind in Whispering Oaks, the Curious Cup was fairly big, and it served two purposes: the first was to sell coffee, tea, and assorted muffins freshly baked every day; the second was to sell . . . well . . . *curios*. I'm not talking small knickknacks for the coffee table; I'm talking works of art—paintings from local artists, handmade jewelry, sculptures crafted from wood and clay, crystal figurines, Native American dream catchers, and an assortment of New Age items. Customers came in either to grab a cup of coffee or to shop for a gift. While cruising the aisles or trying on that gorgeous lapis lazuli necklace, they could munch on muffins and—on Tuesdays and Thursdays—cinnamon scones. After getting that sugar fix, they had the rare opportunity to purchase herbs, stones, and incense sticks that would aid them in the casting of love spells.

Not sure what gift to buy for Grandma? There's no rush! Have another cup of coffee and take your time deciding. Technically, the Curious Cup didn't have a specific closing time. Aunt Fin made it a habit to hang out while customers considered their selections. Sometimes that meant eating dinner right at the front counter—coffee and a leftover muffin, of course—instead of heading home at a reasonable hour.

You can imagine my face when *that* bit of news was broken to me. I mean, get real.

Complaints aside, I liked the Curious Cup. It had been in business for five years and had become a fixture in the town. People enjoyed the mix of the simple and the esoteric. There had never been anything like it in the town's stale history, and customers ran the gamut from bored housewives and old ladies to young newlywed couples and teenagers my own age. Don't get me wrong; there weren't any crowds lined up down the street waiting to get inside, but Aunt Fin did turn a profit every year.

The Curious Cup was a white-shingled ranch house that had long before been converted for commercial use. Nearby were a real estate agency—though I couldn't imagine it making more than three cents a month—a yarn store, a mechanic, and a hot dog and beer joint that moon-lighted as a bridal salon in winter months. Yes, you read that correctly.

The Curious Cup was by far the most interesting place on the quiet lot. Its front door was decorated with gold and blue trim, and colored lights hung in long strands down the front windows. One particularly large pane of glass was frosted in the shape of a crescent moon. Inside, the scarred wood floors opened up directly to the front counter, which stretched ten feet across; barstools and three small tables invited customers to sit their butts down. So the coffee shop part resembled a coffee shop. Yay. Beyond it, however, was an entirely different world. Five paces past the muffin tray, you were standing in an en-chanted forest or a forgotten corner of the magic kingdom of Narnia from *The Lion, the Witch and the Wardrobe.* Four short aisles held the curio items. Crystals and gems sparkled beneath the hanging bulbs, and the hardwood changed to black carpet in the blink of an eye. On the ceil-ing was a mural of the ocean meeting the purple twilit sky. In the intricate design, I spotted the Greek goddess Artemis holding a bow and arrow.

"Wow," I said, standing in the middle of the floor. "You've really done a lot in here since the last time I visited."

"A whole lot," Aunt Fin agreed. "Business has been good. I'm glad you like it." She disappeared into a back room, then came out holding two aprons. She put one on and tossed the other to me.

Ugh. A stinky, stained apron. I stared down the front of

it—fading yellow and red patchwork, my friends—and nearly barfed.

"Don't just stand there," Aunt Fin said. "Don't you know how to make coffee?" She pointed to the three huge machines sitting just behind the counter. "First one is regular, second is decaf, third is special blend."

"What's the special blend?" I asked, pulling the apron over my head.

She smiled. "A secret. It's sort of a hazelnut-cinnamon-chocolate infusion with special powers."

"Can you elaborate on that?"

"I only use water that I've charged beneath the moon, and you'll find it in one of the clear jugs beneath the counter."

I wanted to ask her what the shit that meant, but I merely shook my head and started brewing the coffee. I was feeling weak and sluggish and sad. More than anything, I wanted to head back to my little bedroom and go to sleep. And then the strangest thing happened. I popped open the silver canister that held the special-blend coffee grounds, I caught a whiff, and I experienced the most powerful surge of energy on the planet. It was like a jolt of electricity to my brain. I shook my head as the blood in my veins started pumping.

"Aunt Fin!" I called out. "What the hell *is* this stuff?"

She poked her head out of the back room, where she was busy preparing muffin mix. "Why? You don't like it?"

"It's amazing!" I told her. "In like one second flat, I got totally awake."

She smiled. "Just wait till you drink a cup. That's the power of Mother Earth, Ruby."

I shot her a mean look. "Why did you just call me that? I told you—"

"I know, I know—new name." She rolled her eyes. "We'll think of something."

For the next twenty minutes, I watched the coffee machines perk to life while I dragged a mop across the floor. Then I went into the back room, which was a neatly kept combination of stocking shelves and kitchen. Two stainless steel stoves occupied the farthest corner, and beside them was a deep sink. The other three-quarters of the room held dozens of cardboard boxes in all shapes and sizes. As Aunt Fin worked her magic on the muffins—corn, blueberry, and orange blossom—I started rummaging through the boxes. The packing slips were interesting: they had return addresses from India and Egypt, Morocco and New Zealand. Until that moment, I hadn't known that half the merchandise was shipped from overseas. The newest batch of religious objects was from Medjugorje, a small town in the former Yugoslavia; the multitude of sparkling rosary beads and angel figurines was beautiful.

"You like?" Aunt Fin asked over her shoulder.

"These are awesome," I said. "How do you choose this stuff? It's all so . . . great."

" 'It is art that makes life, makes interest, makes importance . . . and I know of no substitute whatever for the force and beauty of its process.' " She folded her arms across her batter-stained apron and stared at me smugly. "Who said that?"

"Henry James," I replied automatically.

"Yes! That's my girl! I *knew* you'd know!"

Hello? Until two weeks before, I'd been a total book freak. Of course I knew. But that didn't make me feel any better. I shrugged and went back to perusing the boxes.

And that was when my heart stopped.

At the very bottom of the first stack was a big rectangular box, and through its open flaps I caught sight of a book. No. Not *a* book. About two dozen of them.

A box of books.

Hardcovers, paperbacks, shiny jackets and horrible words such as *New York Times Bestselling Author* and *The National Bestseller.*

Books, goddamn it. Books!

Exactly what I never wanted to look at again for as long as I lived.

Seeing them there—and recognizing the names of several popular authors—made my blood boil. What the *hell* was *this* all about?

I whirled around. "Aunt Fin!"

She turned. "Yes, girl-without-a-name."

I pointed down at the box. "What the hell are those doing here?"

At first she looked confused. Her eyes went from the shiny paperbacks to me, then back to the paperbacks. But realization finally dawned on her, and she bit down on her lip. "Oh, darn. I'd forgotten about that."

"About what?"

"Oh, Ruby, I know this is going to suck, but . . . well . . .

last month, long before this whole scandal happened, I decided to start selling books. Not a whole lot of them—just the really popular ones."

I scowled, and I didn't bother to hide it.

"The nearest Barnes and Noble is over an hour away, by Fredonia, and I wanted to offer my customers as much variety as I could. I *swear* I'd forgotten about it."

More scowling. "Where are the copies of my book? I know you ordered some."

"I did." She wiped her hands on her apron. "They must be in one of those boxes off to the left. I . . . I was planning to do a whole display. I . . ."

"Well . . . just *forget* it!" I screamed. "I don't want to see copies of my book, not ever again. So get rid of them!"

"Oh, honey, I know." She took the fedora off her head and wiped the sweat from her brow. "I'll take care of it. I promise. Please don't be upset. You won't even have to ring up any of these other books. Is that okay?"

Like, no, lady—it's not okay. But what other choice did I have? I stormed out of the back room as the coffeepots started hissing.

* * *

The first customer of the day walked into the shop at exactly 10:00 a.m. I was standing by the coffee machines, counting change in the cash register, when the door opened with a whoosh. It was such a deliberately powerful pull, so noisy and forceful, that I jumped back. The sudden rush of air sent the pile of napkins on the counter flying to the floor.

The girl who stepped into the store was short and scrawny and slightly impish. She was dressed in blue shorts and a white tank top, and her blond hair fell to her shoulders in a blunt bob. The expression on her face was intense, almost hostile. And behind huge outdated black glasses were the beadiest eyes I had ever seen.

I stared at her from my place behind the counter. In those few silent moments, I didn't know whether to smile or to fling a blueberry muffin at her and make my escape.

She didn't move. She didn't even blink. She just stood there, looking like Dirty Harriet on crack. Then, all of a sudden, she scratched her head and said, "Hi."

"H-hi," I stammered. I hadn't realized how tense she'd made me. My hands were balled into fists at my sides, and a lump had sprouted in my throat. But in an instant, all the tension left me. Her voice was thin and mousy—harmless. And when I studied her more closely, I saw the pimples on her cheeks and the two buckteeth jutting over her lower lip. She was about my age, give or take a year.

Just then, Aunt Fin came out of the back room, wiping her hands on a dish towel. She took one look at the girl and smiled. "Hi, Rabbit!" she said cheerily.

Rabbit?

"Oh, hi, Finny," the girl said with a sigh, as if relieved.

Like Bugs Bunny? Or the Easter rabbit who drops eggs in the grass? Hello?

"You opened up a little later today, huh?" the girl asked.

"Just a little," Aunt Fin replied. "Get you your usual?"

Rabbit? What kind of a mean joke was that?

"Sure," the girl said. She turned her eyes toward me again and stared.

"Oh dear!" Aunt Fin exclaimed, slapping a hand to her forehead. "Here I am, standing around like everything's the same, when of course it's not." She came over and put a hand on my shoulder. "Rabbit, this is my nie—"

I poked her gently in the ribs.

"—*nice* cousin, Rrrrrr—"

I gave her left foot a stomp.

"—rrroom. I . . . uh . . . *room* temperature is bad in here today, isn't it?" She made a pretense of fanning herself.

Rabbit watched the odd exchange without flinching.

"So stuffy, so humid." Aunt Fin cleared her throat nervously. "Sorry. I just hate it when the air-conditioning is slow. Anyway, Rabbit, like I was saying, this is my cousin."

"Hi," Rabbit said again.

"Hi," I said again. "I . . . I guess it was weird coming in and seeing me standing here, huh?"

She shrugged. "A little. It was kind of a shock. Thought maybe Finny had sold the place without telling anyone."

"Nah, no chance of that happening." I walked to the edge of the counter, feeling somewhat less awkward. Beside me, Aunt Fin was pouring the special-blend coffee into a Styrofoam cup. "Um, so is there anything else I can get you? I mean, besides the coffee and whatever else Finny is getting for you?"

Rabbit took a step toward me. The intense stare and the rigid posture had left her. With her thumb, she jammed her big glasses further up the bridge of her nose. "Nah, I usually stick to my routine."

"Cool," I said.

She cocked her head to one side. "So, you got a name?"

I felt my hands ball up again. The question was innocent and very normal, but it hit me with the force of a fist. I froze and for a single moment wondered if she had a microphone hidden somewhere beneath her shirt. Or if behind her seemingly harmless disposition lived a psycho-bitch like Samantha Golding.

"Here we go!" Aunt Fin called out, jumping to the rescue. She put the cup of coffee down on the counter and winked at Rabbit. "Special-blend coffee, like always. And I even added a little incantation while I was pouring it for you. Your energy levels should be up all day long."

"Thanks." Rabbit dropped a dollar bill on the counter. Now her brow furrowed suspiciously. "Aren't you gonna finish the introduction, Finny? I still don't know your cousin's name."

Strike one, I thought. *This girl already knows something is wrong here.*

"Oh!" Aunt Fin said. "How silly of me. Rabbit, please meet my cousin . . ." Her eyes searched the walls and the floor and the ceiling desperately. She was looking for a clue. Then her gaze landed on the one-dollar bill sitting on the counter, George Washington's face staring at us. "Georgie!" she blurted. "Yes! My cousin, Georgie."

I forced my lips into a smile. A *totally fake* smile, I should add. Georgie? *Georgie?* Was I suddenly a cousin of

Elsie the cow? Why couldn't I be Tiffany or Lindsay or Paris? I mean, *really. . . .*

Rabbit shot me another look. This time it softened quickly, and I saw a glimmer in her eyes. "Nice to meet you, Georgie. What grade you in?"

"I, uh . . . I just finished my sophomore year."

"I just finished my freshman year. It sucked. But then again, what else would you expect in a town like this?" She guzzled some of the coffee. "Oh, wow. This stuff is *strong* today. I swear, if it wasn't for this magical blend stuff, I would've never passed algebra. It's my worst subject."

"Mine too." As the tension seeped out of my body, I found myself inching closer to the counter again.

Aunt Fin, breathing a sigh of what I knew had to be relief, turned toward the back room. "You know where to find me if you need me, *Georgie.* See you later, Rabbit."

My eyes narrowed at Aunt Fin. I gave her one of those we'll-talk-about-this-tonight looks.

"Later, Finny." Rabbit leaned over the counter and drank more of the coffee. Despite the strangeness of the past few minutes, she seemed comfortable and at ease just hanging out. Unlike me, she wasn't self-conscious. She didn't seem to care whether I liked her either.

But I *did* like her. I liked that she wasn't a snob or an introvert. And I liked that she was totally bizarre. "So . . . is Rabbit your real name?"

"No, my parents weren't *that* nuts. My real name is Wilma. Wilma Dooney. But everyone's called me Rabbit since I was a little kid." She glanced at her watch. "Eh, damn. I'm gonna be late. I work part-time on Main Street, at the general store. You been in there yet?"

I shook my head. "What do you do there?"

"Bullshit. Cashier, floor sweeper, salesclerk. Whatever keeps old man Watson out of my hair." She picked up the cup. "You should stop in later on. I'll be there till six tonight."

"I'll try," I said. "I'll be here till whatever time."

She started toward the door, then stopped and looked at me. "If you get bored later, me and a few of my friends are getting together down by Lake Redson tonight. Ya know, just to hang out and stuff. Not much to do here otherwise."

I nodded so as not to be rude. Hanging out with a bunch of other teenagers was exactly what I *didn't* need. As nonchalantly as possible, I said, "Thanks. Maybe if I have the time, I'll try to find my way to Lake Redson."

"I'll come by Finny's place tonight and pick you up," she replied matter-of-factly. Then Rabbit pushed the owlish glasses up on her nose and yanked the door open with a thundering whoosh. In the next instant, she was gone.

Over the River,
Through the Woods

"It'll be good for you," Aunt Fin said.

We were standing in the kitchen, feeding Waffle and Pancake—they liked being fed by hand—and arguing about my plans for the night.

The plans *I* didn't want to go through with.

The plans *I* had never agreed to.

I liked Rabbit's direct approach to forming new friendships, but I felt as if my privacy had been invaded. What if I had more important things on my agenda? What if I just wanted to do cartwheels in my underwear all night? I mean, do you go around telling strangers you'll pick them up three minutes after meeting them?

I fed Waffle the last of a beef biscuit and reached for another. "Don't you think I should be the one to decide what's good for me?" I said to Aunt Fin's back as she rinsed lettuce in the sink. "I'm tired. I'm upset. I didn't come here to create a social life. I came here to hide, remember?"

"Rabbit's a nice kid, and she's got a brain," Aunt Fin replied. "I know she can be a little pushy, but that's just her way. And eventually, Ruby—I mean, Georgie—you're going to end up meeting people in this town no matter how long you stay or how much you want to live beneath the radar. It's inevitable. I think the fact that it's happened so soon is a good thing."

"But I haven't even been here twenty-four hours!"

"Life—the universe, the cosmos—doesn't think about time. Certain things just happen, and you just have to go with the flow."

I sighed. "What the shit does that mean?"

Aunt Fin dropped the bunch of lettuce leaves onto a paper towel and turned to look at me. "It means that you're going to Lake Redson with Rabbit tonight, because there's a reason for your going. And watch your mouth, Georgie. I don't like the brown word."

"Well, just so you know: I happen to *feel* like the brown word." I looked away, not wanting her to see how watery my eyes had suddenly gotten. I shook the second biscuit in Waffle's face, hoping he'd eat the damn thing faster. The new me: full-time cashier and part-time dog feeder. Talk about a lofty life.

Aunt Fin started to mix a salad dressing that looked

like a cross between seaweed and sewer water. "I know you're in a negative state of mind because of all that's happened," she said. "But moving to a new place to start a new life means forgetting your old one. Or at least trying to forget it. No one here will recognize you or bring up that silly scandal. You're Georgie O'Dell now, right? Not Ruby Crane? Well, then, go out there and find out who Georgie is. Maybe she'll like hanging out at Lake Redson with other teenagers her own age. Maybe she'll like getting to know new people."

And maybe I'll win the Pulitzer Prize for fiction tomorrow. I wanted to tell Aunt Fin that her little speech was as worthless as a burp, but that would've been just plain mean, and she didn't deserve a sassy response. I held my scowl in place. Then I went to the freezer and pulled out the pint of strawberry ice cream I'd picked up on the way home. I tore it open with a grunt and grabbed a spoon from the counter.

"That's really not a healthy dinner," Aunt Fin said. She gathered her lettuce leaves in a deep bowl and poured the yucky dressing over them.

I plunged the spoon into the pint, then brought it to my mouth. "Georgie O'Dell doesn't mind having a big old butt," I told her sarcastically.

*   *   *

Rabbit showed up precisely at 7:00. She banged on the front door and smiled when I opened it.

"Hey," I said.

"How's it going?" She was dressed in the same drab clothes, and she pushed her glasses up on her nose in what I realized was a trademark gesture.

"Do you want to come inside?" I was hoping she'd say yes and we'd end up drinking coffee or soda on the couch instead of hanging out with a group of people who might make me nervous—who might recognize me or start asking too many questions.

But she shook her head. "I'm allergic to cats," she said. "I love Pancake and all, but if I get within a foot of her, I'll start sneezing. It's one of those things that come with the total nerd package."

I didn't know what to say to that. It made me feel kind of sorry for her. In all honesty, Rabbit *did* fit that nerd/geek stereotype. With her big glasses and buckteeth, she was pretty much the poster girl for it. I'm not saying that in a mean way. I'm merely stating a fact. I had known girls like her back home in Manhattan, and life hadn't exactly been easy for them. The teasing, the cruel jokes. The only difference between them and Rabbit was that Rabbit had an air of confidence about her, an edge that made her seem anything but vulnerable. I wondered if it was a natural part of her personality or a trait she had acquired as a result of a rough childhood.

I grabbed my Yankees cap from the couch and pulled it down backward over my head, letting a few jagged strands of hair stick out. "I'm leaving!" I screamed to Aunt Fin. "G'bye!"

She hurried out of the kitchen a moment later. "Have

fun," she said to me. "Don't do anything crazy." Then she fixed her eyes on Rabbit. "Georgie's curfew is the same as yours, okay?"

Rabbit nodded. "No problem. We're only going to the lake; then we'll be back."

We ran down the front steps and across the lawn. It wasn't until we reached the corner of Main Street that I realized we'd be walking to Lake Redson and not using some modern mode of transport . . . like, say, a bus or a car. Given the humidity, I wouldn't even have minded riding on the back of a deer. But no: off on foot we went.

"Um, hey, Rabbit?" I broke the silence. "How far is the lake?"

"A couple of miles."

I stopped walking and stared at her. *"Miles?"*

"Yeah, why?" She stared back at me. "Is that too much? It really isn't as far as it sounds. We'll take a shortcut."

I wiped the sweat from my brow, then followed in step with her.

"So, are you from New York City, like Finny?" she asked.

I felt my stomach knot. "Yes," I said after a long, uncertain pause. "I am."

"Wow, that's awesome. I've always wanted to go down to the city, to Manhattan. I hear it's wild."

"It is." Looking around at the meager expanse of Main Street, at the hulking treetops and dirt roads, I felt my first pang of homesickness. I never thought it would be possible to miss concrete and smog, screeching taxis and the drone of helicopters. But there I was, standing in a perfectly peaceful country setting, wishing for urban chaos not even twenty-four hours after leaving it.

"So, how long are you staying here?" Rabbit asked.

Good question. "I'm not sure," I told her. "Maybe the whole summer."

"Oh, cool. Then you'll totally become one of *us*." She laughed.

So did I. "What's that mean?"

"A crazy small-towner, I guess. You'll get used to the ordinary and slow grind. It'll be pretty hard for you, being from the city and all, but it's possible. Finny got used to it. So did my dad."

"Your dad's from the city?"

"Boston, not New York. But still. He came here when he was twenty and just stayed 'cause he met my mom."

"So you've been here your whole life, I guess."

She made a sour face. "That's the sad truth. Most of the families in Whispering Oaks have been here for generations."

"But where does everybody work?" I asked. "I mean, there aren't many places in this town."

"You're right about that. My mom works ten miles over in the next town, Derryville, which is a really industrial place. Lots of factories and garages and crap like that. She works in a food factory. My dad manages the supermarket on Main Street."

"You have any brothers or sisters, or are you an only child too?"

"One brother. Older. His name's Nick. He's a freshman

in college, in Rhode Island. I miss him sometimes. Not all the time, but sometimes."

I nodded as we continued walking. The sweat was pouring so thickly down the sides of my face I didn't bother to wipe it. The stretch of Main Street had fallen away behind us, and now we were hanging a right past the bus stop and the town hall. Ahead of us was the beginning of the forest. I gulped when I saw that massive wall of green.

But Rabbit headed straight toward it. "This is the shortcut," she said. "Just follow me."

"Are you sure?" My voice cracked.

"Yeah. I do it all the time. I know it looks a little scary, but trust me, it isn't."

It looked more than scary. It looked, in fact, like the beginning of a jungle: towering trees, mounds of wild bushes, branches high above that stretched and tangled until they closed the sky's path. The moment we stepped into the brush, the soft light of early evening dissipated and an eerie darkness swam over us.

"We call this the Whispering Woods," Rabbit said, shoving at leaves and shaking pine needles from her shirt. "Partly because of the name of the town, but also because of the legends."

"What kinds of legends?" I shoved a huge spiderweb out of my way and, grossed out, swatted at the mosquitoes buzzing around my face.

"Oh, ya know, the usual creepy kinds," Rabbit said offhandedly.

Given that we were traipsing through shadowy woods

just an hour before sundown, I didn't want to hear anything particularly creepy, usual or not. I kept one eye on Rabbit's back and the other on the slick, rutted ground.

"Sometimes late at night, if you're walking down by the end of Main Street, you can hear whispers coming from these woods," Rabbit continued. "Like, totally real voices. It's creepy."

I gulped. That was all I needed to make my stay in Whispering Oaks complete: disembodied voices. I said, "It sounds like it's probably just the wind in the trees."

"Maybe. Maybe not."

Suddenly, the woods gave way to a clearing, and we were standing in a small open field dotted with daisies. The sky reappeared. So did the soupy light. The contrast was so striking I gasped.

"Hey," I said, "this is really pretty. Is this, like, a picnic area?"

"Ha! Don't you wish! People here don't come into the woods to picnic; we do it in our backyards because we have so much land. My mom usually has a big summer picnic at our house in July. You're totally invited, by the way." Her voice echoed in the surrounding woodland.

"I am?"

She looked at me, and her lips curved in a slight surprised smile. "Sure. Why do you sound so shocked? We're friends, aren't we?"

Somewhere behind us, branches rattled.

I looked up at the sky as dusk began its descent in the west. I wondered how on earth we were ever going to get back to Main Street come nightfall, but I didn't bother voicing my concern. There was something about Rabbit that I trusted. I realized it right then, as we stood in the clearing in the middle of nowhere. Until that moment, I'd been reluctant to think of her as a possible friend. Maybe I was even suspicious of her motives. But that was the New York girl in me. Back home in the city, my every thought for the past year had centered on how I looked, how I sounded, how I acted, how I walked into the cafeteria at the beginning of fifth period. I'd been obsessed with other people's opinions of me and convinced that those opinions had the power to make or break me. But none of that seemed to matter here in Whispering Oaks. Or, at least, it didn't matter to Wilma Dooney, aka Rabbit. In fact, I felt more secure with her than I ever had with the people I'd thought were my friends.

"Y-yeah," I stammered. "We're totally friends."

"You okay?" she asked. "You're not scared or anything, are you? Being here in the woods?"

I shook my head. "No, no. I'm fine. I guess I'm just not used to things here yet, that's all."

She frowned. "That's my fault. You probably think I'm nuts for being so friendly and all, but that's just how I am. That's how most of us are here in town. It's our way, I guess you could say. When I saw you this morning in Finny's shop, you looked kinda scared, out of sorts. I don't blame you for that. I'd be scared coming to a new place too. I just hope you don't feel like I'm rushing you into anything, or being a pain in the ass."

I felt a bubble of guilt well up in my chest. All those crazy thoughts I'd had about her that day . . . "No," I said again, "I'm fine. Everything's cool. I . . . I really appreciate you . . . ya know . . . being the way you are. Friendly."

It was a mushy, girly, Hallmark kind of moment. I half expected Rabbit to hug me, or Bambi to trot by us in the grassy clearing. But neither happened.

Another big rustling of branches snapped us both back to reality.

I spun around and saw a figure striding through the woods—a tall, big-bellied man dressed in jeans, work boots, and a blue T-shirt. He had gray hair and little eyes. In one hand he held what appeared to be a walking stick; in the other was an ax.

You can imagine what went through my mind. Small town. Big woods. Crazy man with a sharp object.

We're totally dead.

Before I could gasp, Rabbit shot the man a stare and crinkled her nose. "Ugh," she said, coming close to me. "That's Frank Canker, probably the most hated person in town. He and his wife, Nancy, own just about everything—from the factory my mom works in to the general store to the building Finny's shop is in. And everything in between. They're gross, mean people. And they're slave drivers."

"Slave drivers?"

"Yeah. He works all his employees to the bone, cheats them out of overtime, and skimps on giving them good health insurance." She curled her lip in disgust as she stared at him. "He's just a big pig."

"So he's going to chop us up into a million little pieces?"

I asked, my voice tinged only slightly with sarcasm. The rest of my tone was serious.

"I doubt it," Rabbit said. "But someone should knock him in the head with a blunt object soon. I can't imagine what he's doing walking through the woods. He's such a weirdo."

To me, Frank Canker looked like a middle-aged man who exercised too much with a fork and a spoon. Minus the ax, he would've appeared pretty usual. But we were two girls in a secluded area, and I didn't like the vibe I was getting.

Rabbit read my mind. She cocked her head and said, "Let's get going. It's only about another mile to the lake."

I took one step and heard a huge twig snap beneath my foot. The sound echoed everywhere.

Frank Canker turned and saw us. And practically growled. "What are you kids doing here?" he shouted from across the clearing, and came toward us.

My stomach bounced into my throat. I was about to say *We're leaving right now, don't be upset, that's a lovely shirt you're wearing and please don't chop our heads off,* but Rabbit didn't give me the chance.

"*Excuse me?*" she shouted back, planting both hands on her hips.

Frank Canker stopped about three feet from us. Sweat dripped from his forehead, and up close, he looked a lot like a pit bull. There was something cradled in the crook of his left arm—a poster or a thick sheet of paper. "You heard me, young lady. What are you doing here?"

Rabbit gasped. Her contempt for the man was coming

off her in waves. "I'm taking a goddamn walk!" she shouted. "You got a problem with that, Canker?"

"You watch your mouth, Wilma Dooney." He pointed at her with the walking stick. The ax, thank goodness, remained still at his side.

"Don't tell me what to do, old man."

"I should have the right mind to tell your momma about that sassy mouth of yours."

"Go ahead and tell her!" Rabbit shot back. "You think I'm afraid of you?" She shoved her glasses up on her nose with a grunt.

Maybe you're not afraid, I thought. *But I am.*

"Just for your information," she continued, "you don't *own* the woods, Canker. Anyone can walk in here. Did I ask *you* what *you're* doing here?"

Frank Canker didn't like Rabbit's attitude. He flushed a vibrant shade of red and shook the stick at her. "One day, Dooney, that smart mouth of yours is gonna get you into a lot of trouble! Now, I demand to know what you're doing here!"

"And I demand that you shut up!" she screeched back.

Frank Canker gasped, and his little eyes widened. The thing beneath his arm fluttered to the ground. "I'm not kidding, Dooney! First thing tomorrow morning, I'm gonna tell your momma what a disrespectful thing you are! Talking to your elders that way! Talking to *me* that way!"

Rabbit, undaunted and unmoved, twisted her lips into a wry grimace. "Eh, blow it out your ditty bag."

Silence followed. I figured Rabbit and I were both headed for a shallow grave, so I decided to spend my last few minutes on earth acting polite. I needed a few virtue points on my get-to-heaven passport. I cleared my throat and said, "Um . . . hi, Mr. Canker." I bent down and picked up the thick sheet of paper. I gave it a quick glance and saw what might've been the sketch of a map.

His head snapped in my direction, but his eyes held that enraged, incredulous stare. He reached out and snatched the map from my hand.

"I . . . um . . . I'm Georgie O'Dell." I cleared my throat. "Nice . . . uh . . . hi."

He didn't seem to like me either. If he'd been remotely impressed by my cordial greeting, he would've at least nodded. Instead, he looked back at Rabbit. "Seems like your little friend here has *manners.* Unlike *you.*"

"My friend has manners because she doesn't *know* you," Rabbit snapped. "Now, if you don't mind, we'll just be moseying on to wherever we want, because the woods belong to everybody." She stuck her chin up, flung her head to one side, and started walking again.

I was afraid to cross in front of Frank Canker because . . . well . . . because I didn't want to end up on his barbecue grill that night. But I swallowed my fear and finally took a step. I managed to feign a smile as I followed Rabbit past the clearing, around a rock quarry, down a steep embankment, and through another clearing. I huffed and puffed the whole way. I didn't dare turn around to see if Frank Canker was somewhere behind us.

"Rabbit," I finally said. "What was that all about?"

"Oh, puh-lease," she answered. "It was about justice. It was about showing a bully that I'm not afraid of him. That's what it was about. He actually has the nerve to wonder why all the teenagers in town disrespect him. He treats everyone like a dog, but he expects us to like him."

"Yeah, but . . . you could get yourself into trouble talking to him like that," I said. "He looked really pissed off."

"He looks like that all the time. And so does his wife. He was probably burying a body out here."

Lovely thought. As much as I wanted to know more about Frank and Nancy Canker, I changed the subject. "Is this how you usually get to the lake to hang out with your friends?" I asked Rabbit. "You walk this much every night?"

"No. I usually get a ride. And I don't go down to the lake every night. I only go like two or three times a week. I can only take so much of the hanging-out thing. Truth is, I'm kind of a loner. Plus, I'm a really bad liar, so I can't get away with smoking or sneaking beers. I tried it once—chugged a beer—and when I got home, my mom smelled it from downstairs. She and my dad gave me hell for that. I was grounded for two weeks."

"So then, I guess Lake Redson is where all the teenagers hang out?"

"It's the only place we can really cut loose. We used to hang out in the parking lot at the town hall, but then Sheriff Onofrio chased us out of there. Said we were getting too rowdy, which was totally not true. There aren't enough of us in this town to get rowdy."

A lake. A parking lot. Those were the designated hot spots for the teenagers in Whispering Oaks. No cafés or museums. No concert halls. No friggin' street corners, for that matter. The picture was grim. On all my past visits to Whispering Oaks, I'd known the town was graveyard dead, but I hadn't really cared, because home was always a few days away.

But now things were different.

Now I was facing the possibility that *this* might be my home for a long while. The thought of hammering nails into my toes seemed vaguely more appealing.

I was about to ask Rabbit how much farther we had to walk when I felt the breeze brush against my face. It was soft and warm, like the faintest touch. Looking up, I saw branches shivering and leaves rustling. And then I heard it—the unmistakable whispering sound, as if the wind were speaking.

I froze. Right there between an oak tree and a pile of mossy rocks. A chill raced up my spine. "Uh . . . Rabbit?"

She stood three feet ahead of me, solid as stone. Her hands formed fists at her sides. She turned around slowly and looked up. Then she gulped. "See what I'm saying?" she asked quietly. "You can hear it, can't you?"

I nodded. "What the hell—"

A second gust swept by, tapping us with its gentle fingers. The whispering rush was everywhere. If my eyes had been closed, I would've thought it was a voice calling out to me from the growing shadows.

"What is it?" I asked, my voice cracking. I nearly hugged the oak tree for protection.

"That's the legend—the one you didn't want to hear about."

"Well, I think I just heard it."

Rabbit stared up again as the leaves skittered down in a cloud of green. She stepped closer to me, visibly spooked.

I stepped closer to her, *completely* spooked.

We were huddling against the tree when a third burst of eerie whispers echoed through the woods. My heart leapt into my throat. I peered through the trees and bushes and tall blades of grass. I should have been looking for something scary, but I was really looking for a place to hide.

Rabbit was biting the nails of her right hand nervously. "We can't just stand here," she said. "We have to keep walking. It'll be dark soon."

"I know, but I can't move. I'm too scared."

She frowned. "So am I. Honestly, I've never heard the whispers sound so loud. I've heard them before, but not like that. It was freaky. It was right here, spinning around us."

"Rabbit," I said, my voice breaking again, "please don't take this personally, but . . . like . . . shut up."

She smirked. "Sorry. But listen: it's quiet now. I think the ghost—I mean, the wind—sorry—is gone now. Here, just hold on to me and follow. We're only like two or three minutes from the lake. Seriously, Georgie. We can do this."

I wanted to stay there, hunched like a purse-sized dog in the underbrush, but Rabbit sounded insistent again. Reluctantly, with trembling hands, I reached out and grabbed hold of her arm. I wasn't exactly reassured. Rabbit was about twelve pounds soaking wet, and my fingers circled her wrist like a big bracelet.

We took firm, fast steps, continuing in silence until we got to a narrow path that cut right through the middle of the forest. Trees flanked it, but straight ahead I could see the surface of what had to be Lake Redson shimmering pink and gold as the sun inched its way to the horizon.

"See? We're almost there," Rabbit said. "It's really not that—"

Her words stopped abruptly as a body jumped out from behind one of the big evergreens. In the instant before I screamed, I caught a glimpse of the boyish face and the broad shoulders, the wide eyes and the joker's grin. Whoever it was apparently thought it would be funny to scare us into complete submission. He was shouting and making goofy faces as he charged toward us.

But Rabbit found no humor in the little stunt.

A second after jumping back in fright, she went into defense mode: she crouched, raised her hands into position, and then gave the guy a lightning-fast karate chop to the stomach.

"Oh!" I heard myself gasp in shock. My fear shifted in a flash. I never thought I'd be afraid of a scrawny girl with big glasses and a nondescript hairdo, but go figure.

The guy let out a guttural "Ugh!" as he doubled over.

That was when I saw the regret on his face and knew the joke had bombed.

"Take that!" Rabbit cried. Turning into Madame

Samurai, she kicked her knees up in a jump, and her left hand shot out like a rocket, catching the guy in the forehead. She made a collection of ungodly sounds— *"highhhhh-yaaahhhh"* and *"eeeeeeek-mahhh"* and *"whooooaaaaaa-sakamaaahhh"*—before realizing she'd done some damage.

The guy was lying on his side on the ground, moaning.

I stared across the length of his bent body at Rabbit, my eyes wide with shock. I felt my jaw drop.

Rabbit was breathing hard. Her hands were still in a karate-chop position.

"Jesus, Rabbit," the guy said, shaking his head. "What the hell is wrong with you? Why d'you always have to beat the shit outta people?"

People? I thought. *As in plural? Little Rabbit? This has to be one of those hidden-video jokes, right?*

"Who is . . ." Rabbit straightened her glasses, which had nearly flipped over her nose during her ninja counter-attack. She peered down at the guy as he hoisted himself into a sitting position. Recognition flashed in her eyes. "Goddamn you, Jacob Chatterley!" she said.

Jacob Chatterley had one hand on his forehead and the other splayed over his stomach. He looked up at her and sighed.

Anger rose in Rabbit's cheeks—bright, red, dangerous anger. Her hands balled up again, and her lips sealed together as she frowned.

The words *short homicidal maniac* flashed through my mind.

"Why do you *always* have to play one of your stupid practical jokes?" she ranted.

Jacob dusted the dirt off his white shorts and mimed her words.

"Why?" she continued. "Getting the shit beat out of you serves you right! I swear it does."

Jacob staggered to his feet.

"The next time you do that, Jacob Chatterley, I'll karate chop you below the waist!"

Jacob Chatterley, I realized, was quite cute.

"Okay, okay," he said. "I'm sorry. My fault. Just don't hit me again."

Rabbit let out a long sigh. The tomato red of her cheeks was beginning to fade.

I didn't know what to do—Jacob Chatterley was a stranger, and I had just realized that angering Rabbit could land me in the critical care unit at the county hospital—so I just took a small step forward and cleared my throat.

That was when Jacob turned and stared at me.

And I mean really *stared*. A hard, long, silent stare that made my heart skip a beat. It wasn't a look of surprise or fright or friendliness. It was one of those pensive looks people give you when they think you're going to say something mean . . . or when they think they might've seen you somewhere before.

Which, of course, totally freaked me out.

The five seconds of silence that stretched between us felt like five years. In desperation, I glanced at Rabbit, who was searching her hands for damage they might have suffered during her counterattack. All around me, the woods were still. I would've welcomed any sound at that point—an airplane, a damn rattlesnake, even the eerie whispers in the wind.

He kept on staring.

Please don't say it, I thought. *Please don't ask me if I'm that girl who was accused of plagiarism, the girl from the newspapers and the television clips. Please don't tell me that I look like her.* I tried clearing my throat again, but no scratchy noises broke the silence.

I couldn't turn and run. I couldn't pretend that his eyes, glittering with suspicion, weren't locked on me. There was nothing to do but meet his stare head-on and accept my fate.

So I did.

And then Jacob Chatterley took a step toward me, cracked a little smile, and said, "Hey."

The Lake of Lost Dreams

After studying me like a moldy piece of bread, or a damp gym sock left baking in the sun, he had only one word for me.

Hey.

Hey?

Hey.

Okay, then: hey.

Well, it was better than *liar* or *plagiarist* or *loser.* Those were a few of the lovely nouns I'd thought he was going to utter. Fortunately, he'd displayed his conversational side and proven his gift for articulation with one syllable, which was fine with me.

"Hey," I answered.

Jacob Chatterley looked like a Buddhist punk. He was tall and lean, with a black Mohawk running down the middle of his shaved head and a diamond stud in his right nostril. His eyes were the deepest blue I had ever seen. There were three earrings in his left ear—two silver hoops and a small cross—and they caught the glint of the setting sun as he shifted his weight from one foot to the other. He was wearing a gray shirt emblazoned with the Wheel of Life, a classic Buddhist symbol.

"Oh my God!" Rabbit said. "See how nervous you got me, Jacob? I forgot to introduce you to Georgie. . . ." She cocked her head at me. "Did you say your last name was O'Dell too?"

"Yeah," I lied. "Like Finny."

Rabbit nodded. "Right. Jacob, this is Finny O'Dell's cousin, Georgie O'Dell. She's staying here in town for a while."

"Pleasure to meet you." Jacob stuck out his right hand.

I took it, gave it a quick shake. My palms were sticky. "You too," I said.

"Jacob's my first cousin," Rabbit explained. "He's sixteen but acts five. He's also the town clown."

"Hey," he shot back at her. "I am not."

"Oh, please." Rabbit rolled her eyes. "You are too. He's done it all, Georgie: left frogs on teachers' desks, put underwear on flagpoles, left bloody handprints in my bedroom on Halloween. My childhood was hell because of him."

"Your childhood was *fun* because of me," Jacob said.

"Nick never paid any attention to you, and your folks are always working. Hadn't been for me, Rab, you wouldn't even know what a practical joke is."

"That's, like, forty percent true." She winked at me, then slugged him in the arm.

Jacob stopped rubbing the spot on his stomach where Rabbit had karate chopped him. Looking at me, this time with a lot less intensity, he said, "So, what brings you to the sprawling town of Whispering Oaks, Georgie O'Dell? Let me guess—the excitement?"

I laughed. Is it just me, or is sarcasm sexy? "I needed some time away from the city," I told him. "My parents are going on a long vacation, and I think maybe they want to be alone. So I called Finny and asked her if I could crash with her for a while."

"And Rabbit found you and now she's an instant best friend," he said. "Right?"

"Right." I gave Rabbit a thumbs-up.

Jacob nodded toward her. "My cousin, the mayor."

"More like your cousin, the bodyguard." I mimicked one of Rabbit's karate moves. "If I'd known you could do that, I wouldn't have been so scared back there."

"Well, my karate isn't something I talk about. It's just something I *do*. A girl's got to know how to protect herself from psychos like Jacob Chatterley." She stuck her tongue out at him.

"What were you afraid of?" Jacob asked, his tone turning serious.

I glanced at Rabbit.

Our eyes met.

We both looked down.

"Come on," Jacob prodded. "What happened?"

I felt his eyes on me. Then I felt his hot fingers poke my arm. When I looked up, he was making a funny face, crossing his eyes and sticking out his tongue.

"Did you see a monster?" he asked in a high-pitched voice.

"No, you moron, we didn't see a monster." Rabbit crossed her arms over her chest. "We heard the whispering in the wind, just back there, past the second clearing. I mean, we really heard it. Scary as hell."

"Scary as hell," I agreed.

Jacob exaggerated peering over our shoulders and into the wooded acres Rabbit and I had just crossed. "Now, lemme see . . . oh, wait, look! I see someone running around in a white sheet. Oh, damn—it's a fake ghost."

Again, Rabbit slugged him. "You're asking for it today, Jacob!"

The smile that his lips broke into was wide and pretty damn perfect—nice white teeth, two dimples. I was thinking maybe I'd found the town hottie.

"It's true," I said quietly. "We definitely heard some strange whispers. I've never heard anything like it in my life. Seriously."

"He believes us, Georgie," Rabbit said. "He's heard the whispering too."

I stared at him. "You have?"

He nodded. "Sure. We all have. I know it's real."

"If you want to know about the legend," Rabbit told

me, "Jacob is the one to ask. He knows *everything* about the history of the town. He's a genius."

"I'm not a genius. Stop telling people that." He looked up at the trees, scanning them for . . . something. Then he looked at me. "Do you wanna know about the big bad scary legend in Whispering Oaks?"

In truth, I wanted to know more about *him*. Just the basic stuff: whether he was single, what kind of music he listened to, when he would be taking off his T-shirt, etc. But I couldn't come out and say that. So I said the next best thing: "Sure, Jacob. As long as you tell it *slowly*."

He smirked. I think he got the hint.

*   *   *

It was full dusk by the time we reached Lake Redson. Crescent-shaped and surrounded by acres of woodland, the lake was a small body of water that looked like it offered little in the way of recreation. There were no boats docked on its placid surface, no big Adirondack chairs to lounge in. Its grassy shores were dotted with tree stumps, daisies, and the occasional can of beer. The mountain range fanned out in the distance, cutting a jagged path across the dark blue sky.

The evening hang-out session was in full swing. There were about twenty teenagers parked on the grass. Cigarette smoke spiraled in the air, and the sound of laughter drifted up from every little group. A radio was playing. Several cars were parked all the way to the right, where, according to Rabbit, a winding narrow road led back to town.

My nerves spiked again when I saw all those unfamiliar

faces. *You're Georgie O'Dell,* I kept reminding myself. *Don't let the name Ruby slip out. Don't speak unless someone speaks to you. Don't talk about books. Georgie O'Dell is not a reader and she's certainly not a writer.*

Inwardly, I sighed. I was getting impatient with Georgie O'Dell. She and I had known each other for only a few hours, and I wasn't sure I liked her. Standing on the shore of Lake Redson, I was a stranger in a strange place, an outsider with nowhere else to go. My first instinct was to talk about books, or writers, or reading. From there, I'd be able to take a conversation anywhere. I was angry that I had to block that part of myself out. But I knew it was necessary. All I needed was for one person to say *Did you hear about that sixteen-year-old girl who plagiarized most of her first novel? Talk about an asshole.* I wouldn't be able to handle my own reaction.

Rabbit led the way down to the biggest group of teenagers. One of them—a short, chubby guy with purple hair—was kneeling beside a stack of broken wood and crumpled newspaper. I watched as he brought a match to the mound and got a bonfire going. Several others turned, beer cans and cigarettes in hand, as we approached.

"Hey, everybody," Rabbit said. "I want you all to meet my new friend, Georgie O'Dell. She's Finny's cousin. She's staying in town for a while, and she's from Manhattan."

The response was immediate. Even before I could open my mouth, the greetings came. There were a "Hey, Georgie!" and a "What's up, Georgie?" and a "Welcome to town, Georgie!" The guy who was building the bonfire, Jason Sydney, shook my hand. So did his twin brother,

Oren, and one of Oren's friends, another marginal cutie named Eric Warner. Two girls, MaryAnn Conner and Kimmy Peterman, waved with their cigarettes. Their conversations didn't stop because I had entered the picture, but they acknowledged me, which was more than I'd expected.

"Hi," I said back. "I'm fine, thanks. It's nice to meet you."

I was taken aback by the instant acceptance. What was this—a town filled with *Little House on the Prairie* clones? The guys were polite and respectful. The girls had offered me genuine smiles, and girls are never nice to each other. There were no intimidating stares, no comments muttered under their breath. And definitely no flashes of recognition.

MaryAnn Conner, short and round, with long black hair and a diamond stud in her left nostril, came up to me and said, "Oh my God like I've always wanted to visit the city but my parents won't let me go and they won't drive there not even for a weekend but I tune in to all of the Manhattan radio stations because the music's the best and do you ever go to nightclubs back home?" Her eyes popped wide open as she awaited my reply.

It had to be the longest run-on sentence in grammatical history. As her words tore through my brain, I imagined commas and semicolons and periods falling blessedly into place.

"Not really," I told her. "I'm still too young to go to nightclubs, but I did sneak into one a few months back."

She puffed on the cigarette. "Really? You must see a lot

of famous people when you live in the city because of Broadway and everything and all the movies that are constantly being filmed there and even the soap operas oh my God have you ever seen a movie being filmed?"

"MaryAnn, give it a rest, will you?" Jacob said. "Georgie's gonna need some aspirin for a headache if you open your mouth one more time."

MaryAnn clucked her tongue at him. "Shut up, Jacob."

Oh, yay, I thought. *An actual sentence.* I looked at MaryAnn and smiled. "I've seen a few movies being filmed. But that's kind of inevitable when you live in Manhattan."

She beamed at me.

Rabbit tugged my arm and handed me a can of soda. She chucked a bottle of water at Jacob.

I sat down on the grass, tired from the long walk, from the scare in the woods, and from the bumpy bus ride the night before. But I wasn't thinking about sleep. I was thinking that I suddenly felt comfortable and more at ease than I had in several days. I didn't know why. It was a strange realization. Maybe it had to do with my being emotionally burnt out. Maybe it was the result of one of Aunt Fin's positive energy spells tearing up the cosmos. Or maybe, I told myself, it was from the refuge that only a place like Whispering Oaks could offer—a refuge that was both welcoming and mysterious.

The crackling bonfire illuminated the dusk like a swarm of fireflies. High above the mountains hung a sliver of moon, as thin and delicate as a shard of glass. Two birds crisscrossed the sky where the treetops met. Then the stars bled through the canopy of darkness, a wild array of twinkling lights unlike anything I had ever seen.

The nights aren't like that in the city. From the top floor of a high-rise, you can glimpse the jagged skyline and the faraway ribbons of traffic gliding across the Brooklyn Bridge. You can even see the Statue of Liberty shining in the harbor. But the night sky is invisible in Manhattan, eclipsed by the millions of lights shining on the streets below. You can't look up while you're standing in Times Square and spot Orion's belt shimmering in the heavens. The city has its own beauty, its own chaotic romance, but there was something downright intoxicating about sitting beneath a star-filled sky on a summer night.

I popped open the can of soda and felt Jacob settle beside me. I didn't look at him but kept my eyes on Rabbit, who was talking to MaryAnn down by the water's edge.

"So," Jacob said, "I guess it's better here, right? Without the freaky whispers?"

"I'd still like to hear what this legend is all about," I told him.

"Hmmm . . . I don't know. You seem like you get spooked easily." He chugged water from his bottle while staring at me out the corner of his eye. A smile tugged at the corners of his mouth.

"I'm a New York City girl," I said. "I don't spook that easily."

"Good answer." Those perfect white teeth came into view again. "And by the way, I'm sorry if I scared you before—ya know, jumping out of the woods like that. Rabbit's right, no matter how much I pretend to disagree with her. I really am a practical joker."

Sitting so close to him made my heart beat faster. I could easily have done the appropriate thing and kept our relationship on a platonic level—I hadn't come here for a social life, remember?—but the sky was so beautiful and my mind was at ease for the first time in a long while, so I decided to take a chance. And besides, I was still figuring out who Georgie O'Dell was. She was revealing herself to be a risk taker. So I said, "All those practical jokes must really drive your girlfriend crazy."

The expression on his face changed, softened. "It annoys my *imaginary* girlfriend," he said jokingly. "But since she only exists in my head, I can tune her out when she starts complaining. It remains to be seen whether an actual, live girlfriend would be driven crazy by my practical jokes."

Single. Somebody get Georgie a net. I tried to look as though the news didn't affect me one way or the other, but I felt a slight heat rising in my cheeks.

"How about you?" he asked. "When's your boyfriend coming up to visit from New York City?"

For a split second, a picture of Jordan Lush flashed in my mind . . . and then the picture turned into a target, and I mentally shot it with an arrow. "I don't have one," I said simply.

"Huh. I thought you Manhattan girls went through us guys like Kleenex."

"Not always. Some of us move more slowly than others."

"That's what girls say when they wanna play hard to get."

My jaw dropped. "That's so not true."

"Sure it is. But that's okay. I live by a single belief when it comes to girls."

"Oh, really?" I raised an eyebrow. "And what's that?"

" 'What is better than wisdom? Woman. And what is better than a good woman? Nothing.' "

My heart stopped. Totally ceased to function. I mean gone. We're talking flatline here, people.

I recognized the quote Jacob Chatterley had uttered, but I couldn't believe he—or *anyone*, for that matter— knew it. "You read Chaucer?" I blurted.

His eyes widened. "Yeah. That quote is from *The Canterbury Tales.* You know it?"

"Of *course* I do." I felt like I'd been hit in the face with a hardcover copy of *War and Peace.* I couldn't stop the excitement—the sheer joy—from taking over. Cute. Confident. A mischievous grin. *And* a reader. What were the odds? When my heart started beating again, I said, "I read all the time. I read everything. I . . . um . . . I love books."

So much for Georgie O'Dell and her illiteracy.

"Cool," Jacob said. "Same here. Let's see if you know this one: 'Silly things do cease to be silly if they are done by sensible people in an impudent way.' "

"Jane Austen," I automatically replied. "That's from *Emma.*" My voice dropped into one of those dramatic, breathless whispers. I lost all sense of time and place. There were only Jacob and I and the books that held the universe together.

He was smiling broadly again. " 'If you really want to hear about it, the first thing you'll probably want to know is where I was born. . . .' "

"J. D. Salinger," I said. "*The Catcher in the Rye*. That was too easy."

"I know."

" 'Last night I dreamt I went to Manderley again,' " I quoted, praying he would recognize the line.

Squinting in thought, he locked his eyes on mine. He made a show of looking confused.

Please, I prayed, *don't break my heart. Tell me you recognize that line.*

He must have caught the anticipation on my face, because after a few more seconds, he snapped his fingers and said, "*Rebecca*. First line of the book."

See? The world really is a beautiful place.

"That's my favorite novel," I told him. "I've read it seven or eight times."

"I liked it," he said. "But I have too many favorites. I don't think I could choose just one. You ever read *A Separate Peace*?"

"Yes."

"How about *To Kill a Mockingbird*?"

"It's another favorite of mine."

"*The Heart Is a Lonely Hunter*?"

"I read it."

"Pretty depressing," he said. "But it was realistic. I had a hard time getting through that one."

"Yeah, but there's something haunting about the way Carson McCullers wrote. She's hard to forget."

Jacob drained the last of his water, then set the empty bottle on the grass. "So then, I guess you have a room full of books back home in Manhattan, right?"

My bedroom. My bookcases. My dusty paperbacks. I had sworn off them, and no matter how much my love of books showed, I would never again turn those yellowed pages. "I have more books at home than I know what to do with," I admitted. "Books are my obsession, I guess you could say."

"Well, you won't find many of them around here," Jacob said. "The stupid local library is about the size of my kitchen, and the old librarians never stock anything new."

"How's that possible? I'm pretty sure that libraries are required to keep up with what's being published." The words flew past my lips, and I immediately regretted speaking them. I was talking too much. I was straddling the fine line that separated Ruby Crane from Georgie O'Dell, and that was dangerous.

"Maybe so," Jacob said, "but there's not enough funding to make our library a good place. There never has been. And the really shitty thing is that there isn't a Barnes and Noble, or even an independent bookstore, anywhere near here. You either order your books online, or you just forget about reading altogether."

"That's really horrible," I said, genuinely saddened. "I

mean, what do you people *do* here? Rabbit told me you guys mostly hang out here at the lake, but what about your parents? And what happens when you get tired of sitting here talking with everyone night after night?"

Jacob shrugged. "Not much else we can do, unfortunately. Most of us don't have cars, so it's tough to drive out to the next county. Finny's shop is the best thing in town, and we all try to hang out there every now and then, but browsing four aisles and drinking coffee gets boring too. As for our parents—well, when they wanna cut loose, they go down to the Higgins Bar and drink away their depression."

"That's really sad."

"Sad or not, it happens to be true. We're a community without culture. I swear, if it wasn't for being able to order books and movies online, I would've drowned myself in the lake a long time ago."

I looked at the groups of teenagers loitering at the lake's edge. Most of them were lighting up new cigarettes or reaching for more stolen cans of beer. This was the extent of their recreation, because they didn't have any other choice. Who could blame them for wanting to get drunk?

"There has to be *something* to do in this town," I said, exasperated. "Doesn't your high school have extracurricular activities? The debate team? Track? A football team?"

"Don't you wish!" Jacob laughed. "There are exactly two hundred and six students at Whispering Oaks High. Up until ten years ago, the county used to bus us over to Derryville High because it's bigger, but then shit happened—

money, politics, red tape—and we ended up getting our own little dump of a building to call a school. The teachers try their best, but there's nothing to do." He looked away. "It's just us and the lake. The lake of lost dreams."

"What?" I asked.

"The lake of lost dreams," he repeated. "That's what we call this place. All we ever seem to do when we hang out is bitch about how boring our lives are. Nobody thinks about the future until after they leave Whispering Oaks." He picked up a rock and skimmed it over the bonfire and into the water.

"How long has this place been called the lake of lost dreams?" I asked.

"A long time. It actually has something to do with the legend, but even without the legend it would be the lake of lost dreams. Mainly because we're all so . . . lost."

"Don't you want to change that?" I said, prodding. "Maybe there's a way to make it the lake of new promises or something."

He frowned. "I doubt it. It's been this way for too long. Why? You got any ideas, New York girl?"

"Maybe." I hugged my knees to my chest and tried not to meet his eyes. I watched a flock of birds jet over the tree-tops again, their wings like shadows against the sliver of white moon. The silence between us was comfortable.

"So, do you believe in ghosts?" Jacob asked.

"I don't know," I told him. "I've never given it much thought. Do you?"

"Yeah, I do. Not in all cases. But in some cases."

"That's cool. I kind of expected that from you."

"Why?" He cocked his head to one side.

"Because you're open-minded, curious. I get the feeling that you like to explore things, really think about them. That you don't . . ." I swallowed hard over the lump in my throat. I didn't want to say it, but I just had to. So I did. "That you don't judge a book by its cover."

He nodded. "That's pretty funny, Georgie."

"What is?"

"That we've only known each other a short time and you've already figured a big part of me out. There aren't many people who've been able to do that. Mostly, people look at me and they think I'm kind of freakish—ya know, my hair, my piercings. Or they just think I'm this completely crazy practical joker who's never grown out of his childhood." He paused, holding my gaze. "Most people don't want to know all the other stuff about me."

"Well, most people are stupid." I knew I had gone too far in spilling my literary guts to Jacob, speaking to him as the old book-loving Ruby and not the new antiwords Georgie, but I didn't worry about it. Something told me that I was safe in this crowd. That I had found a place where I could be liked and invisible at the same time. And, strangely enough, I didn't want the night to end.

"So, tell me about this legend," I said.

Ghosts

"It's kind of a sad story," Jacob began, folding his arms over his chest and shifting his body so that he faced me directly. "And sort of scary. It's one of the things you learn early on when you grow up here."

"Well, I'm here now," I told him. "And I might be here for a while. I think I should know what everybody else knows—especially since I heard the whispering in the woods myself."

"Okay, okay." He nodded, then stared out at the lake. "It's all about a girl named Mattie Dembrook," he began. "She lived here, in Whispering Oaks, over a century ago.

According to the legend, Mattie came here around 1884, when she was seventeen years old. She was apparently an orphan, and she came here to work as a housekeeper in one of the big hotels that were popping up all over the place. This was when the Adirondacks was a chic vacation place. All the rich New Yorkers had mansions here.

"They say that Mattie Dembrook was beautiful—milk white skin, dark eyes, and long reddish hair. That summer, she appeared on the doorstep of the Deer Heart Hotel, carrying only a satchel and an old gray shawl. No one knows where Mattie began her journey or why, but she was accepted at the Deer Heart and began working as a housekeeper right away. It was obvious from the beginning that she wouldn't be a normal staff member. She knew how to read and write, and was clearly educated."

I lost myself in the cadence of his voice. As inconspicuously as possible, I inched my way closer to him, until our knees were touching slightly.

"The Deer Heart had eighty-five rooms," Jacob continued. "It used to stand right there, straight across Lake Redson. Now it's just open field. But back then, the hotel catered to a rich group of people, and from its highest floor, there was a distant view of Lake Placid. Summer was high season, and you can imagine the hordes of people who came—more people than we have in town today, for sure. It was really a golden time, with lots of parties and rich people walking around.

"But for Mattie Dembrook it was a totally different experience. It was the poor who staffed the lodges and hotels, and they were all underpaid, overworked, and isolated from the beauty that the wealthy guests enjoyed all the time. She didn't swim in the lake or go boating. She didn't go on picnics with her family or friends. Most days, she woke up before dawn; she swept the floors in the kitchen and wiped the grime from the counters. Then it was on to the rooms. She made beds, changed sheets, washed down windows and hard oak banisters until the palms of her hands probably ached.

"The funny thing, though, is what the legend says about Mattie," Jacob went on. "She was supposedly a really high-spirited girl—ya know, funny and optimistic and not much of a complainer. Apparently, she got into trouble a lot because she was always talking and making jokes with the other girls who worked as housekeepers or waitresses. She was known for her sense of humor, and she was supposedly unpredictable in a lot of ways."

"How?" I asked him. "What did she do?"

Jacob shrugged. "People say she did things that made her a little bit of a celebrity in town. Once, when she was cleaning the room of a really rich couple, the husband put his hand on Mattie's butt when his wife wasn't looking; Mattie threatened the man graciously, but her warning was enough to make him steer clear of her for the rest of his stay at the hotel. Another story is that Mattie dove into Lake Placid on a stormy night with all her clothes on to save a drunken man from drowning. It's also a well-known fact that she would leave her room to take long walks in the woods after midnight. No one ever knew what she did in the woods, but people say she stole food from the pantry to feed the deer, squirrels, and coyotes. Basically the people of Whispering Oaks had never known anyone like her."

The bonfire popped and crackled beside us.

"It might not sound like much," Jacob said. "But you have to understand that Mattie's defiant attitude—her unpredictability—was a really rare thing for girls over a century ago, especially poor girls who had no family history, or at least no history they would speak of. They were expected to be quiet little mice, running around and breaking their backs, incredibly grateful just to have a roof over their heads. But Mattie was confident because she was educated. She was also beautiful, and that didn't go unnoticed."

"I was just about to ask you if she had a boyfriend," I blurted out, maybe a little too eagerly.

But Jacob didn't seem to mind. He smirked and went on with the story. "So the story goes that late in the summer of 1884, Mattie caught the eye of seventeen-year-old Eamon Whitfield. Eamon came from a wealthy, blue-blooded New England family. The Whitfields owned one of the huge summer cottages not far from the Deer Heart Hotel, and they spent their days lounging around and swimming in the lake. Eamon spotted Mattie outside the hotel one evening and was instantly taken by her beauty. He saw past the wrinkled housekeeper's clothes and all that, and Eamon and Mattie began to meet in the woods or beside one of the creeks that ran past the hotel. Eamon would wait for Mattie to finish work so that he could walk with her in the woods at sunset. Nobody really thought their relationship was serious, but all that changed when Eamon was caught leaving Mattie's room early one morning."

I heard myself gasp. So the pretty housekeeper and the nineteenth-century hottie were getting it on. "*That* must've been a total scandal," I said.

"Oh, yeah," Jacob agreed. "The Whitfields were embarrassed, and the thought that Eamon might have actually gone that far with 'the help' totally rocked the boat. What would happen if she got pregnant? Eamon's life would change completely, and the Whitfields weren't going to put up with that kind of scandal."

"So what happened?"

"Well, the bond between Mattie and Eamon wasn't easy to break. It wasn't a typical teenage romance; it was a real, passionate love affair, and back then, teenagers getting frisky with each other wasn't as accepted as it is now. One newspaper described Eamon as having been 'sick with love' for Mattie. In another article, employees of the Deer Heart Hotel claimed that Mattie did nothing but talk about Eamon and their plans for the future. And, of course, before long the entire town was talking about the forbidden romance between the rich boy and the maid.

"You can imagine it, right? All those rich old ladies talking up a storm. The Whitfields were mortified, and when they demanded that Eamon end the relationship, he just ignored them. He spent every waking moment outside the Deer Heart Hotel. He brought Mattie flowers and presents. Supposedly, he even stood beneath her bedroom window and recited poetry—Byron, Longfellow, Shakespeare.

Now, here's where the story gets *really* interesting—especially for me."

I stared into his eyes and inched a little closer to him. "Why?"

"Because Mattie Dembrook and Eamon Whitfield both loved to read," he said. "People say it's what cemented the bond between them."

"Seriously?"

"Yeah, seriously."

My heart started pounding in my chest again. I was picturing the story in my mind, every last detail. I couldn't help feeling all sappy and warm inside. It sounded impossible, almost made up, but as I sat there listening and staring into Jacob's eyes, I knew the story was true.

There was genuine passion in his expression. Intensity. The same look I'm sure I have when I talk to people about *The House of Mirth* or *Pride and Prejudice*. Even when I used to talk about *The Heart Stealer*. It's the look of excitement and confidence. Of completeness.

"So what happened?" I asked again. "Did Mattie and Eamon end up beating the odds?"

"No, they didn't," he answered sadly. "And that's where the story goes south. By the end of the summer their relationship had grown to obsessive proportions. They were inseparable. Then one night two employees of the Deer Heart reported seeing Mattie and Eamon beneath a willow tree. They saw him bend down and ask Mattie to marry him.

"That very same night, Eamon gave Mattie a gift that

would become the most important part of their legend: a rare first edition of Shakespeare's collected works, stolen from a shelf in the Whitfield family's extensive library. The book was one of Mattie's favorites."

"A *first edition* Shakespearean volume?" I nearly screamed. "Are you kidding me?"

Jacob shook his head. "The book was published in 1623, a Whitfield family heirloom passed down through the generations."

"Today that edition would be worth . . . like . . . millions of dollars," I said, stunned. "What happened to it? What happened to *them*?"

"Well, the news got out fast. Early the next day, the whole town was buzzing about the marriage proposal," Jacob said. "His mother, Mary, was angry and embarrassed—especially when she discovered that the prized Shakespearean volume was missing. Eamon confessed to giving it to Mattie, and his confession was exactly what Mary needed to put an end to their relationship. She went straight to the police and accused Mattie of stealing it."

"But that's not fair!" I protested. "If Mattie didn't steal it, why should she be accused?"

Jacob frowned. "The Whitfields were a powerful family. But anyway, that was the night of August twenty-fifth, and a huge storm blew in. Then the wind started and it was so strong it snapped branches from trees. Eamon was desperate to save Mattie from being arrested, so he snuck out of the Whitfield cottage and began a long, dangerous hike to the Deer Heart. Some people say he planned to take Mattie and run away and elope, but nobody knows for sure." Jacob paused.

"Don't tell me," I said. "Eamon didn't make it?"

"No. People always say that Eamon Whitfield was so determined and driven by love that he would definitely have made it to Mattie that night—if not for an accident. A tree fell in the middle of the storm, trapping him as a flash flood ripped through the woods. Eamon's body was found early the next morning."

That got me. The story was new to me, but I felt like I knew Eamon and Mattie. Maybe it was the way Jacob told the story—with such feeling and sincerity—or maybe it was simply that I liked hearing a good romance.

"The legend says that Eamon died crying out to Mattie from the forest," Jacob explained. "And that Mattie, alone in her room at the hotel that night, actually heard him— not necessarily his voice, but his heart. Lying in the middle of the woods, Eamon knew he was going to die. And when the news finally broke all over town, Mattie Dembrook apparently lost her will to live. Some say she died of a broken heart right there in the Deer Heart Hotel; others claim she left Whispering Oaks at night, taking both the memories of their romance *and* the rare, expensive volume of Shakespearean works. But the most widely believed theory is the one the newspapers reported two days later: that Mattie saw a ghostly image of Eamon in the woods behind the hotel and, in a mad rush to join him, threw herself into Lake Redson."

I gasped as Jacob uttered the last bit of the story. "She died?" I said. "Mattie actually killed herself?"

"That's what most people believe," he replied solemnly. "Witnesses—other girls who worked at the Deer Heart— said that they saw her diving into the lake, and that she never surfaced. But the interesting fact is that Mattie Dembrook's body was never found. The lake has been dragged three times in the past century, but no one's ever pulled up any remains." He stared out at the lake again, peering through the darkness. "Mattie didn't leave a physical sign of her existence, but legend has it that her spirit roams the woods from dusk till dawn, in and around Lake Redson. When the wind whispers through the trees, they say it's really Mattie trying to find Eamon, calling out to him from her heart, reciting the poetry they both loved. Even today, on a fairly regular basis, people here in Whispering Oaks say they've spotted Mattie walking in the woods, or floating over the surface of Lake Redson in the foggy glow of the moon."

"What about the book?" I asked. "The rare edition of Shakespeare?"

Jacob shook his head. "It was never found. Supposedly, Mattie's room at the Deer Heart was searched in the days following her and Eamon's deaths, but no sign of the book. And two years later, the Deer Heart Hotel burned down. There was nothing left but ashes. And open land. Lots of open land."

Sitting beside the smoldering bonfire, I felt a chill run up my spine. I had heard the whispering in the wind earlier with Rabbit. I *knew* I'd heard it. That eerie, ethereal sound echoing through the woods—Mattie Dembrook, or a natural phenomenon?

"Have you ever . . . seen anything out here?" I asked Jacob quietly.

"Once I thought I did. It was a couple of months ago. I was on my way here to hang out, and I parked my dad's car further back on the road because it had rained that day and there was a lot of mud and when I get his car dirty, he makes me wash it. I started walking towards the woods—it was dusk—and then I heard the whispering and I got pretty freaked out. Weirder than that, though, is what I saw down there on the north side of the lake." He pointed in the darkness to the narrow lane. "It was a split second, but I think I saw someone moving through the trees. I thought I saw long hair and a white dress."

Goose bumps. I kissed my good night's sleep goodbye. "And what did you do?"

"I ran like a little girl." He laughed. "I was freaked out for days after that. I mean, we all kind of believe the legend about Mattie and Eamon haunting the woods, but to actually see it? Damn. I don't think I want to go that far."

Same here, kiddo. The last thing I needed was a ghostly sighting to make me second-guess my sanity. Having my life pulled out from under me once was enough, thank you very much. I said, "Has anyone ever looked for the book? I mean, if it's true, if there really was a rare edition of Shakespeare's collected works from the sixteen hundreds . . . we're talking a major find. Major bucks."

He shrugged. "I think the book was stolen from Mattie's room after she died," he told me. "Maybe it was even delivered back to the Whitfield family. But no one's ever launched any kind of official search, if that's what you mean."

"That's what I mean."

"Where would you look? The hotel's gone, and the Whitfield cottage, which is a good two miles away from here, was sold and resold a dozen times. First it was a bed-and-breakfast, then it was a private residence, then it was a school, and now it's a private residence again."

"How do you know so much about this stuff? All the little details. Is it just what you remember from hearing the legend as a kid?"

"No. My parents own the *Whispering Oaks Gazette,* which is the town's answer to the *New York Times.* Ya know, all the juicy stuff that happens in this town. Anyway, my parents are amateur historians, and my mom loves ghost stories. Every year for the past God knows how many years, they've run a special section in the paper around Halloween. They've collected a lot of stuff on Mattie and Eamon."

"Did they ever find out where Mattie came from? Her past?"

"Nope. No records. But the Whitfield family is still going strong. They're like billionaires. They don't hang in this area anymore. Now the rich people from New York party in the Hamptons and South Beach, right? I guess you'd rather be partying in one of those places right about now, huh?"

"No." I answered him quickly. I stared him straight in

the eyes. The dying embers illuminated the short space separating us. "I don't want to be anyplace but right here."

Ha. Georgie O'Dell was starting to assert herself, and she was doing a good job of it.

Jacob Chatterley blushed.

*   *   *

Rabbit told Jacob in no uncertain terms that it was his responsibility to get us home safely. "The fact that I even have to *ask* you is mind-boggling," she said to him as we walked around the edge of the lake toward the narrow road where the cars were parked.

"Chill out," he snapped. "I was going to offer to take you home. I wasn't going to, like, *leave* you guys here or tell you to walk back through the woods."

"Well, you should still be more gentlemanly," Rabbit said jokingly. "*Asking* would have been the nice thing to do."

Jacob sighed and rolled his eyes.

Walking in step with Rabbit, I sensed a slight change in her demeanor. There was something whimsical about her now, something more playful in the way she talked and walked and glanced at me. She had loosened up. And it didn't take a genius to figure out what was happening.

Rabbit was a smart girl. I could tell that beneath the frail, thin, birdlike surface was a big brain and an even bigger radar. She was a keen observer, the type of person who never missed anything. She had spent the last two hours chatting with her other friends, purposely leaving Jacob and me alone. But I knew she'd been watching from her perch at the edge of the lake, catching all the subtle hints and smiles and wide-eyed stares that had passed between us. Those were the obvious signs of attraction, the hot little flags anyone would notice. The more visceral ones, however, weren't quite as easy to spot. But Rabbit had spotted them. She knew that Jacob and I had found a connection. She obviously *sensed* it, and she seemed happy about it.

Jacob's car—or, more accurately, his dad's car—was an old Saturn coupe the color of earwax. He unlocked the doors by touching a button on his key chain, then walked around to the driver's side and climbed in. "Not exactly a Ferrari," he said. "It'll do though, right?"

I instinctively went to crawl into the backseat, but Rabbit grabbed my arm and pushed me toward the front one so that I could sit next to Jacob.

"I mean, *really,*" she muttered. "Duh."

I bit down on my tongue to keep myself from laughing, then hopped in.

Rabbit followed.

"Now, should I take the scenic route home?" Jacob asked, glancing in the rearview mirror. He gunned the engine. "To show our guest the nighttime beauty of Whispering Oaks?"

"He's being sarcastic," Rabbit snapped from the backseat. "There *is* no scenic route, Georgie. Just trees and dirt and dark sky."

"I figured as much."

"Did you like the lake?" Rabbit asked.

"Yeah, I had a really great time. I learned about the legend." Out the corner of my left eye, I watched as Jacob threw the car into gear and started driving. I might've seen a nervous twitch in his lip, but I wasn't sure.

"So does that mean you believe it?" Rabbit sounded hopeful.

"Yes, I do. Totally."

"Good." She clapped her hands delightedly. "Maybe we'll go ghost hunting next week."

Um, maybe not. I wasn't all that interested in catching a hazy glimpse of Mattie Dembrook or Eamon Whitfield. I was, however, eager to get my hands on that lost edition of Shakespeare's collected works. Had there really been such a glorious treasure in Whispering Oaks? That thought was almost as intoxicating as the thought of kissing Jacob.

I know—it sounds like I was moving too fast. Hanging out with a guy for a few short hours and already wanting to lock lips with him is usually the mark of a minor slut. But, I swear, if you were sitting next to Jacob, if you saw his bright eyes and his perfect smile . . . well . . . you'd probably accept your fate of becoming a minor slut and pucker up too.

The ride back to Aunt Fin's house took about seven minutes. It consisted of a bumpy trek up the narrow, winding road, then a straight drive to Main Street. Painfully short. As Cherry Pine Road came into view, I felt my stomach knot a little bit, the realization that the night was ending hitting me.

The car rolled to a stop in front of the house. The living room windows were lit up, and Aunt Fin's Native American wind chimes were chiming. "Well," I said, kind of meeting Jacob's eyes but not really meeting them at all, "thanks for the ride. I'll, um . . . I'll see you soon, I'm sure."

He nodded, cracked a nervous smile.

Say something, I thought. *Say "Yeah, I'll see you tomorrow night, right?" Say anything.*

But he didn't.

I popped open the door. I climbed out and started up the walkway to the house, Rabbit falling in step with me.

"I swear, men are just mentally incapacitated," she grumbled.

I laughed. "What makes you say that?"

We were standing in the shadows of the front porch, and Jacob was a mere silhouette through the windows of the car. "I thought my brilliant cousin would've at least had the sense to drop me off at home first," Rabbit said. "Or *say* something to you. Jeez, he's really a shit-for-brains sometimes. Which bugs me, because he's so damn smart."

"It's okay," I told her, trying to sound cool about the whole thing. "Really it is. I just got here, ya know?"

"He likes you, Georgie. I can totally tell." She shoved her glasses up the bridge of her nose. "And I hope you like him too."

I didn't know how to answer that, but I knew that the dreamy, enchanted look on my face—in my eyes—was obvious.

"I guess I'll see you tomorrow," Rabbit said. "I'm going

to work at the general store, as usual. I'll pop in for my coffee around ten."

"I'll be there." I watched as she started back down the walkway toward the car, a skinny shadow blending into the darkness. "Rabbit?" I called after her.

She turned and stared at me.

"Thanks," I said. "Ya know—for everything."

She smiled.

A moment later, I heard a shuffling sound coming from the car, then a quick thud. I saw Jacob's silhouette disappear from the window. Then I saw the outline of his head as he got out of the car and stood against it.

"Georgie?" he called out.

"Yeah?" Slightly stunned and totally confused, I watched as he ran up the walkway, past Rabbit, and to the front porch. Ran like he was racing to a finish line. Or chasing after something he didn't want to let out of his sight. He didn't just *walk;* he *ran.*

He came to a stop three feet from me, breathless, and our eyes met and he said, "I just wanted to tell you that . . . well . . . I mean . . . I'll see you tomorrow night, right?"

Remember the dramatic moment in *Jane Eyre* when Jane realizes that she's hot for Mr. Rochester? The longing? The yearning heart? Well, I felt a lot like that—minus the whole Victorian thing that would have required me to act like a prim and proper lady. And minus the drab clothing Jane was likely wearing on that gloomy, overcast day in Britain.

"Yeah, Jacob," I replied, meeting his hopeful stare.

"You'll see me tomorrow night." I waited a few seconds, letting the silence between us do its wonderful wordless thing.

The look in his eyes told me he understood.

I opened the front door and stepped into the house. I stood there, staring at the hardwood floor, listening as his and Rabbit's footsteps shuffled back to the car. Then the engine thrummed again, and they were gone.

I found Aunt Fin in the living room. She was sitting cross-legged on the couch in front of a bunch of burning votive candles. The soft light cast a glow across her face, and when she glanced up at me, it was with a knowing smile.

"You look like you had a nice time," she said.

"I did," I admitted. "You were right—going out was good for me." I took off the Yankees baseball cap and chucked it onto the couch, letting the messy and chopped-up strands of my hair fall where they might.

"I'm so glad to hear that. I was sending you good vibes, Georgie."

"Well, they worked." I kissed her good night, then went up to my room. I was tired. I was wired. But more than anything, I was eager to surrender myself to sleep, and to whatever sweet dreams awaited me.

Life, Uninterrupted

It's going to sound cliché, but the weeks really did pass in a slow rhythm. I got used to the sounds of the country, to the birds in the early morning and the crickets at night, to the echo of a single car driving slowly down a dusty road. I got used to people calling me Georgie O'Dell.

I think my first big lesson revealed itself after I had spent only a week in Whispering Oaks, and the lesson was all about change—not that it can happen so suddenly but that we can get used to anything if we have to. I had to get accustomed to a bunch of nice people and a relatively serene existence. It was a lucky break—initially, at least.

After such a Gothic descent into hell, I had expected nothing less than the requisite flames and accompanying scars, but what I found in Whispering Oaks was a sanctuary, a little slice of heaven that welcomed me with open arms.

At the Curious Cup, my duties took on more meaning. The simplest tasks became a strange sort of therapy, and I wiped down counters and swept the floor and dusted objects without the slightest hint of anger or reluctance. It felt good to move and sweat. I didn't check my reflection in the mirror twelve times a day or worry about who might have been making comments about me. No one did. Appearance wasn't what people in Whispering Oaks noticed when they met you. Instead of sweeping their eyes over your mismatched outfit, they held your gaze with a smile and asked if you were enjoying the weather. They talked about their dogs and their new favorite recipes. The mundane was the norm, and I liked that just fine.

I met Aunt Fin's array of interesting customers one by one. There was old Mr. Fuller, who at eighty-three still looked and sounded like a recent retiree; he had a thick mane of white hair, and he walked three blocks to the Curious Cup every day for a blueberry scone. I got used to storing his cane behind the counter and listening to his stories about the years he'd served in World War II. Three Purple Hearts and a medal for bravery. His wife, Helen, had died a decade before, and his children had moved out of Whispering Oaks in search of better jobs.

Lisa Marie Keating came into the shop twice a day for coffee; she was thirty-six, with short blond hair and the stained teeth of a smoker. Born and raised in town, Lisa had only left once, for a two-week vacation in London. She was married and had three kids, and when she laughed, her lungs sounded like a motorcycle revving up.

There was the S.M.C.—Single Moms Club—a group of women who came to the shop on Wednesday nights to sit at the counter, drink tea, and bitch about the bad men who'd left them and the good men they were hoping to find. They considered themselves nice Christian ladies, but they didn't hesitate to ask Aunt Fin for love spells or any kind of moon ritual that would help them land husbands. The potential-husband pool in Whispering Oaks wasn't very large. Most of the men in town were married.

One of my favorite customers was Lynn Bodders, the town beautician. Lynn was short and chubby, and her hair was a mix of different shades of blond and brown. She reminded me of an Easter egg. Lynn had been born in Rochester—her idea of a big, flashy city—and then she'd fallen in love at eighteen, moved to South Carolina, and spent the next twenty-five years cutting and curling old ladies' hair in her basement. She always came into the shop like a shell exploding, waving her hands and saying "Hellll-oooooo, Ms. Georgie!" before slapping them down on the counter in a prolonged beat. With amazing precision, she tapped out Rolling Stones and Tina Turner songs. Pink hairdresser's apron, white shorts, and a bright red T-shirt—that was Lynn. She'd moved to Whispering Oaks three years earlier and had no intention of ever leaving.

To be perfectly honest, I kept quiet while working at

the Curious Cup. It wasn't that I didn't talk to people—I did. It was just that I wanted to be more of a listener, a sponge. I had spent the past year being the center of attention. It was nice to be chilling out in the background. I got asked a lot of personal questions. Everyone wanted to know what home was like, how long I'd be staying in town, if I preferred lakes and fields to Times Square. I answered politely, then always managed to steer the conversations in another direction. There were even rare, mind-blowing moments when I had to remind myself that a girl named Ruby Crane had existed once upon a time. That she'd written a novel, been sort of famous, and then fallen from grace like a dead bird at target practice.

Of course, reality came rushing back whenever the phone rang: Mom made a habit of calling four times a week at exactly 9:30 in the evening. Our conversations consisted of my listening silently and her talking about how much better it would be for me to "recover" at home in the city. I really didn't want to hear it. In fact, I spent those long minutes sitting on the couch with the phone pressed to my ear, making stupid faces that Aunt Fin disapproved of. I mean, I love Mom and all, but why do parents forget that we have our own minds? That we can make our decisions?

When the calls ended, I usually sighed and rolled my eyes. And that was when Aunt Fin always said the same thing: "If you don't want to speak to your mother, maybe you should try writing letters to her."

It was an idea, but not a very good one. If there was

another lesson I'd learned since I'd come to Whispering Oaks, it was that I still didn't trust my own words. And maybe I never had.

* * *

Rabbit and I had developed a ritual. Three afternoons a week, we met for ice cream at Banana Split, the small candy shop at the far end of Main Street. One Wednesday, on what otherwise would have been a boring afternoon, I walked into the general store—and right into the middle of a fight.

"I will *not*!" I heard Rabbit yelling from one of the side aisles. "Do you hear me, Watson? Do you?"

I bit down on my tongue to keep from laughing out loud. Rabbit and Mr. Watson argued about everything—where to stock the new groceries, how to turn the air conditioner up higher, when she would take her lunch break. According to Rabbit, Larry Watson was a difficult man to work for. He was stubborn and wore a perpetual scowl. He had been running the general store since the Ice Age. He didn't believe in progressing with the times, so the cash register was still one of those clunky models from the 1960s that creaked whenever you touched the big buttons.

I walked farther into the store as Rabbit sighed and clucked her tongue.

"No, that's all wrong!" she was saying. "You're just making a mess!"

"Um . . . hello?" I called out. I made my way to the aisle where Rabbit and Mr. Watson were standing. From the looks of it, they were arguing about where to stock the newest shipment of Oreos. Clearly, Rabbit wanted to put them beside the refrigerator that held milk, but for some odd reason, Mr. Watson thought cookies belonged smack between toilet paper and hair spray.

"Hey," Rabbit said, shooting me a glance. She sighed again as Mr. Watson began lining up the boxes of Oreos in a neat row.

"But don't you see that what you're doing is wrong?" she snapped. "Oreos go with milk—not hair spray!"

Mr. Watson stared at her and sneered. "I'll stock things where I want!" he told her sharply.

"Fine!" She crossed her arms over her chest. "But God help you if you ask me to change your little display tomorrow! I already know where I should stick those boxes!"

I laughed—one of those piggish, unladylike snorts that pop out of your nose unexpectedly.

Rabbit looked at me. "Come on," she said. "Let's go."

"Go *where?*" Mr. Watson suddenly shrieked. He stared both of us down and moved his lips as his dentures slipped.

"It's noon," Rabbit told him. "And I'm going for lunch."

"You'll go for lunch when I tell you to!" he shouted. "And now is not the time!"

Well, Rabbit didn't appreciate that at all. "The nerve you have, old man!" she screeched at him. "This dump would be a bunch of fire logs if it wasn't for me! And just so you know, it's *illegal* to deny me a lunch hour when I work a full eight hours. I'll have a lawyer in here tomorrow if you're going to violate my human rights! Do you hear me? I won't stand for abuse in the workplace! That's why unions were created!" And with that, she shoved her glasses into place and stormed out of the store.

Mr. Watson looked as though he'd shit a solid brick.

I stood there offering him a sorry look, but he didn't seem impressed. The grandfather/granddaughter relationship he and Rabbit shared was totally unhealthy, and I wasn't about to get in the middle of it. I turned and walked out of the store.

*　　*　　*

"Can you believe that?" Rabbit asked, leaning against a streetlamp. "That old guy is nuts."

"You, um . . . you should really try not to fight with him," I said. "It doesn't really solve anything."

"Yeah, well . . . welcome to my life." She frowned and rolled her eyes.

We started walking down Main Street. There weren't any cars, and there certainly wasn't any foot traffic. Even on a hot summer day, Banana Split was empty. Not that it had space for more than three people—in all, it consisted of two small rooms: one held the ice cream freezer and a small table, and the other was a bathroom. Ellie, the woman who ran the shop, was sweet and quiet and just a little bit plump. She didn't say anything as she prepared a large brownie sundae for me and Rabbit.

We took our seats at the table and dug in. As usual, we

spent the first three minutes of our ice cream time pigging out. That was something else I had grown to appreciate: the comfortable silence. Rabbit and I didn't always need to fill up the minutes with conversation. We both understood that there was something to be said for enjoying each other's company.

That, of course, didn't stop her from talking about what was on her mind.

"So, what's going on with you and Jacob?" she suddenly blurted with her mouth full of whipped cream.

I nearly choked on a chunk of brownie. "What do you mean?"

"Just that. Are you two an item yet or what? I mean, it's about time, don't you think?"

I opened my mouth to speak, but no words came out. I wasn't offended or even taken aback by Rabbit's prying. In fact, I couldn't blame her for asking. "I'm not sure," I said. "But whatever we are, I like it."

Her mouth twisted into a wry grin. "I don't buy that. And neither does Jacob. He's totally into you."

Her words made my heart pound.

Jacob and I had been seeing a lot of each other. It wasn't anything crazy or obsessive but rather a slow friendship. One night, we ate dinner at the diner. Another night, we sat in Aunt Fin's backyard and played cards and listened to music. I learned a lot more about him. Jacob was the youngest of five kids, and he was the only boy. His sisters were all married and living in different parts of the country. He told me that growing up in his house was a lot like growing up in an all-female psycho ward: lots of emotions and crying and fights. He didn't get much attention, but he got a lot of encouragement to do his own thing. From the time he was a little kid, he said, he'd always rebelled against conformity, against doing what was expected of him. He didn't love school or play well with his classmates. He didn't watch cartoons. Once he hit junior high, he spent a lot of time hanging out by himself, reading, writing, going for long walks in the woods.

I liked that he was a loner. Being your own person— especially with piercings and a Mohawk—wasn't easy in a place like Whispering Oaks, but Jacob believed in what he called the biology of identity. He said we're all born a certain way, with specific likes, dislikes, passions, and fears, and that denying any of them is denying nature. It's a disservice to ourselves and to the world around us. He just didn't feel comfortable in ordinary clothes or an ordinary haircut. What some people considered odd or freakish or even downright dangerous he often felt drawn to. He held the distinction of being the first person in the history of Whispering Oaks to sport a Mohawk.

I dug my spoon into the brownie sundae and swirled it around the bowl. "Has he said anything to you about me?"

"He always asks me if I've seen you," Rabbit said. "Like you're the president or something. I swear, I'm surprised he doesn't salute when you walk by."

I laughed at that. "We talk about a lot of things when we hang out."

"Yeah, that's nice. But have you ever talked about turning up the heat?"

"Rabbit!" I blushed. The smile that spread across my lips was unstoppable. It happened whenever someone mentioned Jacob Chatterley.

There was one afternoon when he'd walked me home from work. It was a Wednesday, and it was nearly a hundred degrees. We walked down Main Street, purposely bumping into each other and letting our arms and hands touch. By the time we reached Aunt Fin's house, we were both sweaty and probably a little . . . well . . . let's just say we were both probably thinking about skinny-dipping in Lake Redson. Suddenly, Jacob stared me straight in the eyes and said, "You're really pretty, Georgie."

I was taken off guard. I didn't know what to say. I looked up at him. I saw the honesty on his face, heard the tenderness in his voice. I had never experienced either of those things with Jordan Lush—or any guy, for that matter. It was the first time Jacob had really opened up to me. I mean, like, let it all come through without any of the hesitation or suggestive, sexy jokes that usually passed between us. "You're pretty hot yourself, Jacob," I whispered back. And I thought, *Kiss me, kiss me, kiss me!* It would have happened, too, if Aunt Fin hadn't come stumbling onto the front porch to let Waffle out for his daily sniffing around on the lawn. I wasn't really all that upset about it, though. I'd seen what I needed to see in Jacob's eyes, and I knew that our first kiss was inevitable.

Rabbit finished up her side of the sundae, then drew a napkin across her mouth. "I know it's none of my business, but I just think you and Jacob would make a really great couple. You two have so much in common. And I *know* he has the hots for you, because Jacob isn't the type who talks a lot, but lately, he's been talking about nothing but you."

"I think I'm guilty of that too," I admitted. "Finny told me this morning that I've been talking about him a lot."

"We're talking about him now, aren't we?" Rabbit smiled. "I just think it's really cool that, because of you, Jacob hasn't been spending so much time down at the lake with the rest of the crowd."

I ate another spoonful of ice cream. "I don't really mind the lake, but I know what you mean. It's not exactly an interesting place."

"Tell me about it. You think I'd go to the lake of lost dreams if I had someplace better to go? Puh-lease."

"You don't *have* to go down to the lake every night, Rabbit," I told her. "You could come to Finny's house and hang out with me."

"I know." She turned and stared out the window. "These days, anything seems better than that lake."

The lake of lost dreams.

I hadn't wanted to accept that dismal description of life in Whispering Oaks—especially for the kids in town. But it was true. Slowly, surely, I came to understand what it meant. I saw it in Jacob's eyes, on Rabbit's face. I heard it in MaryAnn Conner's endless sentences. In the way Jason Sydney talked about wanting to stay drunk for the rest of his life.

At the lake of lost dreams, the only dream ever discussed was the one of leaving town. And I knew all about that.

The Kiss

It was a Saturday, nearly a month after I had arrived in Whispering Oaks. The afternoon rush at the Curious Cup was over—ten people in total—and I was wiping down the front counter when Jacob walked in.

He was dressed in cutoffs, a white shirt, and flip-flops. Not exactly an Armani poster boy, but still cute enough to make my heart do a cartwheel. His Mohawk was straight up and jet-black, a perfect complement to his blue eyes.

I'm gushing, right?

"Hey, you," he said, closing the door behind him.

"What's up?" I dropped the damp rag and leaned on the counter.

As usual, Jacob stood in place for a few seconds and just stared at me. It was a habit of his I'd noticed. He did it all the time—in his car, at the lake, walking down Main Street. I assumed it was a way for him to collect his thoughts before speaking, and he always had a lot to say.

We were still just friends, but there was a vibe between us that screamed attraction. I joked with him more than I did with any of the other guys I'd met in town, and he joked with me more than he did with the other girls. Like when I asked him if he was ever going to show me the tattoo on his chest, or when he asked me if I wanted to go skinny-dipping in the lake. Funny. Okay, maybe a little trashy. But the banter worked. I think we both would have preferred a nice long kiss, but for some reason it hadn't happened yet, and I wasn't going to rush it.

"Want some coffee?" I asked him, reaching for the pot.

"Eh, not really. Maybe some of that herbal tea infusion stuff Finny keeps in those magic jars instead?" He came to the counter and sat down.

"Which magic infusion tea? The one that turns you into a wolf or the one that turns you into a bird?"

He feigned indecision, arching his eyebrows and cupping a hand over his chin. "Hmmm. Better make it a wolf. In case I need to run through the woods for food tonight."

"Now, there's a coincidence," I said, loading herbs into a cup. "I was planning on doing the same thing tonight."

"Awesome! You feel like hunting deer or elk?"

I added a spoonful of sugar to the peppermint-lavender tea, gave it a stir, then set the cup down in front of Jacob.

He took a sip. "Amazing," he said. "You know just how I like my tea. Sweet tea from a sweet girl. Now, this is what I call a nice afternoon."

See what I mean? I felt my cheeks starting to blush.

Jacob reached into the pocket of his shorts and pulled out a crinkled white envelope. "I wanted to bring you this," he said. "I thought you'd find it interesting."

"What is it?"

He opened the envelope and yanked out several folded sheets of paper. "These are articles on Mattie Dembrook and Eamon Whitfield, clips from the *Whispering Oaks Gazette* from over the years. It's mostly Halloween paranormal stuff, but there are interesting historical facts about the story, and the legend."

I gathered the pages in my hands and began glancing through them. "This is great," I told him. "I've been thinking about Mattie and Eamon ever since you told me their story."

"I know. You seem as fascinated by them as I am. I told my parents that I want to write a piece on the legend this year for one of the autumn issues of the *Gazette*."

"That's a great idea."

"You think so?" He perked up. "I wanted to know if you'd help me do the research."

"Sure. I'll help you." I paused and leaned a little closer to him on the counter. "What did you have in mind?"

Jacob took a long sip of the tea, staring at me over the rim of the cup. "It would be a lot of time alone. I mean, just the two of us."

Did he think I would object? "We could do that," I said. "We'd probably make a good team." Playing it cool . . .

He cleared his throat. "Maybe we could take a ride out to the county historical society up in Killinger Falls. It's about an hour from here. It's . . . it's a really pretty town. Right on the river, with lampposts and old houses and . . ."

I reached for the rag again and wiped at invisible stains on the counter. "Sounds like a date," I said.

"Yeah. I know. About time, right?"

I didn't meet his eyes, but I was blushing.

"We could go out to eat first," he continued. "So it would be, like, three-quarters fun and one-quarter actual research."

I liked what I was hearing. "So . . . um . . . do you know exactly what it is you want to research?" I glanced up to see him smiling, then quickly lowered my eyes again. A moment later, I felt his hand on my chin. I was startled, but I didn't jump back or jerk my head away.

I looked up.

Jacob was standing. The tips of his fingers grazed my bottom lip as he pressed his warm palm against the side of my face.

My heart was booming like a thunderstorm, and I think I even saw flashes of lightning—but that might've just been the heat pulsing throughout my body.

It was time for the Kiss.

He leaned forward.

I leaned forward.

His eyes started to close.

My eyes started to close.

Everything around me disappeared as I slid my hand across the counter and linked my fingers with his and—

And then the door opened with a resounding whoosh.

The.

Door.

Opened.

Just like that.

Whoosh.

Can you friggin' believe it? After that perfect moment?

Whoosh.

We both jumped back. Jacob quickly lowered himself onto the stool he'd been sitting on, and I grabbed the damp cloth and gave it a skid across the countertop.

Aunt Fin walked into the shop, carrying two big boxes.

Aunt friggin' Fin. I'd forgotten all about her. She'd gone down to the general store for more paper coffee cups and had promised to be back soon.

The anger I experienced was monumental. I actually knew, in that moment, what it felt like to be a human land mine.

"I think we're due for a storm," she said, lowering the boxes in her arms and looking at me. "It's so cloudy out—" One glance was all it took. She saw my jaw-clenched face and Jacob's nervous fidgeting and she knew, right then, that she had no damn business walking into her own store.

It was going to be *my* kiss. And *that* superseded the issue of ownership.

"Oh," she said. "Oh . . . I was . . . I'm sorry. I . . . I was just taking these boxes into the back room. Excuse me."

"Here, Finny. Let me help you with those." Before she

could protest, Jacob jumped from the stool and grabbed the boxes from her arms. He turned and carried them into the back room.

When he was well out of earshot, I planted both hands on my hips and gave Aunt Fin a guttural, nostril-flaring, dragon's-breath sigh.

"I'm sorry," she whispered. "I didn't know."

"Didn't you at least *sense* it?" I snapped. "With all that psychic energy flowing around you?"

"My chakra points are completely off-kilter," she said. "I haven't had a chance to meditate or perform an aura-cleansing on myself in days, otherwise I would have *absolutely* felt desire emanating from the front door."

The funny thing was that Aunt Fin truly meant what she said. Every last strange word. She came to my side and jabbed me with her elbow. "But way to go, girl. He's such a cutie."

"Be *quiet.*" I folded my arms over my chest and pouted, like I did when I was three.

"Your mom and dad called me about an hour ago," she said quietly. "They're not too happy that you've been avoiding them."

Sigh. "I've been *busy.*"

"Well, busy or not, you'll call them tonight as *soon* as you get home. I know they have a tendency to dredge things up from the past, but they mean well, Ruby."

"*Georgie!*" I whispered, though it was really a barked whisper.

Aunt Fin cupped a hand to her mouth, then bit down

144

on her fingers. "I'm sorry. Oh, I promise to keep my mouth shut. I do. I promise."

"Good."

Jacob came out of the back room, wiping his hands on his shirt. "Those boxes were a little dusty, Finny, so I set them down on the floor. I hope that's okay."

"It's fine," she assured him. "Thank you so much. And now I really have a lot of work to do in the back room." She started toward it, then came to a dead stop and faced us. "The work I have to do is very far back in the back room. It's, like, in the back-back. So if you need me, Georgie, you'll have to come and get me, because I won't hear or see a *thing* that goes on out here."

"Actually," Jacob said, "I have to get going myself. It *does* look like a storm's about to hit, and I should help my mom secure the storm drains just in case." He looked at me and frowned.

I frowned back.

He started to wave good-bye, then suddenly said, "Oh, wait a minute," and reached into the back pocket of his cutoffs. He pulled out a book and handed it to me.

"What's that?" I asked.

"It's a gift," he replied. "You'll see why. Take it."

I reached out and grasped the heavy paperback in my fingers. It was a shiny new copy of Shakespeare's collected works.

"It's not exactly a rare edition," he said, "but it's the best I could do via Amazon. I'm sure you already have it at home."

Tears sprang to my eyes. *Okay, heart, I give you permission: melt.* "No, I actually don't have this one," I told him, my voice trembling a little as I met his soft stare.

Aunt Fin slipped quietly into the back room.

"Good. That makes me feel better." He shoved his hands into his pockets and shifted his weight from one foot to the other.

"Jacob, this is the sweetest gift anyone's ever given me." I placed the book on the counter and ran a finger over the glossy cover. "I really mean that."

Then I looked into his eyes.

There was no need for coordination or planning or little details. It felt natural this time.

I leaned into him and our lips met and held. I pressed myself into his chest as his hands slid down my arms and around to my back.

Fireworks. The kiss would have pulled Rip Van Winkle wide-awake.

It only lasted a few seconds, but the electricity coursing through my body would likely last a few days.

He pulled away from me, his eyes still closed. When he opened them, he turned, then started out of the shop. But he didn't leave. He paused at the door. Finally, he turned back and said, "Read sonnet eighteen. It's my favorite."

And he was gone.

I stood there for a long while, rooted to the spot. My head was spinning. My lips were tingling. The electrical current surging through my blood made me feel hot all over. In the event of an evening power outage, no one had to worry: I'd glow brightly enough to illuminate the entire state.

I picked up the book and found sonnet 18.

Shall I compare thee to a summer's day?
Thou art more lovely and more temperate:
Rough winds do shake the darling buds of May,
And summer's lease hath all too short a date:
Sometime too hot the eye of heaven shines,
And often is his gold complexion dimm'd;
And every fair from fair sometime declines,
By chance, or nature's changing course, untrimm'd;
But thy eternal summer shall not fade,
Nor lose possession of that fair thou owest;
Nor shall Death brag thou wander'st in his shade,
When in eternal lines to time thou growest:
So long as men can breathe, or eyes can see,
So long lives this, and this gives life to thee.

A tear trickled down the side of my face.

As I read the sonnet a second time, something happened inside me. A click. A kick. A boom. A seismic shift in the foundation of my safe and secret world. And I knew that everything was about to change all over again.

The Passion

I hadn't expected it quite so quickly—I hadn't expected it at all, actually—but life's strange little twists often come without any warning. In the blink of an eye, everything can change.

I'm not just talking about Jacob and the kiss here. I'm talking about what happened as a *result* of Jacob, the kiss, and the inanimate paperback clutched in my hand.

It took a few minutes for my body to readjust to planet earth. I leaned against the counter for support and let the heat pulse its way out of me flash by flash. All the usual good stuff happened: the room spun, the floor felt like it was tilting, huge glittery spots swam in the air. I kept replaying that one moment over and over in my head—the one of Jacob closing his eyes and puckering his lips at the same time.

After three long weeks of trying to make the kiss happen, it happened in the most unanticipated way. I would never have imagined that we would lock lips in the Curious Cup. For some reason, I had pictured us getting a little busy in the woods, or down by the lake, or somewhere dark. But the magic moment came as I was standing there in a stained apron, smelling a little too much like eucalyptus incense and coffee. Go figure. Somehow, though, it was perfect.

I liked Jacob more than I'd realized. No one had ever made me feel so wired and drained at the same time. Before Jacob, there had been only one other—the lying sack of shit better known as Jordan Lush—but not even Jordan, with his spectacular looks, had managed to produce such a fiery response with a kiss.

I wasn't mystified by that. In fact, I completely understood it. I was attracted to Jacob's mind as much as I was to the rest of him, which meant I didn't need to see his face to know how I felt. I would probably never get bored talking to him. I *wanted* him to keep on talking.

And I knew he felt the same way about me.

After convincing myself that my new life in Whispering Oaks would be devoid of anything even remotely recreational, I was falling in love. I had never experienced that feeling. Everything else paled in comparison to the dizzying rush.

A part of me—maybe the most important part—had

been jump-started back to life by that one kiss. I was still likeable. I was still cute—even if I had a bad haircut. And, despite the cover of a new name, I was still *me*.

And the sonnet. Was there ever a more romantic expression of love than a sonnet? Shakespeare's most tender thoughts, meant to be passed from one lover to another. I mean, *seriously*. Can you blame me for getting all dramatic and buttery? A sonnet, people. A *sonnet*.

"Georgie?"

Aunt Fin's voice broke my reverie.

I turned around.

She was staring at me, a worried look on her face. "Honey? Are you okay? Oh, God . . . I'm so sorry about walking in and—"

"It's okay," I said. "Really, it is. Everything . . . worked out."

Aunt Fin grinned. "You mean . . . he kissed you?"

I blushed, dammit.

"Ha!" She did a little dance and slapped her hand down on the counter. "Did you see stars and fireworks? Oh, listen to me. Of course you saw stars! A kiss is a gift from the cosmos, and from the angels of the cherubic realm."

Whatever that meant. I couldn't help being embarrassed, so I started looking for the damp rag again.

"So, was that your gift?" Aunt Fin said, gesturing at my hand.

I was still holding it. The paperback copy of Shakespeare's collected works. The book was clenched in my fingers like a good-luck charm. I stared down at it, then nodded. "Yeah. He knew I'd love it," I said quietly, maybe a little dreamily.

Aunt Fin was beaming.

That was when I remembered the *other* feeling that had arisen in those moments immediately following the kiss, while I'd been reading sonnet 18. It was the feeling of pure joy. I was *holding* a book—smoothing my fingers down the length of a page, letting my eyes dance over the print, listening to the words echo in my mind. And I didn't want to throw up.

I hadn't held a book in more than a month. I hadn't read a paragraph or a sentence; I'd barely even read a title. Now I looked down at the book in my hand a second time. I felt it as I'd never felt an object before. My heart was beating furiously. My eyes were watering. This was the same rush I had experienced when I'd kissed Jacob only minutes before. The same eagerness. The same sense of overwhelming rightness.

"Honey?" Aunt Fin was standing beside me. "What is it? You look a little . . . out of it."

Slowly, I put the paperback down on the counter. Then I walked past Aunt Fin and into the back room. I went directly to the boxes I had found on my first day there. The boxes I hadn't wanted to see or even to acknowledge.

The boxes of books Aunt Fin had planned on selling at the Curious Cup.

They were stacked against the refrigerator, piled with newspaper and dented cartons. I knelt down and pulled open the first one. Ten shimmering paperback copies of the hottest romance novels. I plunged my hands into the second box and found ten glowing copies of bestselling mysteries and thrillers. Next I found the young adult and children's books, followed by three volumes of poetry. Then I was wrapping my hands around the classics. I was relieved to set my eyes on pictures of Emily Dickinson, Walt Whitman, Charlotte Brontë, James Joyce, and Oscar Wilde.

Gathering several copies of the books in my arms, I stood up and ran back out to the front of the store. I unloaded my shipment onto the counter.

"What . . . what are you doing?" Aunt Fin asked hesitantly.

"You wanted to sell these books," I said excitedly. "But you didn't. Because of me, right? Because I told you I never wanted to see another book again, right?"

"Right. But that's okay. You don't have to—"

"I know I don't have to," I said, cutting in. "I *want* to. I *need* to. I didn't realize it until now, until just a few minutes ago, but, Aunt Fin—I can't give up books. I can't just forget about reading, about how great things were in my life before . . . and things were great because I was always able to escape in a book, in a story. That was what made me happy. That was really the only thing that made me happy." I tore off the apron and flung it onto the rack. "I know I sound crazy—"

"No, you don't." She stepped forward and put her hands on my face. "Ruby, you sound completely *normal*.

And I knew you'd come back to it! To tell you the truth, I'm surprised it took you this long."

"I'm surprised it came back at all," I answered.

"Why? Don't you see what's happening? Geography doesn't change things. Being here in Whispering Oaks, assuming a new name . . . it's what you feel is necessary right now because of what happened. But no matter where you go or who you become—Georgie O'Dell, Ruby Crane, whatever—your heart will stay the same. Sure, you could discover new loves, but the old ones never die."

Tears welled in my eyes. "I like it here, Aunt Fin, but I miss a lot of things."

"About home, you mean."

"Yeah." I sniffed. "But I can't go back there. Not anytime soon."

"No one said you have to." She turned and poured herself a cup of the magical-blend coffee. "The point I'm trying to make—the point we're both trying to make, actually—is that you lost yourself because of what happened, and maybe now you're beginning to find yourself all over again."

"I *did* lose myself," I admitted. "I mean, I still don't feel like the person I was, but it's getting better day by day."

She sipped the coffee, then shot me a gentle but penetrating stare. "To tell you the truth, I think you lost yourself *before* the scandal."

Her words shocked me. But, strangely enough, they didn't upset me. I knew exactly what she meant.

Aunt Fin and I had never discussed the whole plagiarism

thing. We'd talked about scandals, about how hard it was being sixteen, about the differences between small-town life and big-city living. The word *plagiarism,* however, had never been uttered. She was waiting for me to bring it up. She was *hoping* I'd bring it up.

But I couldn't. Not right then.

"What are you going to do with all those books?" she asked.

I glanced around the shop and spotted the empty corner beside the last aisle, the one that held unicorn T-shirts, Wiccan spell kits, and assorted gnomes and gargoyles. "I'm going to build a display right there," I told her. "Where can I find an extra table?"

"You sure about this? You sure you'll be okay?"

I glanced down at the gleaming copies of *The Giver, Island of the Blue Dolphins,* and *A Wrinkle in Time.* My heart started pounding again. "Yes, Aunt Fin. I'm sure."

* * *

I worked in silence for two hours, listening as rain tapped against the window and thunder sounded in the distance. The storm kept customers away. Aunt Fin retreated into the back room to catch up on paperwork and agreed not to come out until I called her. I wanted the display to look perfect, as good as any of the ones I'd seen a million times in the big Manhattan bookstores.

First I cleaned and swept the corner beside the last aisle. I picked up little chunks of wax and flecks of herbs and shooed away a dozen spiders. The two black tables

Aunt Fin had given me were scarred and wobbly, but I managed to clean them up nicely. I set them side by side, then brought out all the books, stacking and arranging them until I had a pyramid effect going. I was no expert: they fell at least five times before finally settling into place.

On top and in full view were the romance novels. This was a move calculated purely to generate sales. I thought about the women I'd met in Whispering Oaks and the conversations I'd overheard there in the shop and decided they could all use a little heat. The hunky, bare-chested men on the paperback covers would initiate the sparks; the steamy pages would likely create raging fires.

I arranged the mysteries and thrillers beneath the romance books. I figured the women might want to buy gifts for their husbands or boyfriends, and the dark, suspenseful tales were the best choice. Men generally aren't fans of romance novels. It's been my experience that if a story doesn't contain a high-speed chase or some sort of explosion, most guys lose interest. Best to keep them occupied with mayhem, murder, and cliffhanger endings.

The second table was where I spent the most time. Aunt Fin had ordered a lot of teens' and children's books, and I drove myself crazy trying to find the right display pattern for them. I finally decided to spread them out like a fan in one colorful, organized rainbow. Beautiful copies of *The Phantom Tollbooth, Because of Winn-Dixie, Caddie Woodlawn, Freaky Friday, Harriet the Spy, The Cricket in Times Square, Dicey's Song, Freckle Juice, My Side of the*

Mountain, Number the Stars, The Face on the Milk Carton, Vision Quest, Killing Mr. Griffin, and *I Am the Cheese.*

The three volumes of poetry, along with the classics, I placed upright in the very middle of the crescent, so that Emily Dickinson's face could stare out at customers while they drank their coffee and ate their scones.

I laid all the books out in perfect symmetry. I wiped the last flecks of dust from the covers. Then I stepped back and surveyed my creation.

A more inspirational sight I had never seen.

The entire shop had taken on a new aura, a new look, and a new mission. The Curious Cup would no longer be a place just for curios; if I had any say, the shop would be a destination full of enrichment, of culture and creativity and, best of all, books.

The air even smelled different: slightly dusty, slightly tinged with cardboard staleness. Being there was like standing in a small library that burned incense and scattered potpourri across the floors. Aunt Fin's array of magical tools and blends was a potent perfume, and her vast collection of artful objects shadowed just about everything. But the two tables of books were perfectly placed: anyone who walked into the shop would automatically see them, because they were positioned diagonally from the front door.

At the counter, I fashioned a sign with markers and a sheet of eight-by-ten-inch paper. I wrote NOW SELLING BOOKS in big block letters but then decided to be a bit more creative and mysterious.

I took a fresh sheet of paper from the bottom drawer

of the counter and picked up a black marker. I chose a quote from *Jane Eyre*, which I knew by heart. *It is in vain to say human beings ought to be satisfied with tranquility: they must have action; and they will make it if they cannot find it.*

Ha. The people of Whispering Oaks would understand that one.

On another sheet, I scrawled a quote from *Heart of Darkness*, by Joseph Conrad: *I don't like work—no man does—but I like what is in the work—the chance to find yourself.*

Totally true for me at the moment.

From Abraham Lincoln: *The things I want to know are in books; my best friend is the man who'll get me a book I ain't read.*

I spent almost an hour jotting down as many quotes as I could from memory. I lost myself in that simple act, I guess because it was the closest I had come to writing anything. When I was done, I walked around the shop and hung the sheets up wherever I could fit them, smoothing pieces of tape across the tops and bottoms and sides.

Outside, the storm had passed. I went to the door and propped it open as the last gray clouds disappeared and dusk set in. The day was almost over, but I felt like it had just begun.

The door behind me opened with a clink. I turned to see Aunt Fin poking her head out of the room, one eye squinted shut.

"I'm not looking," she said. "I just need a pair of scissors from behind the counter."

"You can look. Go ahead and open your eyes," I told her.

She did, and she gasped. "It looks amazing! Wow! People will be buying books by the armful!"

"It's not only so people can *buy* books," I answered. "There's a bigger plan here."

"Oh? And what's that?"

I walked to the counter and sat down. What I was about to say wasn't a sudden brainstorm; the idea had formed in my head sometime in the past three hours. "I'm starting a book club."

Aunt Fin's eyes widened. "A book club?"

"And a teen poetry slam," I added.

"A teen poetry slam," she repeated.

"And maybe even a self-help circle for some of the wacko people in this town. That is, if you can order some self-help books."

She stared at me. The expression on her face was both confused and amused. "It all sounds great," she finally said. "But, well, do you think it'll actually work here? You've met most of the teenagers in town, and most of the residents. I've never thought of Whispering Oaks as a particularly bookish place."

"That's exactly why we have to try to do this," I said. "Because the people here have never had the chance to experience the way books—words—can change a life. I mean, Aunt Fin, regardless of what happened to me, I still know that books played a huge role in my life."

"In mine too," she said, running a hand through her mop of long red hair. "I still remember where I was the day I finished reading *The Secret Garden*. I was in the fifth grade, it was January, and I finished reading it while I was on a bus coming home from school. I got lost in that book for days. And even though we lived in the city, your mom and I tried to find our own secret garden somewhere on Lexington Avenue."

That image made me smile. I could totally picture my mom and Aunt Fin knocking on brick walls. "So then, you think it could work? A book club, I mean. A teen poetry night—or just *something* to get the teenagers in this town interested in stuff that doesn't have to do with wasting every night down at the lake."

She nodded reassuringly. "It's worth a shot. But how are you going to get the word out to people?"

Before I could answer, the front door opened and Rabbit walked in.

The Word Out

Without so much as waving or muttering a hello, Rabbit stared across the floor and zoomed in on the two tables. She blinked. She shoved her glasses up on her nose. Then she smiled and said, "Ha! What a great idea!"

I was facing her, leaning my back against the counter. "You think so? The Curious Cup is now Whispering Oaks' answer to Barnes and Noble."

She kept smiling as she followed the posted sheets of paper, reading over the quotes. "Oh my God!" she shouted when she got to the tables. "*The Phantom Tollbooth*! This was my favorite book when I was a little kid!" She picked up a copy and studied it. She flipped open the cover. Racing to the first page, she scanned the opening few lines of the book, then put it back down and set her eyes on another. "*The Giver. Because of Winn-Dixie.* Shit, Georgie, I haven't seen these in years!"

"I didn't know you read," I said, walking over to her.

"I do. I mean, I used to read a lot more. But I don't always get the chance to drive up to the bookstore, and my folks won't let me shop online because they're afraid of giving out their credit card info. When I read, it's mostly stuff Jacob throws my way." She ran a finger over the Emily Dickinson volume. "Whose idea was this?"

"Finny's."

Rabbit glanced over at Aunt Fin and gave her a thumbs-up.

"Yeah," Aunt Fin said, "but Georgie built that whole beautiful display. It's something, isn't it?"

"Totally," Rabbit said. "Ya know, last year I told Mr. Watson that he should order some books and stock them in the general store, especially for those of us who have summer reading to do. We could've just bought our copies easily. But the old ass didn't listen."

"What books are on your summer reading list?" I asked, intrigued.

"*Wuthering Heights* and *Uncle Tom's Cabin.* I've read them. So has Jacob. But we're probably the only ones. The summer reading list isn't a big deal at school. It's not like we have to write reports on the books or anything."

"So, do you think some of the other teenagers in town will be into . . . coming here?"

"To buy these books, you mean?"

"To join a book club, maybe have a poetry slam. Ya know, something a little more interesting than just hanging out at the lake."

She thought about it for a long minute. "I think most of them would be into it, or at least willing to give it a try. Not all of them, though. There're a few who think hanging out at the lake is what life's all about." She crinkled her nose and made a sour face.

"Those are the ones we have to get here," I told her. "If they just tried to read a good book, I'm sure they'd realize how much fun it is. A book can open up a whole new world for a person." I couldn't help grimacing at the thought of the world one particular book had opened up for me, but I caught myself before Rabbit noticed the look on my face.

"I agree with you, Georgie. But not everyone in this town is like you and Jacob. And me, to a certain extent. Most people think reading is a big waste of time."

Ugh. "Still," I said, "I think it's worth a shot. I really believe it's worth a shot. And I want you to help me get the word out."

"Okay." Rabbit nodded toward the front door. "Then let's get started. Everybody's probably already down at the lake, half drunk by now. We might as well start spreading the word tonight."

I looked at Aunt Fin.

"No time like the present," she said.

* * *

We took the shortcut through the woods. By then, I didn't really need to follow Rabbit, because I knew the way by heart. We walked side by side in the twilight. The air was rinsed clean by the storm, the humidity lingering only slightly. The sky was the purplest I had ever seen it.

I kept thinking about what I would say to everybody at the lake. I didn't want to sound like a babbling idiot, but I really wanted them to get what I was trying to accomplish. Back home in the city, starting a book club or a poetry slam or anything even remotely literary would've been easy: one announcement and I'd have had at least a dozen people my age rallying around me for a list of books. But here? I had a feeling it was going to be a challenge.

As we walked through the woods, Rabbit said, "Jacob came by the general store to see me right after he went to see you. He seemed *really* happy. I mean, unusually happy. You know anything about that?"

I didn't meet her stare, but I knew she was giving me one of her knowing smirks. "Maybe," I replied casually.

"Oh, come on, you can't keep me in suspense. Did you two finally kiss?"

I blushed. I couldn't hold back my smile.

"You did!" Rabbit shouted, her voice echoing through the woods. "Ha! I should've known. I've never seen Jacob that happy."

"It was a really hot kiss," I gushed. "I could've kissed him forever."

She put her hands over her ears. "Ewww. Stop. Jacob's like a brother to me."

"Well, you asked!"

"I know, but confirmation of a kiss is enough. I don't need the details." She shoved newly bent branches out of the path as we walked deeper into the woods. "But seriously, I'm really glad you two are finally taking this to the next level. It's about damn time."

"I'm glad I got the chance to know him first," I said. "He's smart and funny and sweet. Just my kind of guy." I nudged Rabbit with my arm. "What about you? Do you have any crushes I should know about?"

She kept her eyes centered on the ground as we walked. "Yeah, I do. But it's not something I really think about much."

"Why not?"

"Because . . . well . . . because it's just not feasible."

"What's that mean?" I asked her, confused. "Anything is feasible between two people if the chemistry is right."

"Exactly. And I'm what makes it not feasible."

"But why?"

"Because I'm ugly."

Her words, so unexpected and harsh, yet stated with such firm indifference, made me gasp. I stopped walking and grabbed her arm, spinning her around. "Why would you say something like that?" I snapped. "*How* could you say something like that?"

She stared back at me, and a soft breeze blew past, lifting her hair away from her face. Her eyes were wide behind the owlish glasses. Her expression might've been one of shock. It might've been one of alarm. But I suspected it reflected plain insecurity mixed with fear.

I didn't take my hand off her arm. "Are you going to answer me?"

"Why do I have to answer?" she asked me in a quiet voice, the quietest I'd ever heard from her. "The truth is obvious just by looking at me."

"No, it isn't," I said fiercely.

"Yes, it is, Georgie. You think they call me Rabbit because I look like Jessica? No—they've called me Rabbit since I was a kid because I have buckteeth and big ears. And I'm scrawny and I wear glasses and I have no boobs."

"Boobs aren't what make a person beautiful," I nearly screamed. "A personality makes a person beautiful."

"In what world?" She shook her head. "Not in the world *we* live in. I'm not trying to put myself down or to get sympathy from anyone, Georgie. I'm just stating a few facts. I look like what I look like, and I've accepted it."

My jaw dropped. I was angry and sad. I would never believe there wasn't a guy out there who'd see who Rabbit was—a smart, sweet, cheerful girl with a genuinely big heart. "So what does that mean?" I went on, my voice growing sharper. "That you never think about falling in love? That you don't want to meet a guy who'll appreciate you and maybe roll around in the hay with you? It means you've *given up* without even trying."

She sighed. She didn't say anything.

"Do you realize what a great person you are, Rabbit? You met me the first day I got here and made me feel like this place was my home. And everybody likes you! You're like the mayor of this town!"

"I know." She clenched her jaw. "But nobody likes me in *that way*. The guys look past me, or I'm their friend. That's just the way it is. Really, Georgie, it's not a big deal. I didn't mean to upset you. I promise, I'll never say the word *ugly* again."

"That's not good enough, Rabbit," I said right away. "I want you to know—to *believe*—that you're not an ugly person. Hasn't anyone ever told you that?"

"Sure. My mom always tells me I'm not ugly. But she's my mom. What else is she supposed to say?"

I put both of my hands on my hips and scowled at her. "You're not getting this, are you? I want you to tell me that you don't believe you're ugly."

"If I say it, will you shut up?" She grimaced.

I sighed impatiently. "Is this why we've never had, like, ya know . . . girly conversations? Why you've never mentioned boys to me, or dating or stuff like that? I thought it was just because you weren't comfortable enough with me to talk about those things yet."

"There's nothing to talk about. I don't have a romantic life, and I don't have any hopes for one."

It was another stab to my heart. "Who do you have a crush on?" I asked her sharply. "Tell me right now. I want to know."

"Or what? Are you going to beat me up?"

"I'm serious, Rabbit!" My voice echoed through the woods.

"What's the point of telling you? It's not going to change anything. I'm not going to pursue him or try to kiss him or anything. And the last thing I want is for you to run around here playing matchmaker."

"I swear, I won't do that." I held up my hand in a promise. "You have my word. But how do you know he doesn't like you? Have you ever even talked to him about it? Or even tried to?"

She looked down at the ground again, kicking away a rock. "Jason Sydney," she muttered.

I searched through the names in my head until I found the one I was looking for. Jason Sydney. The short, slightly chubby sophomore who was always lighting the bonfires at the lake. I had talked to him only a handful of times, and he seemed nice enough. From what I remembered, I was sure he had a beer can glued to his right hand. "So," I said, "what do you like about him?"

"I've always had a little crush on him. Since we were in grade school," she answered. "He's kind of quiet and introverted, but he's . . . I don't know . . . confident. He's always done his own thing, ever since we were kids." A small smile spread across her lips as she seemed to recall memories of Jason Sydney. But then the smile disappeared as quickly as it had come. "But it's just silly. It's stupid to even talk about it. He doesn't like me."

"How do you know?" I pressed. "Have you ever talked to him? Like a serious conversation?"

"Here and there. Last year, at the back-to-school dance, we talked about scientific things. He's into science. But that was about it."

"Whispering Oaks High has a back-to-school dance?"

That was news. In the town the world had forgotten, some-body apparently remembered to turn up the radio.

"It's nothing good," Rabbit said. "But freshmen are, like, required to go. Crazy."

"Who'd you go with last year?"

"No one. I worked the drinks table. Pretty pathetic, huh?"

I dodged the question. "Jason's always the first one to offer you a can of soda when we get to the lake. Always. Haven't you noticed that?"

"He gives everybody a can of soda or a beer. He doesn't like me, Georgie."

I didn't answer her. I figured I had said enough, and I didn't want to make her uncomfortable or seem like a Nosy Nelly. But I couldn't help sympathizing with Rabbit. I couldn't help seeing a lot of myself in her. More than any-thing, I wanted to tell her that I had been a lot like her be-fore the book deal changed my life and brought me into the deceitful realm of popularity. I had never been consid-ered pretty. Everything I had gotten throughout my fresh-man year at Frasier High School I'd gotten because of the limelight. The friends I'd made, Jordan Lush . . . they hadn't known the real me, the Ruby Crane who preferred glasses to contact lenses and a quiet night at home with a book to some A-list party.

Now I was Georgie O'Dell—a nondescript girl from New York City. But more and more often, I was realizing that Georgie had a whole lot in common with Ruby. I was hiding from a scandal, not from my true self. Jacob Chat-terley's attention was proof that the old Ruby wasn't so bad after all. He hadn't kissed me because of my gorgeous face or my perfect body. He had seen something else in me, something that went deeper than appearance.

And I had done the same thing with him. Yeah, Jacob had an adorable face and a great smile, but the whole Mohawk thing was new for me. So were the piercings. I was mostly attracted to who he was inside. I'm not going to lie and forget to mention his great lips, but in all truth, there was so much more to him than that.

I wanted Rabbit to understand what I was saying. I wanted her to know that one day someone would find her beautiful, because she *was* beautiful. Big glasses and scrawny body and all.

Standing in the silence, just beyond the first clearing in the woods, we fumbled for words, for a way to end the uncomfortable conversation comfortably. Birds chirped overhead. Animals—raccoons? deer?—rustled in bushes nearby. The darkness was falling fast.

"So, does this mean you're going to be all weird with me now, because I told you I think I'm ugly?" Rabbit asked me flatly.

"No, of course not." It was my turn to kick a stone across the rutted ground. "But it does mean that I want you to think about what I said. To take it seriously."

"It's a deal."

"Good. Now, how are we going to get the rowdy Lake Redson crowd interested in coming to the Curious Cup for coffee and books?"

Rabbit scratched her head. "When did you say you were hosting this event?"

I shrugged. "How much advance notice should I give people? A week?"

"Oh, please," Rabbit said. "It's not like anyone has to check a social calendar or anything. You can do it as soon as you want."

"Tomorrow night, then," I replied, surprised by my own answer. "The sooner the better."

*　　*　　*

Jacob was sitting alone not far from the bonfire when Rabbit and I reached the lake. The small crackling flames illuminated his profile. It had to be the sexiest profile on earth. Not because of his totally sweet features but because he was hunched over his knees, reading a book, oblivious to what was going on around him.

And there was a lot going on.

Luck was with me: the crowd was bigger than usual. I spotted a few faces I hadn't seen in several days—Tim Corey, Vanessa Kruger, Colleen Morrison, Lonnie Paver— but no newcomers. The teenage population of Whispering Oaks was not a melting pot.

Jacob saw me and stood up. A thin smile creased his face, and he held up his hand in a wave. He wore one of those happy/excited/slightly embarrassed looks that always follow a first kiss.

As I walked over to him, I saw Rabbit make a sharp turn and head down to the water's edge.

"So, does this mean it's your favorite sonnet too?" he asked.

I stopped in front of him and smiled. "It was the best gift anyone's ever given me," I said as I hugged him.

When he drew away from me a minute later, he said, "I'm glad to hear that, 'cause I've pretty much been telling everyone you're my girl now."

How 1950s of him, I thought. But I smiled and said, "That could totally work."

"We might be the only couple in town who reads Shakespeare, but it'll be our secret."

"Funny you should say that." I told him about the book display I had just built and my master plan. "Tomorrow night, I thought maybe it could be an informal thing, like just to get everyone to the shop and browsing and listening to what I have to say. Maybe a poetry reading or something like that."

"Seriously?" His eyebrows arched. There was excitement in his voice. "Can I choose something to read? I promise it'll be something good—maybe a poem, maybe a passage from one of my favorite books. It'll be good."

"You think anyone else would come besides you and Rabbit?" I asked him worriedly.

"Are you kidding? Of course people will come! First of all, it's something to do. Second of all, it's actually a great idea. But it shouldn't only be us—the kids, I mean. Why not tell everybody in town? Like, put up flyers or just get the word out?"

"Eventually, that's the plan," I replied. "But since I don't really expect much to come out of it . . . I mean, I *wish* a lot would come out of it, but I thought it'd be better to start off small."

"Big ideas deserve big promotion," Jacob said.

I turned and looked at the crowd. MaryAnn Conner was talking to Lisa Trina, both of them smoking cigarettes and laughing. Kimmy Peterman, walking back from her father's beat-up Ford Taurus, was chatting on her cell phone. Jason Sydney was sparking one of his small bonfires. I watched as he flicked a lighter to a bunch of newspaper and twigs. Then he went to the cooler a few feet away and began rifling through it. He took two cans of soda, held one, and then went up to Rabbit and handed her the other.

I *knew* I'd caught that little move of his.

Rabbit, engaged in conversation with LaDonna Modine, didn't seem to notice it. She just took the can of soda and popped it open and started drinking.

Suddenly, Jacob started toward the bonfire, taking my hand. "Hey, people!" he called out. "Listen up! Georgie has an announcement to make."

I felt my stomach clench. I had thought I'd never be speaking in front of a crowd again for as long as I lived. My heart did a jumping jack and my palms got all sweaty.

Everybody whirled around at the sound of Jacob's voice. He glanced at me, the bemused expression still on his face. "Go for it," he said.

Taking a deep breath, I stepped up to the bonfire; it was Whispering Oaks' version of a stage and spotlight. *You can do this*, I thought. *You can make them see your point.*

I cleared my throat. "Hey, people," I began. "This might sound kind of strange and all, but . . . well . . . anybody here interested in doing something a little different tomorrow night? I mean, instead of just hanging out here at the lake?"

Silence. Stillness. The caw of a bird as it cut across the black night sky.

Anyone? Anyone?

Suddenly, a hand went up. Then another . . . and another. And before I knew it, I had a few takers.

An Unseen Path

Long after everyone had left, Jacob and I stayed behind, sitting in front of the bonfire. He had stoked it with more twigs and paper and fallen branches, and the little embers burned through the darkness like a lighthouse beacon. It was a cool night, and the air smelled of smoke and wet leaves. Above us, the sky glittered with stars.

"I think you got everyone interested and excited," he said, breaking the comfortable silence between us. "I have a feeling the whole thing—the whole event—is going to be a success."

"I hope so." There wasn't much more to say than that.

In truth, everyone *had* gotten excited by my little speech. I'd been honest and clear about my plan; it was about books and reading, I told them, and there would probably be a lot of talking going on. They didn't seem to mind. At first it was as if I'd spoken Swahili, but as the idea wrapped itself around their brains, they understood what I was trying to do. Jason Sydney waved his hand at me and asked, "So, like, we can read stuff we've written ourselves maybe? Like, to share with each other?" That was a happy moment, because it confirmed my suspicion that there were plenty of teenagers in the town who either read or wrote but just didn't have a place where they could express their ideas.

I nodded at Jason and encouraged him to bring whatever he wanted to the shop. An essay. A passage from his favorite book. Lyrics to a song. Whatever. The idea was to get our minds moving. I explained that I would recommend a book for everyone to read and that we'd get together once a week to discuss it.

At that, MaryAnn Conner gasped. "Oh my God just like they do on *Oprah* I know what you're talking about my mom actually belonged to an online book club last year and loved it for a while but then she said she wished there was one with real people and not just screen names and I mean I think it's a great idea because it's different and it could actually be fun is that what we're gonna do? Is it? Is it?"

I had never wished for an entire case of aspirin before, but right then and there, I would've downed about a hundred tablets.

"So," Jacob said, interrupting my thoughts. "I guess you didn't have a chance to read through those articles I brought you this afternoon, the ones about Mattie Dembrook and Eamon Whitfield."

I turned to look at him directly. "No, I didn't. I was too sidetracked by the sonnet. And the kiss."

He smiled shyly, and when I looked back up at the sky, I saw a million more stars.

"Jacob?" I ran my fingers over his left hand.

"Yeah?"

"Do you wonder if it was like this for them? For Mattie and Eamon?" It sounded like a stupid question, but I meant it.

"I think this is exactly how it was for them," Jacob answered quietly. "They knew from the very beginning that they clicked—even though they knew it was improbable. Kind of like us."

"How are we improbable?"

He tightened his arms around my waist. "Think about it. Here *I* am—born and raised in this small town in the middle of nowhere. But my mind belongs in the city, where there's a lot of culture and diversity. And my whole life, I've always believed that I'd be alone—at least until college, or until I could move away."

He paused and glanced up at the trees, where a flock of birds was fanning out against the black sky. "And here *you* are—this cool and smart city girl," he continued. "And then you find yourself here, of all places—in Whispering Oaks. I mean, what are the odds? When you really think about it, *we* should never have found each other."

I thought about it. He was right, in a lot of ways. We weren't forbidden, just unlikely.

"Be honest," he said. "What would your friends think about me? They'd probably call me a dumb country boy, right?"

"No, they wouldn't," I replied quickly. "They'd like you just fine." But I thought, *What friends? I was exiled from New York City—well, pretty much any big city—and dropped by all the people I thought liked me.* The only friends I had were here, in Whispering Oaks.

I wanted to say those words exactly. But how could I even begin to explain to Jacob what had happened to me? I hadn't explained it to myself yet.

I felt a surge of guilt so powerful that tears burned behind my eyes.

Of all people, Jacob deserved to know the truth. About my identity, I mean. About how I'd once been Ruby Crane and how Ruby and Georgie were really the same person. Inside, at least. Did that count for anything?

Maybe. I wanted to believe that it would.

I closed my eyes. I didn't want to think about the past. Was there even a point in thinking about it? If you become a new person, in a new place and with a new name, does the old one matter? Can't *everything* disappear once you've disappeared?

I asked myself those questions as I sat enveloped in Jacob's arms. But I sure as hell didn't get an answer. Not one that calmed my fears, anyway.

I felt safe with him. But why was I so scared?

Wanting to change the subject, I cleared my throat and

said, "What were the articles about—the ones you wanted me to read?"

"Just biographical stuff on Mattie and Eamon, and some opinions from a couple of local historians about the legend," Jacob answered.

"What kind of opinions? I thought the story you told me was pretty much it."

"It is, but like I said, some people think Mattie never drowned herself in the lake."

Staring out at the lake, I imagined Mattie Dembrook running into the water. "What's your opinion?" I asked him. "You're as much an expert on the legend as anyone else."

"No, I'm not. I'm just obsessed with a couple of ghosts. But for the record . . . I'll tell you what I've never told anybody else."

That got me. I sat up straight and turned to face him. "What?"

He picked up a rock from the ground and skimmed it across the lake; it disappeared into the darkness. "I'm starting to understand what Mattie and Eamon felt for each other," he said quietly. "Why they got so wrapped up in each other. The intensity. The power of it. Now I know why no one was able to break them up."

Thudding heart. Wide, dopey smile. In case you're wondering, I'm describing myself here. I wrapped my arms around his neck and went for another mammoth kiss, determined to hold it until the sun rose.

And then it happened.

A breeze lifted all around us, flowing over the grass

and the lake and swirling through the trees. The woods started whispering.

I broke away from Jacob, but my hands grasped his shoulders tightly. "Oh my God," I breathed, looking up. "That's unreal. Did you hear—"

"I heard it." Jacob gulped.

The breeze grew stiff. It wasn't the wind of a summer storm or a draft coming off the lake; it was something else entirely—something ethereal and eerie and unnatural. The hair on my arms stood up. And as I turned around in search of an answer—a source—another gust pushed past us, extinguishing the bonfire like water dousing a lit matchstick.

The darkness around us was total.

"Jacob," I said. "Um . . . I can't see a damn thing."

"Neither can I. Just stay calm. We'll be fine."

I listened as he fumbled in his pockets for his lighter. I got quick glimpses of him as he tried to reignite the bonfire, flicking the spout again and again. But every time a spark shot from it, the breeze grew stronger. The whispering grew stronger too, pulsing around us until the air was warm on my neck. My heart was drilling through my ribs. I had never experienced a darkness so encompassing. There was no switch I could flip, no bright moon shining in the sky. In all that open land, I felt completely trapped.

Finally, Jacob grabbed my hand and pulled me to my feet.

"What are you doing?" I asked him. "I can't even see your face."

"I know. Maybe another storm is coming. Let's try to make it back to the car."

"We can't see two feet in front of us."

The wind sounded as though it were speaking—one whisper after another, one word after another. If it was Mattie Dembrook, she was talking in complete sentences.

I couldn't hide my fear. I started taking quick breaths. I held on to Jacob as he stepped in front of me and led the way.

But there was nowhere to go.

Right? Left? North? South?

Suddenly and inexplicably, we were lost.

"Wait," Jacob said firmly. "We have to get ahold of our senses. We're just panicking, and that's not doing us any good."

"I think the car is to the right," I told him.

"Well, that's funny. Because I thought it was straight ahead."

Then I saw a blip, a peripheral flash.

Something was moving through the trees up ahead.

"Did you see that?" I asked quickly. "Right over there?" And I pointed like a moron. I felt Jacob freeze beside me. The wind had calmed down, but the whispering continued in small, certain spurts.

"I saw it," he replied. "It was like a . . . flash, right?"

"Yes. Could it have been lightning?"

"Without rain or thunder? The sky is clear. If you look up, you can see the stars. Look, there's Orion."

I wasn't interested in seeing any belt at this point—even if I could wear it. "Let's just get out of here," I said. "Let's just start walking."

So we did. We moved slowly but steadily, dodging tree stumps and branches. I followed Jacob's lead. I kept one hand locked in his and used the other to swat at woodsy obstacles I couldn't see. Within minutes, I knew we had gone in the wrong direction, deeper into the woods and away from the narrow lane where the car was parked. Jacob knew it too, but he didn't say anything. We were both too afraid to admit that we were lost in the dark. Not to mention that we were surrounded by unexplained gusts of wind that sounded way too much like voices whispering directly into our ears.

The strangest thing, though, was how the fear left me little by little. With each step I took, I realized that my hands weren't trembling as much, and that the rapid beating of my heart was slowing down. I kept catching flashes of something in my peripheral vision. I saw the swift, sudden burst of light and felt reassured somehow. Even the darkness lost its threat: it became a sort of cocoon, sheltering me and Jacob from any dangers we might encounter. I didn't know I'd stopped stumbling and batting at branches until Jacob called out my name.

"Georgie?"

"Yeah?"

"What's wrong?"

Talking to him in the dark was strange, but I didn't feel the need to rush on. "Nothing," I said quietly. "Just listen."

"I am listening," he replied. "But right now, I'm more concerned about getting us out of here."

"Can't you hear it?" I said. "The whispering—it's trying to tell us something."

He went silent.

And above us, the trees rattled, and we heard the soft murmuring, listened to it until it formed a word . . .

It sounded as if someone said the word *go* on a long, drawn-out sigh.

"Where the hell are we?" Jacob's voice sounded tense.

"I don't know, but I think we should . . . go," I said, urging him. "Just keep walking. We'll find our way."

I meant it. I felt strangely safe. Protected. I wanted to call out to Mattie or Eamon. I sensed their presence as Jacob and I continued through the woods, sensed it as I'd never sensed anything before. I mean, who *wouldn't* totally freak out in the middle of dark, haunted woods? Only a complete psycho. Or—given how oddly peaceful I felt in those minutes—a psycho having a supernatural experience.

I don't know how long Jacob and I treaded through the woods. I didn't bother thinking about time or praying to be rescued. When the line of trees finally ended and we could see the faint glow of a light burning in the distance, I squeezed Jacob's hand and said, "See? We're . . . somewhere."

We went a few more paces before the wind died down and the whispering stopped. That was when I realized that we had crossed acres and acres only to find ourselves, inexplicably, back in town. Or at least in familiar surroundings.

"Holy spirits," Jacob said.

My sentiments exactly. The light burning in the distance was a candle, and the candle was sitting inside a window, and the window was attached to a white clapboard house that I immediately recognized as the Curious Cup.

*   *   *

"That's quite a story," Aunt Fin said as she poured two tall glasses of iced tea and set them on the counter.

Jacob and I were sitting on the stools on the sales floor. The shop was closed, but Aunt Fin had stayed late to catch up on paperwork. When we'd made it inside, I'd blurted the story out to her. Then I got dizzy and tripped and had to sit down on the grimy floor of the back room. Aunt Fin, even with all her mysterious occult-related beliefs, didn't know what to say. She was astounded by the whole thing.

"What gets me," Jacob said now, after gulping the iced tea, "is how we made it *here*. I've lived in this town my whole life and never made it across the woods like that. I didn't even know there was a direct path from the lake to right here."

"There is," Aunt Fin said. She was drying her hands on a dish towel by the cash register. "Or there used to be. That's what someone told me once upon a time. But I admit that it's strange. The woods are way too thick and uncharted to make a clean cut from the lake to the back door. You're both lucky you didn't run into a mean coyote with an appetite."

"Totally lucky," Jacob echoed.

"Well, I think it was Mattie and Eamon," I finally said. Which, of course, brought on complete silence.

"Seriously," I continued. "I think it was one of them trying to make contact with us."

"Aha!" Aunt Fin smiled. "So that's what the two of you were doing—hunting for the resident ghosts of Whispering Oaks." She gave us a knowing look.

Jacob blushed, then dipped his head back toward the glass.

"Is it really so far-fetched?" I asked. "I mean, think about it. The legend has been around for a long time, and people here in town really believe it. I felt something in those woods tonight. I think I even saw something—those flashes in the woods. Jacob, you saw them too."

"I did," he agreed. "And to be honest, they spooked me."

"It isn't far-fetched," Aunt Fin said. "Not to me, at least. I've always thought this shop—this house—was haunted, so I know what you're feeling."

"What?" I screeched. "You didn't tell me that."

She shrugged. "I've been here a long time, and I've seen and felt things too, things I couldn't always explain. But whatever—or whoever—is here happens to be a good, polite entity."

"What kinds of things?"

"Lights turning on and off, objects moving," she explained. "Once, about two years ago, I found the faucet in the back room running when I came in to start the day. I never use that faucet. But someone turned it on."

"What's the history of this house, anyway?" I asked Aunt Fin. "Do you know anything about it?"

"It's been here for over two hundred years," she told me. "It's been modified and fixed up countless times, of course, and it's served as a private residence, a doctor's office, a veterinary office . . . you name it. The first owners of the house, according to what I've heard in town, were the Liliths. James and Anastasia Lilith."

"And the Liliths," Jacob said, cutting in, "were pretty outspoken. They led the town's first employment strike. That's what my mom says, anyway. She has newspaper clippings about them."

Aunt Fin quickly fixed herself a glass of water with lemon and some sort of shiny leaves, then came back to sit with us at the counter. "Well, now this property and building are owned by the Cankers, and they really aren't the type who care much for ghost stories, or history at all, for that matter."

"*Ugh.*" Jacob made a face, scrunching his nose and sticking out his tongue. "I can't even stand to hear their names."

I thought back to my first night in Whispering Oaks. Rabbit and I walking through the woods and meeting up with Frank Canker. The slave driver. The pit bull. And, according to Rabbit, the big pig.

"Rabbit just loves Frank Canker," I said sarcastically.

"Ha!" Jacob laughed. "Rabbit's his worst enemy. And she has no fear voicing her opinion—right to his face."

"Well, that's how some people are," Aunt Fin said. "Mr. Canker comes in here to collect the rent check from me the minute it's due. I know he and his wife have a bad reputation, but they've really never been mean to me."

Jacob downed the last of his iced tea and slid the empty glass across the counter. Then he ran a hand over his Mohawk and yawned. "Well, they're mean-spirited people, Finny. They don't care about anyone. It's a pity *they* didn't get lost in the woods tonight."

"We didn't get lost, remember?" I tapped his shoulder. "We made it here safe and sound."

"True. But I still don't think I'll be getting a good night's sleep tonight. That was too freaky. I feel like we got pulled into *A Wrinkle in Time*."

"Well, speaking of books," Aunt Fin said, "you have a pretty big day ahead of you tomorrow. Word on the street is that we've got quite a crowd coming here for . . . whatever it is you guys are doing."

Word seriously traveled fast around here. Jacob stood up. "That's true. I've got to get home and pick out the things I'm going to read." He gave me a mischievous smirk. "They're a surprise."

"Wait," I said, "how are you getting home? We left your dad's car down at the lake."

"My folks are at the Higgins Bar on Main Street, and if I don't show up right about now and interrupt them, they'll get flat-ass drunk. We'll handle it."

"Are you sure?" Aunt Fin asked.

"Yeah. It's no big deal. I'm used to keeping tabs on their drinking binges."

It made me sad to hear him say that. "Maybe after tomorrow night, they'll stop kicking back so many beers."

"Ha! That I'd pay to see. But you know what they say: stranger things have happened." He looked at Aunt Fin. "Thanks for the tea, Finny. Now, if it's cool, would you mind turning around so that I can give Georgie her goodnight kiss?"

I bit down on my lip. Totally embarrassing and totally hot.

Aunt Fin winked at me as she disappeared into the back room, herbal drink in hand.

I stood up and collapsed into Jacob's arms. The exhaustion—the weirdness—of the night finally hit me, and I felt like a big, heavy bag of rocks.

" *'Good night, good night! Parting is such sweet sorrow / That I shall say good night till it be morrow.'* "

"*Romeo and Juliet,*" I said. "That was way too easy."

"Okay, then. I'll give you a tough one." He cleared his throat. " *'The voice of the sea speaks to the soul. The touch of the sea is sensuous, enfolding the body in its soft, close embrace.'* "

The words had been beautiful when I'd read the book in the first term of freshman year. Now they sounded more beautiful than ever, falling from Jacob's lips like a prayer. I kissed him once. "*The Awakening,* by Kate Chopin," I said, and kissed him again.

"See you tomorrow."

I walked him to the door and watched him disappear down the walkway and into the night. And then I was alone. No whispers. No wind. No flashes of light seen from the corner of my eye. Only the strange, peaceful feeling that something was happening. Something I couldn't quite explain.

"Mattie?" I whispered into the silence.

Above me, the lights flickered.

A Town Speaks

By late afternoon of the following day, the Curious Cup had been transformed into a "center for integrative and interdisciplinary creativity." Those were Aunt Fin's words, not mine. If you ask me, the shop looked a lot like one of those small independently owned bookstores that deserve a lot more attention than they ever get. The curios and various other items were still prominently displayed, but books were the main focus. All you had to do was step inside to realize that. The two display tables had been moved closer to the center of the floor, and the pages of literary quotes I had written were now outlined in black and gold marker.

Much to my surprise, all the regular customers had heard about the event. I kept reminding myself that news spread quickly in a town like Whispering Oaks, especially if it was *new* news and not the usual small talk.

When old Mr. Fuller came in for his daily baked good, he rested his cane against the counter and hobbled to the display. He bought a copy of *Frankenstein* and told me that it was one of the books he had read while serving in World War II. Lynn Bodders stormed in around eleven o'clock with a resounding "Helllooooo, Georgie!" Her hair was a dark shade of auburn with scattered blond streaks that looked pink in the light. She ordered a cup of coffee, tapped out "It's My Party" and then assured me that she'd be there that night to join in the fun. Patty Naddy, a member of the S.M.C.—Single Moms Club—dropped in and reserved four copies of *Prisoner of My Desire,* a romance novel by Johanna Lindsey. She stared wantonly at the bare-chested guy on the cover before adding lots of ice to her cup of tea.

It was two-thirty when Aunt Fin asked me what the evening's schedule looked like.

A tough question, since I really didn't know. "People are supposed to start arriving around seven," I said. "We'll just play it by ear."

"Do you have any idea how many people are coming?" she asked.

I tried to do an accurate count. Most—but certainly not all—of the teenagers in town would be there. Plus a few adults with their little kids. And then I added two stray cats, just in case. "Maybe fifteen people," I said. "Not more than that."

Aunt Fin nodded, then went about preparing extra coffee and tea, scones and muffins and cookies.

It probably wasn't a good idea to play it by ear, but I had no idea what the night would end up being like. All I knew was that I had high hopes for it. That I believed in it. There was always the possibility, however, that it would be a total bust, and I was prepared for this. Maybe five people would show up and sit there and just stare into space. Maybe there were already a few residents who thought the new girl in town was brain-fried. Whatever the case, I was determined to change things in Whispering Oaks for the better. If I could turn just one nonreader into a reader, my job was done. Two nonreaders into readers? A greater success than I ever thought possible. *Three* nonreaders into readers? Hell, somebody get me a Nobel Prize.

Jacob showed up around five-thirty, carrying a huge covered bowl and a flat metal pan.

"What's all this?" I asked, helping him unload the goods onto the counter.

He was wearing black jeans, a white dress shirt with both sleeves cut off, and black biker boots. His Mohawk looked shinier than usual, as if he'd slicked it with gel. "My mom made some food," he explained. He pointed to the bowl. "The pasta salad she's famous for." He pointed to the pan. "And the brownies she's famous for. She and my dad are coming tonight. When I told them what we were doing, they got pretty interested."

I stared at the bowl and the pan and couldn't believe my eyes. I didn't know what to make of it. Why would Jacob's mom go out of her way to make so much food?

When Jacob saw the look on my face, he said, "You shouldn't be all that surprised."

"I shouldn't?"

He shook his head. "Generosity and friendliness . . . that's the small-town way. I thought you had figured that out by now. You're still thinking like a city girl."

He was right. I hadn't expected so much generosity and friendliness.

"So," he said, "tell me what I should do."

Together, we straightened out the few rows of chairs Aunt Fin had set up earlier, swept the floor again, and wiped down the counters. We found a string of white Christmas lights in one of the back room drawers and hung them from two hooks in the ceiling so that they sparkled above the display tables. We even flicked away the last particles of dust from the shiny book jackets. I moved more slowly than Jacob, mainly because I spent a lot of time staring at his butt and the muscles in his forearms. I felt kind of guilty about that. He broke a sweat, lifting and carrying and stretching. I stood around imagining what he'd look like naked. I confess, my friends, to thoughts of an impure nature.

We were both so consumed with what we were doing— Jacob with organizing the sales floor, me with imagining him naked—that neither of us heard the front door open. It wasn't until Rabbit cleared her throat that I turned and saw her standing there.

And the shock was so great, I gasped.

Rabbit was dressed to the nines. She was wearing funky boot-cut jeans, a black tank top with so? printed across it in red lettering, and a silver choker. She had traded in her flip-flops for black boots. Her face was beautiful: a light shade of red lipstick that drew attention away from her teeth, soft strokes of blush across her cheeks, and a pair of small rectangular glasses that didn't dwarf her features. Her blond hair was full and held just the slightest wave.

"Rabbit?" I said, barely able to get her name out. "Is that really you?"

She cradled a book to her chest and let her gaze dart around the shop. She was either nervous or scared—I couldn't tell which—but the gleam in her eyes was one of determination. "Of course it's me," she snapped. "Why would you ask a question like that?"

"Because you look so . . . different," I said. "You look beautiful."

"Oh, please." She uncrossed her arms. She still wouldn't meet my stare. "It's just the same old me. Nothing's different."

I moved out from behind the counter and walked toward her.

Jacob said, "Hey, Wilma Dooney. You look downright hot."

Rabbit's jaw clenched. "Jacob Chatterley, you *know* I hate it when you call me *Wilma*."

"Yeah, yeah, yeah." He leaned on one of the chairs and shrugged. "Whatever your name is, you still look hot."

Her cheeks flushed, and she kept fidgeting. "Well, it's a special event, so I thought it'd be nice to dress up a little bit. But maybe it was a stupid idea. All this fuss just so I can see the same people I've known for years. And, ya know, it's not like anyone will even notice that I changed my glasses."

"You changed a lot more than that," I said.

"A *little* more," she replied. "Not a lot. I don't want anyone thinking that I've changed a lot just because of how I look."

Staring at Rabbit close up was crazy. It was still her—the same sweet Rabbit with the buckteeth and the intense stare—but it was also a new person. An older person. I saw a girl who had taken a really big risk . . . and won.

Somewhere, she'd probably known that she wasn't ugly, and that love and romance weren't out of her reach. But the fear of being rejected, of being shunned, had kept her from coming out of that shell. It was easier for her to hide in the shadows than to play in the sun, so to speak.

Because I'm ugly. That's just the way it is.

Her words. So flat and firm and indifferent.

And her fear. All that time, she had kept herself hidden from the world because she'd been afraid that no one would notice or care. Or maybe that someone *would* notice and criticize her.

She'd been afraid to fail.

Just like me.

Afraid that what I had inside wasn't good enough.

"Hey." Jacob touched my arm. "You okay?"

I blinked back to reality and said, "You look really beautiful, Rabbit."

She finally cracked a smile. "Thanks. I . . . I wouldn't have done it if it wasn't for you."

"Really?"

"Yeah."

"Why?"

"Because of what you said to me last night, I guess. And also because of tonight."

"Tonight?"

She nodded at the display tables and the chairs. The books. "It's the first fun and important thing we've done in this town in ages. I don't think you realize what you're doing. Other people might've thought about it, but nobody had the guts to actually do it."

Hearing Rabbit's words, seeing the change in her—the night was already a success as far as I was concerned. "So, are you going to read something for the crowd tonight?" I asked.

She tapped the book cradled in the crook of her arm. "Yeah. I've got my poem."

"That's all you need," I said, and put my arm around her.

*　　*　　*

They came: Kimmy Peterman and her mom, Joyce; MaryAnn Conner and her parents, Alan and Jessica; Jason Sydney and his two older sisters; Lisa Trina and her mom, Cassie; Billy Burns and his father, William; LaDonna Modine; Pam Covington; Ellen Watson; Jimmy John Petrillo.

Jacob's parents, Aidan and Rochelle, waved at Aunt Fin as they walked through the front door. Rabbit's mother, Laura—the spitting image of Rabbit, by the way—took a seat in the back of the room as quietly as possible. Then came Lynn Bodders, Lisa Marie Keating, the members of the Single Moms Club, and Mr. Fuller with his copy of *Frankenstein.*

One by one, they stepped through the doors of the shop and began reading the quotes plastered on the walls, pointing and smiling and commenting to each other. Everyone marveled at the display, crowding around the tables and snatching up copies.

What got me was that they all seemed so damn happy to be crowded into the shop. With each other. Staring at quotes they'd probably heard but couldn't really place. And I thought, *It's so easy to do this, to come together and just chill out. What's the big deal?*

But it *was* a big deal. A huge deal. Whispering Oaks hadn't been resuscitated in a long time.

The buzz of conversation on the air was tremendous. I watched as Aunt Fin worked the floor: she went from person to person and thanked them for coming; she motioned to the books; she pointed at me while answering questions.

Jacob was standing at a makeshift podium, arranging several sheets of paper. Rabbit came out of the back room balancing a tray in her hands—scones, cookies, brownies. She was joined by Kimmy Peterman, who took it upon herself to make sure everyone got a cup of coffee or tea and a taste of Rochelle Chatterley's famous pasta salad. Just behind the podium, Billy Burns was setting up his guitar.

Things went on like that for nearly forty-five minutes, until Aunt Fin began directing people to their chairs. The event was standing room only. Aunt Fin went up to the podium, plastered on a smile, and waited for silence. When it fell, she said, "I want to thank you all for coming to the Curious Cup tonight. It's actually our first official event . . . an evening that celebrates books, poetry . . . the written word." She cleared her throat. "I have to admit: this was not my idea. I give credit to a member of my family, a very special member who came here to live with me just recently. Many of you already know her." She glanced at me.

Everybody glanced at me.

"Georgie is sixteen years old, but she's really a lot older in her soul," Aunt Fin continued. "She already knows a lot about herself, but she's learning more every day. I don't have any doubts that her future will be bright. Tonight, she and her friends—all of them fine members of the Whispering Oaks community—will be expressing their passion for . . . well . . . for living creatively! And so without further delay . . ."

There was a big round of applause as I made my way up to the podium. My heart started hammering in my chest. For a split second, when I looked out at the crowd, I flashed back to that awful moment at the American Literature Club: a happy occasion . . . and danger lurking just around the corner. But I pushed the thought away quickly. *No*, I thought, *this is a new place, a new experience, a new beginning. Georgie O'Dell does not have a past.*

I cleared my throat, then reached under the podium,

where I'd stored my copy of *Rebecca*. The silence in the shop was huge. The air was still. And yet there was an awesome feeling circulating everywhere, an electrical current that invigorated me.

" 'Last night I dreamt I went to Manderley again,' " I began. " 'It seemed to me I stood by the iron gate leading to the drive and for a while I could not enter, for the way was barred to me.' "

For nearly five whole minutes, I read. I lost myself in the beautiful cadence of the words, in the lush descriptions, in the journey that transported me to the Gothic realm of *Rebecca*. And the audience came with me. I knew it. I saw it on their faces when I finished and looked up: everyone had the dreamy look that comes only in a moment of complete surrender, when you've given yourself over to the magic of transcendence.

There was no applause, just a steady stream of silence as Rabbit made her way up to the podium, clutching a hardcover to her chest. She kept her eyes cast downward as she leafed through the pages.

"I'm reading a poem by my favorite poet, Emily Dickinson," she said. "I like Emily because I think her poetry does a lot of things: it can scare you or make you sad, it can make you laugh or cry . . . but most important of all, it makes you think. Emily was a recluse. She never got married. She actually never even left her home except for a handful of times. She devoted her life to her writing. A lot of people probably thought Emily was weird, but when her poetry was published after she died, they were all pretty shocked, because they realized that she knew a lot about life. The old saying 'You can't judge a book by its cover' applies well to her and to her life. I admire her for being true to herself."

Then, in a strong voice, Rabbit read the poem she had selected:

Hope is the thing with feathers
That perches in the soul,
And sings the tune—without the words,
And never stops at all,
And sweetest in the gale is heard;
And sore must be the storm
That could abash the little bird
That kept so many warm.
I've heard it in the chillest land,
And on the strangest sea;
Yet, never, in extremity,
It asked a crumb of me.

She waited a long moment before closing the book, giving that last powerful line the opportunity to impact the crowd.

I was standing off to the side, out of sight of everyone. I watched as a smile curved Jason Sydney's lips. His eyes followed her back to her seat.

Rabbit's mother was crying. Tears spilled down her cheeks and she wiped a wadded tissue across her chin. "I didn't know," she whispered to Lynn Bodders. "I had no idea my Wilma liked poetry, or that she could read with such feeling. I really didn't know."

Jacob stepped up to the podium next. He pulled several crinkled sheets of paper from his back pocket and smoothed them out on the hard wooden surface. His eyes found me and held me for just a moment. "I'm going to read one of my favorite poems," he said. "I used to read it a lot when I was a little kid, just because I loved the way it sounded—like a song. It's by Lord Byron." He gave his throat a good clearing, then began to read:

She walks in beauty, like the night
Of cloudless climes and starry skies;
And all that's best of dark and bright
Meet in her aspect and her eyes:
Thus mellowed to that tender light
Which heaven to gaudy day denies.

One shade the more, one ray the less,
Had half impaired the nameless grace
Which waves in every raven tress,
Or softly lightens o'er her face;
Where thoughts serenely sweet express
How pure, how dear their dwelling place.

And on that cheek, and o'er that brow,
So soft, so calm, yet eloquent,
The smiles that win, the tints that glow,
But tell of days in goodness spent,

A mind at peace with all below,
A heart whose love is innocent!

As his voice trailed away, most of the women in the room dabbed at their eyes and started to sniffle.

I saw Jacob's parents clapping proudly as he smiled and stepped away from the podium, leaving it open for anyone else.

Not even a few seconds had passed before MaryAnn Conner shot to her feet.

Please, I thought, *use the periods!*

She was her bouncy, bubbly self, staring wide-eyed at the audience, clutching a thick paperback in her right hand. "I'm going to read from *A Tale of Two Cities* by Charles Dickens because I found out last night that it's my mom's favorite book and when she told me and gave me this copy I started reading it and I think it's really awesome I stayed up late and spent most of today trying to get through it I mean it's not the easiest reading but I understand what's going on and I'm so glad that I've started it so anyway"—she cleared her throat quickly—" 'It was the best of times it was the worst of times . . .' "

Nearly three minutes of breathless hyperbole that made my head spin. Somewhere, Charles Dickens was turning over in his grave. But you couldn't get angry or annoyed with someone like MaryAnn. Her enthusiasm was genuine and heartfelt and infectious. She left the audience smiling and clapping and even took a little bow before leaving the podium.

Jason Sydney and Billy Burns went up next. Billy settled into a chair with his guitar, and it was obvious from the way he and Jason were conferring with each other that they had rehearsed their performance earlier in the day. "Um . . . hi," Jason said. "I'm going to read a little bit from a really cool poem called 'The Highwayman'; it's by an English poet named Alfred Noyes, and, um . . . for those of you who don't know, Alfred was born in England in 1880, and he published his first book of poems when he was only twenty-one years old. He, uh, he actually taught at Princeton University for a few years, where I really hope to go to college one day, and, well, I really think the poem is awesome. And Billy here is going to be playing a tune we worked out together, okay?"

Billy gave a quick nod. He looked down at the guitar, placed his fingers on the strings, and strummed the first few notes. Soft, slow, high.

Then Jason started reading:

The wind was a torrent of darkness among the
gusty trees,
The moon was a ghostly galleon tossed upon cloudy
seas,
The road was a ribbon of moonlight over the purple
moor,
And the highwayman came riding—
Riding—riding—
The highwayman came riding, up to the old inn-
door.

He'd a French cocked-hat on his forehead, a bunch
of lace at his chin,
A coat of the claret velvet, and breeches of brown
doe-skin;
They fitted with never a wrinkle: his boots were up
to the thigh!
And he rode with a jewelled twinkle,
His pistol butts a-twinkle,
His rapier hilt a-twinkle, under the jewelled sky.

Billy changed the tune on his guitar, and the notes rose and fell steadily, sounding a lot like a horse's hooves galloping across rutted ground. Jason smiled and swayed his head along with the melody. He continued reading:

Over the cobbles he clattered and clashed in the
dark inn-yard,
And he tapped with his whip on the shuters, but all
was locked and barred;
He whistled a tune to the window, and who should
be waiting there
But the landlord's black-eyed daughter,
Bess, the landlord's daughter,
Plaiting a dark red love-knot into her long black
hair.
And dark in the dark old inn-yard a stable-wicket
creaked
Where Tim the ostler listened; his face was white
and peaked;

His eyes were hollows of madness, his hair like
*   mouldy hay,*
But he loved the landlord's daughter,
The landlord's red-lipped daughter,
Dumb as a dog he listened, and he heard the robber
*   say—*
"One kiss, my bonny sweetheart, I'm after a prize
*   to-night,*
But I shall be back with the yellow gold before the
*   morning light;*
Yet, if they press me sharply, and harry me through
*   the day,*
Then look for me by moonlight,
Watch for me by moonlight,
I'll come to thee by moonlight, though hell should
*   bar the way."*

Jason stopped reading, but Billy went on playing. The last minute of the tune was especially haunting—a series of high fast notes followed by low, deep ones. The effect sent tingles up my spine. The applause was spontaneous.

"Encore!" Lisa Marie Keating yelled.

Lynn Bodders stuck her fingers in her mouth and whistled like a freight train.

Other readings followed: Kimmy Peterman read from her favorite children's book, *Anne of Green Gables*. Lisa Trina read from *Julie of the Wolves*. LaDonna Modine and Pam Covington took turns reading from *The Outsiders*.

Ellen Watson read from *The Color Purple*. Jimmy John Petrillo read from *Holes*.

I studied the faces in the crowd. Everyone seemed generally stunned by the presentation. By the fact that something so moving and artful could be happening before their very eyes. Here. In Whispering Oaks.

Aunt Fin got up and went to the podium. The look on her face reflected a mix of excitement and pure ecstasy. She led another round of applause, then pulled a tattered sheet of paper from her pocket. "I just want to leave you all with one final thought—and one that I hope will stay with you for the rest of your lives. It's a poem by Emily Dickinson, so Rabbit will certainly identify with it!" She smiled. "But I'm sure you all will." And then she read the short verse:

> *There is no Frigate like a Book*
> *To take us Lands away*
> *Nor any Coursers like a Page*
> *Of prancing Poetry—*
> *This Traverse may the poorest take*
> *Without oppress of Toll—*
> *How frugal is the Chariot*
> *That bears the Human soul.*

After that, everyone started mingling again. But the night didn't end. In fact, it pretty much began at that point. The two display tables were ransacked, nearly all the books snatched up. The romance novels went the fastest. The poetry volumes disappeared. Aunt Fin worked the register like a madwoman as dollars flew and receipts scrolled out.

I watched it all from my own corner, stunned and drunk with happiness. When people approached me—Rabbit's mother, MaryAnn's parents, Lisa Marie Keating, Lynn Bodders, even old Mr. Fuller—I didn't know what to say. They congratulated me. They reached out and patted my shoulders. I saw their lips moving but didn't really hear the words they uttered. I didn't need to. I knew from the looks on their faces that they had been positively punched by the readings.

But then I *did* hear something.

I heard Lynn Bodders say, "I'm inspired! These past few years I've been so busy and caught up with life that I haven't had a chance to sit down and enjoy a book the way I used to when I was a kid. But now that's all going to change. I'm buying up a few books tonight and I'm going to spend my evenings reading. Happily and peacefully. Just reading. How about that? Hellllooooo, Georgie!"

I spotted Jacob in the middle of the crowd.

He pointed to the front door.

I nodded and began sifting through the crowd. Outside, the night was balmy and fragrant and calm. The sky was flooded with the moon's silver light.

Jacob met me on the walkway. He slipped his arm around my shoulder and drew me to him. "Well, looks like you're a big hit in the country, city girl," he whispered in my ear. "None of this would've been possible without you." He pulled back just a few inches and caressed my face. "In fact, I think you belong here, Georgie O'Dell. Right here, in Whispering Oaks."

I let those words swim through my brain. I liked the way they sounded, the way they felt. And I liked all the possibilities they promised. "I'm glad you think so," I whispered back. "Because I'm not leaving."

The Beginning, the End

It started with that one magical night, but it didn't end. For days afterward, a sort of literary renaissance overtook Whispering Oaks. You couldn't walk down Main Street without someone stopping and talking to you about what they were reading or what they wanted to read next. At the diner, people ate burgers with one hand and balanced paperbacks in the other. Lynn Bodders curled hair and brightened highlights while discussing *Treasure Island,* her new favorite book, by Robert Louis Stevenson. Mr. Watson, not as grumpy as usual, was reportedly caught reading a Danielle Steel novel on his lunch break. And, for the first time in years, the Higgins Bar was only half full on Thursday night.

I mean, it wasn't like a sudden circus of reading robots, but books had definitely become the new pastime. The adults were only half the story. Most of the teenagers got into it too, and nights at the lake weren't the same. There was constant talk of writing and reading, of maybe taking a drive out to the big Barnes & Noble an hour from town to browse the aisles in search of books Aunt Fin couldn't order or restock immediately. Everyone was eager to schedule another night of reading, or performing, or just getting together to start a book club. Most of the guys wanted to read dark, mysterious stuff. The girls, of course, leaned more toward books with a hint of romance or stories that held some promise of love. It was good to see those little disagreements stir: they were loud and heated and passionate and, for once, had nothing to do with beer or bonfires.

Almost overnight, the Curious Cup became known as the local bookstore. Aunt Fin and I took orders for more titles and had to widen the display to three tables. I was constantly making recommendations to people for what they could be reading. The members of the Single Moms Club raced through the romance novels; they sat at the counter and drank coffee and stared at the muscleman covers with wide, gleaming eyes. I felt kind of bad for them. In the heat of midsummer, reading romance novels can be dangerous: they raise blood pressure and send hearts racing. Fortunately, no one suffered a cardiac episode while chilling at the shop. I put out copies of

Madame Bovary and *Valley of the Dolls,* and they flew off the shelves.

The following Tuesday night, Jacob, Rabbit, and I built a bonfire at the lake and invited the usual crew to join us for an impromptu reading of Edgar Allan Poe's "The Raven," not only because it's my favorite poem, but also because Jacob thought it'd be fun to take advantage of the full moon blazing in the sky. So we gathered in a circle as the breeze swept over us and the lake shimmered silver and white. I sat beside Jacob. Our arms were intertwined. I stared at the faces surrounding me and caught the unmistakable glimmer of exhilaration in their eyes. Things hadn't been that way before the reading. Once the lake of lost dreams, it was now a lake of new possibilities, a place where books could be read in the shade of an oak tree, where poems could be written in the amber glow of dusk. I had never believed that a single night—or a single event, for that matter—could alter the course of so many lives, but the proof was alive and well right in front of me. The power was in the books, the words.

"Georgie knows the whole poem by heart," Jacob said, nudging me. "But she doesn't want me to tell anyone."

"Really?" Rabbit asked. "You've read it that many times, huh?"

I nodded. And I noticed that she was sitting next to Jason Sydney.

"Oh my God I so want to hear that poem I know it's totally scary and I'm gonna freak out but I read *The Tell-Tale Heart* in eighth grade and loved it go ahead and recite it, Georgie. Okay?"

MaryAnn Conner, ever breathless and full of wonder.

The fire crackled. The moon shimmered in the trees. I closed my eyes and began reciting the poem:

> *Once upon a midnight dreary, while I pondered,*
> *   weak and weary,*
> *Over many a quaint and curious volume of*
> *   forgotten lore—*
> *While I nodded, nearly napping, suddenly there*
> *   came a tapping,*
> *As of someone gently rapping, rapping at my*
> *   chamber door.*
> *" 'Tis some visitor," I muttered, "tapping at my*
> *   chamber door—*
> *Only this and nothing more."*
> *Ah, distinctly I remember it was in the bleak*
> *   December;*
> *And each separate dying ember wrought its ghost*
> *   upon the floor.*
> *Eagerly I wished the morrow;—vainly I had sought*
> *   to borrow*
> *From my books surcease of sorrow—sorrow for the*
> *   lost Lenore—*
> *For the rare and radiant maiden whom the angels*
> *   name Lenore—*
> *Nameless here for evermore.*

After reciting half the poem, I paused and took in the amazement on their faces—not there because I'd recited it by heart but because the words had chilled them to the core. There we were, sitting at the lake . . . in the same place . . . in a different place. Nothing about the landscape had changed, yet the words had transformed our surroundings.

I continued reciting the poem to the last eerie line. And that was when I saw Rabbit cowering in the shadows . . . and Jason Sydney's arm slip firmly around her shoulders.

*　　*　　*

The Single Moms Club had officially become the Reading Moms Club. I kid you not. The women of Whispering Oaks had created an elite little clique, deciding to devote two hours every Friday night to the discussion of romance novels. That happened at a small round table beside the book display: seven chairs crammed closely together, seven heads bent over cups of coffee, tea, or soda, seven minds joining forces to find a way to incorporate lusty prose into their everyday lives.

Keeping my usual post behind the counter, I tried not to listen in on the discussion that evening. Which, of course, was very hard. I have no problem with hearing people talk about sex, but when those people are your parents' age . . . well . . . let's just say *eeewwwww.* I occupied the time by going over the new book orders that were scheduled to arrive the next day. I also counted the cash in the register and logged the amount in Aunt Fin's daily plan sheet. Since the addition of books to the shop's roster of items, income had literally doubled.

At six o'clock, Jacob strolled through the door. His and

Rabbit's moms had both joined the reading group. He wasn't scheduled to pick up Mrs. Chatterley for another hour, but I wasn't surprised to see him. He leaned over the counter and planted a kiss on my lips.

"So, any plans for the night?" he asked, lowering himself onto a stool.

I frowned. "I promised Aunt Fin I'd help her clean up the house and give the dog a bath," I told him. "How about you?"

"Nothing, I guess. My nights aren't any fun unless you're with me."

"Flattery will get you everywhere." I poured him a glass of iced tea and set it before him. "You're more than welcome to come over and help, if you want."

"I just might do that." He sipped the tea. "So, you still haven't gotten a chance to read through those articles I left you, huh?"

The articles. The afternoon we first kissed. I felt like a total moron. "I swear I didn't forget about them," I said. "It's just been so busy—you know, with the books and all. Have you started writing your article on the legend yet?" I asked.

"No. I need to do some more research. That's why I want you to read. Because I need your help. After what happened to us the other night, I'm not sure what I believe anymore."

I leaned over the counter. "Maybe Mattie wanted to be here to see the greatest literary event in the history of Whispering Oaks. She was a booklover, after all."

"Very funny. You're lucky you're beautiful when you're sarcastic."

"How about this: if you forgive me for not reading the articles, I'll go on a research mission with you tomorrow. Deal?" I said.

"Deal." He smiled. "I promise it'll be fun."

"As long as we don't end up lost in the woods again, I'm down for whatever."

"I ain't makin' no promises."

The front door opened with a whoosh, and Rabbit stormed in. She was wearing white Capri pants and a pink shirt, and the new, smaller glasses let her big eyes shine through. She huffed and puffed her way to the counter. Dropping onto the stool beside Jacob, she threw an ugly glance at the moms' table and then followed it up with an ugly glance in my direction.

It caught me off guard. I froze.

"You're in *big* trouble, missy," she said, pointing a finger at me.

"I am?"

"Yes. You are."

My mouth fell open. My heart did a cartwheel in my chest. The fear that seized me was more powerful than anything I'd ever felt. *Please don't tell me you know. Don't tell me you've found out. I can explain. Really, I can.* "Why?" I finally forced the word out. "What'd I do?"

Jacob sighed and swiveled around on the stool. "I know what this is about, and I'm about to die laughing."

"Shut up, Jacob!" Rabbit yelled. "A lot of help you are."

"Well, what did you want me to say?" he shot back. "It's not a big deal."

Rabbit crossed her arms over her chest and scowled. "It's a very big deal. A big, gross, disgusting, embarrassing deal."

"It is not."

"That's because it didn't happen to you."

I banged my hand down on the counter. "Will one of you please tell me what's going on? I really have no idea why I'm in trouble."

"Fine," Rabbit said, "I'll tell you. It's all your fault that I almost died of embarrassment today. This whole book thing has gotten out of hand."

I was still completely confused. "What?"

"Oh, yes I did. And you want to know why?" She huffed again and leaned toward me. "Because today, I came home from work earlier than usual and heard . . . I heard . . . my parents . . ." She shivered. "Ugh. It's so gross."

"Just say it," I said, urging her.

"I heard my parents getting all frisky with each other in the living room," she said. "I mean, like, *getting it on*. Doing it."

Oh my God. There's such a thing as too much information. I didn't know what to say, so I looked at Jacob.

He was stifling his laughter.

"Um . . . Rabbit?" I finally said.

"What?"

"How is that my fault?"

She clucked her tongue. "It's your fault because my mom has been spending every last minute reading romance novels, getting hot and bothered and fantasizing about dirty things."

Jacob laughed harder.

Rabbit slugged him in the shoulder.

"Wait a minute," I said. "So what if your mom is reading romance novels, and so what if your parents are . . . ya know . . . having fun? Maybe they haven't had fun in a long time. That's a good thing, isn't it?"

Rabbit stared at me. The scowl loosened ever so slightly.

"Think about it," I continued. "How were they before your mom started reading romance novels?"

"Miserable," she answered. "But I liked it better that way."

"Rabbit, you know you don't mean that," Jacob snapped.

"No, I don't," she said, relenting. "But I swear, if I catch them taking a dip in the love pool one more time, I'm going to forbid my mom to read another romance novel."

"I think you'd have a hard time winning that battle." I pointed to the moms' table, from which a crescendo of laughter had just risen.

"Look at them," Rabbit said. "Happier than ever. Laughing and carrying on with those romance novels. I've never seen anything like it."

"Neither have I," Jacob said. "And it's not only here. I took a peek inside the Higgins Bar last night, and it wasn't its usual hopping self. I think a few people have traded in beer bottles for books."

Rabbit nodded. "MaryAnn told me her mom's been reading every night instead of going to the bar like usual."

"It's called the power of books," I said. "And from what I understand—or from what I'm assuming—you've experienced that romantic power yourself these past few days, Rabbit."

She peered at me over the rims of her glasses. She blushed.

A half hour later, the Reading Moms Club broke up. Jacob kissed me good-bye and promised to call me later on. Rabbit stayed behind, helping me clean up.

"Okay, now we're alone in here," I said. "Are you going to tell me what's going on with you and Jason?"

She gathered teacups and wiped crumbs from the tabletops. "We're, ya know, talking a lot more."

"I saw the way he slipped his arm around your shoulder the other night at the lake."

A reluctant smile played on her lips. "He walked me home after that. Told me I looked pretty."

"You see? I *knew* it. I told you all you had to do was talk to him." I flung a damp washcloth across the room and watched it drop onto the register with a splat. "So what are you two going to do now? Did you ask him out?"

"Are you crazy? I think men should be the ones to ask women out, not the other way around."

"That's totally not true," I argued. "But just think of it this way: what would Emily Dickinson do in this situation?"

Rabbit carried the teacups and glasses to the counter and set them down. "Emily Dickinson never left her house!

She'd probably have just written a poem about the situation. That's what she would've done."

I smiled. "Exactly."

"You're saying I should write Jason a poem?"

"I'm saying you should write a poem for yourself—but share it with Jason. You'll have him in the palm of your hand in no time."

She frowned. "Oh, I don't know. I mean, I'm just glad that we're talking more. He actually told me I looked pretty. None of it would've happened if it wasn't for you, Georgie. You're not leaving anytime soon, are you?"

The question knocked me off balance a little. I stared at Rabbit, saw the hopefulness in her eyes. Not too long before, I might've given a nonchalant answer or avoided the question entirely. But now I knew the answer. "No," I said, "I'm not leaving anytime soon."

"Good."

Just then, the door opened, startling us.

And Frank Canker stepped over the threshold.

He looked the same—the big belly, the beady eyes. Tonight, however, he was dressed in blue slacks and a white shirt. And there was no ax in his hand, thank God.

"Um . . . hi," I said.

"Is Finny around?" he asked in a gruff voice.

"Sure," I answered. "I'll get her for you." I hesitated a second, studying Rabbit's reaction.

She didn't say anything as Frank Canker looked at her. Instead, she pinched the stems of her glasses between her thumbs and forefingers, slid them down the bridge of her nose slowly, and met his gaze head-on.

Hatred, people. I'm talking a demonic stare here.

I knocked on the door of the back room and cracked it open.

Aunt Fin was sitting at her small corner desk. She glanced up at me and smiled. "Mr. Canker is here to see you," I whispered.

She stood up and walked out onto the main floor. "Oh, hi, Frank. What brings you here?"

"Can we talk in private, Finny?" he asked her flatly.

"Of course." She waved him into the back room, then gave me an I-have-no-idea-what-this-is-about look.

The door closed.

"Did you happen to get a whiff of him when he walked by?" Rabbit asked quietly.

"No. Why?"

She pinched her nostrils. "He smells like kitty litter."

I bit down on my tongue to keep from laughing. "I wonder what he wants," I whispered. "I've never seen him in here."

"He probably wants some sort of spell or incantation that will make him halfway attractive," Rabbit said. "Someone should tell him that Harry Potter doesn't live in Whispering Oaks."

For ten minutes, we busied ourselves with cleaning the rest of the shop. We folded up the table the moms had used, straightened up the display, and then went into the aisles and began dusting off the various curios and art pieces that hadn't gotten enough attention in the past week.

When the door to the back room opened again, I got the shock of my life.

Aunt Fin emerged holding a wad of tissues to her nose, sniffling as tears ran down her face.

Behind her, Frank Canker looked somber.

"Oh my God!" I shrieked, running to her side. "What happened? Are you okay?"

She took my hand in hers. "Oh, I'll be okay. It's just . . ."

"What?" I asked urgently. "What is it?"

"Finny? Is everything okay?" Rabbit leaned over the counter.

"No," Aunt Fin said, weeping. "It's . . ." She looked at Frank Canker. "It's just terrible. Terrible." She sniffled and dragged the tissue across her nose.

"*What's* terrible?" I snapped.

"The shop is closing at the end of the month," she said.

"*What?*" Rabbit and I screamed in unison.

Aunt Fin nodded. "It seems that Mr. Canker . . . is bulldozing the property here in order to build new offices for his company, and . . . and that means that we have to leave."

"But . . . that's impossible!" My voice shot through the ceiling.

"Oh, honey, it's possible." Aunt Fin pulled another tissue from her pocket. "And unfortunately, it's not my decision."

"Unfortunately," Frank Canker said, cutting in, "I need this space as quickly as possible. I know it's been a great shop for the town, but this doesn't mean you can't move somewhere else."

"Oh, Frank, you know that's impossible," Aunt Fin told him. "There's no other place for me to go in town, and I'll never be able to move all my merchandise somewhere else without losing a ton of money. I really just can't believe this. I've never been so upset in all my life."

Rabbit came over and threw an arm around Aunt Fin. As if Frank Canker weren't standing two feet away from us, she said, "That's just so disgusting. I'm sure if you had the strength, you'd totally slap someone."

Aunt Fin chuckled.

I was too shocked to say anything. I felt as if the floor had snapped in two. As if I'd been struck by lightning. The Curious Cup? *Closing?* After so many years? After giving this town a little bit of personality?

After everything that had happened in the past week alone?

How the hell could that be?

I spun around and faced Frank Canker. "Wait—isn't there anything else we can do?" I pleaded. "Can't you give us more time? Reconsider your options?"

"I'm afraid that's not possible," Frank Canker said. "I need this space and I need it quickly. There's nothing that can be done."

"But . . . you don't understand," I said. "All the important things that we've been doing . . . Do you know what's going to happen to this town if this shop goes?"

"I'm sure Whispering Oaks will get along just fine," he said.

I grabbed him by the arm and pulled him toward the display. "Look here for just a sec. You see those tables? They were stacked high with books just a few days ago. Now they're almost empty. That's because people are reading; they're happy, and it's all because of this shop."

He didn't seem to care. He glanced at his watch as I waited for him to answer me.

I grabbed a book off the table—*The Adventures of Tom Sawyer*—and held it out, waving it in his face. "Do you see this, Mr. Canker? It means a lot to this town right now. You can't just close us down."

"I can do whatever I want," he snapped. "This is my property and I'm the one who decides what will become of it. Now, if you'll excuse me . . ."

He turned and walked out of the shop.

I stared at Aunt Fin, my jaw on the floor. The big pig had completely ignored me, and I was enraged. Blown away. I would never believe that the Curious Cup was closing in just a few short weeks. In that moment, as I stood beside a weeping Aunt Fin and a pale Rabbit, I swore that it wouldn't happen. Because I wouldn't let it happen.

I ran outside. "Mr. Canker! Wait!"

He was halfway to his car, a bright blue Mercedes. "What is it now?" he snapped.

"I'm trying to tell you what's been going on here," I said. "Book clubs have been started; all of my friends here in town are reading; even some of the elderly people are getting involved. The point is . . . the Curious Cup is an important place. You'd be doing the town a huge disservice by closing it."

"I think I've heard enough, thanks."

"Maybe you *haven't* heard enough," I shot back. "You

just can't do this! The shop is a great place for everyone in this town."

He whirled around. "Now, you listen to me! *I'm* the owner. I can do whatever I want to do. That shop will close its doors in a few weeks and that's it."

"But—"

"But nothing!" he yelled. "It's over and done with. Where does a girl your age come off thinking she can speak to an elder like that? Like she knows what's best?"

"But I *do* know what's best!" I shouted back. My voice had reached a high pitch. I was raging, freaking mad. The polite way of doing things hadn't worked; it would never work with someone like Frank Canker. I couldn't control my anger.

"You do *not* know what's best!" he said. "You or your crazy little friend. Now, if you were smart, you'd go in there and start helping Finny pack her bags and her boxes."

"Books, Mr. Canker," I said sharply. "We're talking about books here. Does that mean a single thing to you?"

"No, it doesn't. And I've heard enough from you. I don't care about your stupid books or *any* book that anyone is reading!" He zapped the alarm on his car and went toward it.

The rage—the heat—had boiled over in my blood. I was on fire. And I totally lost it.

"Mr. Canker!" When he looked at me, I pivoted my body around halfway and jutted my butt out into the wind. I was still clutching the paperback copy of *The Adventures of Tom Sawyer* in my right hand. I slapped it against my ass and screamed, "You can just *kiss my book*!"

Go Ahead: Kiss It!

And just like that, it all ended.

Or at least we were told it would all end.

Aunt Fin and I spent most of that night pacing the floor of the shop, trying to come to grips with what was happening, trying to find ways to make it *not* happen. She pulled out all her paperwork and documentation and rental receipts. She went through the contracts she had signed with Frank Canker line by line.

He did, in fact, have the legal right to kick the Curious Cup to the curb. He had the right to ruin our lives and change the whole new dynamic of the town.

But why now? I wondered. *And why at all?*

"That pig can't do this!" Rabbit screeched, banging her hands on the counter. "He has no right! He can't violate us this way! This shop is the best thing this town has; he can't take it away from us!"

"But he *can,* Rabbit," Aunt Fin said sadly. "And that's exactly what he plans on doing."

Her eyes already glassy, Rabbit shook her head and fought to hold back her tears. "There has to be something we can do," she whispered. And when neither Aunt Fin nor I said anything, she stormed out the front door and into the night.

I didn't run after her. I didn't try to stop her or calm her down. How could I do any of those things when I felt like crying myself?

Long hours followed. Aunt Fin and I didn't speak as we made our way home, walking up the lonely stretch of Main Street hand in hand. At home, the house held us like a cold jail in the darkness—me pacing the floor of my bedroom, Aunt Fin pacing the floor downstairs. In no time at all, the sun came up over the treetops in the east.

*   *   *

"There were rumors of this happening," Aunt Fin said as she moped around the kitchen, Waffle and Pancake at her heels. "A long time ago, people were talking about the Cankers getting ready to bulldoze Star River Road and a lot of their properties. And I guess now it's really happening."

"But why so urgently?" I asked her for the millionth time. "After all these years, shouldn't he have to tell you why he's turning your life upside down?"

The answer—sadly, shockingly, maddeningly—was no. Frank Canker was under no obligation to be polite or professional or even civil about the shop's closing. All he had to do was wave his hand and sign certain papers to put his plan into motion. And that plan, as far as Aunt Fin knew, was to do away with most of the structure that housed the Curious Cup. To turn it into dust. In its place would rise some sort of modern building where Frank Canker could plot the rest of his real estate ventures.

The Curious Cup, as of that morning, was a doomed business.

Even as I opened the front door of the shop and flicked on the lights, as I prepared coffee and warmed up scones and muffins, I couldn't accept it. I felt as though I were walking through a nightmare. My movements were sluggish. My eyes were watery. And my heart was breaking. I stared across the store at the objects Aunt Fin had collected over the years, at the colored candles and the incense sticks, at the dream catchers and the beautiful Native American wood carvings.

I stared at the books.

In that moment, I flashed back to the night of the reading and saw Rabbit and Jacob and MaryAnn and Jason standing at the podium. The magic had continued—with the Reading Moms Club, with all of us sitting around the bonfire with "The Raven."

Was it possible that all that positive energy—all that change—would be gone in just a matter of weeks? And what about Jacob and Rabbit? What about our friends?

Would everything go back to the way it was before the books?

The lake of lost dreams. All that open, empty darkness. All that promise lost to plain unfairness.

We had taken the first steps. We were just beginning.

Now we were facing the end.

I walked to the display tables and stared down at the books. *Sense and Sensibility; The Last of the Mohicans; Where the Red Fern Grows; A Tree Grows in Brooklyn; The Pigman; Fahrenheit 451; The House on Mango Street* . . .

I sighed as the first tear slipped down my face. I didn't want any of the magic to end.

Taped to the walls still were the sheets of paper on which I'd written some of my favorite quotes. One in particular jumped out at me. That powerful and passionate line from *Jane Eyre: It is in vain to say human beings ought to be satisfied with tranquility: they must have action; and they will make it if they cannot find it.*

I pulled the sheet off the wall and held it in my hands.

It is in vain to say human beings ought to be satisfied with tranquility . . .

The anger welled up inside me again. As sharp as a dagger. As jarring as a bomb blast. The emotion seized me in a single instant and I knew what I had to do.

Exactly what I had never done before.

The power is in the words.

My own words.

I went to the drawer beside the cash register, pulled out a few sheets of paper and a pen, and began to write.

226

By now, many of you have probably heard about what's happening here in Whispering Oaks. The imminent closure of the Curious Cup has taken us all by surprise, not only because the news reached us so quickly and unexpectedly but because it means a certain new way of life is coming to an abrupt and unfair end. For the past several years, you have enjoyed the Curious Cup for what it has always been: a stopover on your morning walk to work, a gift shop for that last-minute present, a place where tea and fresh scones can be enjoyed all year round and where the specially brewed coffee is literally out of this world. You'll also find good conversation and a welcoming smile here. Indeed, when Finny O'Dell opened the Curious Cup, she did the residents of Whispering Oaks a favor, and she has lovingly catered to your every need. It is not premature to say that the Curious Cup has become a vital piece of the fabric that makes this town a safe and loving corner of the world.

Last week, a new dimension was added to the shop's mission of service. Many of you noticed the new books on display here, the wonderful copies of classics and contemporary novels, of poetry and children's books. This was not a strategic sales move aimed at boosting revenue. It was, rather, an action of concern, responsibility, and true passion. For too long, the residents of Whispering

Oaks have been denied one of the greatest pleasures in life, and that is the pleasure of finding strength, courage, happiness, and healing in the power of the written word.

Many of you have already experienced this.

You came last week to the town's first-ever literary event. You saw your children express their hopes and dreams and creativity through prose and verse. You laughed and cried and applauded because the words moved you. You returned the very next day to purchase books because what awakened in you that night was a force too powerful to ignore. You were able to revisit and recapture the true feeling again and again every time you read the words or turned the next page.

This is the magic of words. This is the priceless journey of a story. And the journey has no end, because the tale lives on forever.

How many of you have spent the last few days lost in a great book? Think about it right now. Raise your hands. Salute the characters who have spoken to you, the writers who have given you a passport to a new place. Your mind opened, your soul sang, your heart embraced that journey.

Will you disagree with me?

Last week, life in Whispering Oaks took a turn for the better. I saw it in my friends at Lake Redson. I saw it in the customers who stopped by the Curious Cup just to peruse the book display at the back of the shop. I'm not speaking only of the books themselves, but of where they brought us.

There's been a change in this town. A shift in the way we think. In the way we view self-expression and the need for books and literature in our lives.

And so I ask you now: Do you want it to continue? Do you want long, dark, boring nights at Lake Redson, or at a bar, or at home on your couch? Or do you want those nights to be filled with thought, imagination, and excitement?

I think I know your answers to these questions. And that's why I'm writing to you. That's why I'm trusting once again in the power of words. That's why I'm PROTESTING the imminent closure of the Curious Cup. I'm taking a stand for books, for wonderful evenings spent gathering in the back of our shop, listening to poetry and music. I'm PROTESTING the return to an old and uninspiring way of life. I'm PROTESTING the careless disregard for the residents of Whispering Oaks.

I am urging you to join me in taking a stand. Tell Frank Canker that the Curious Cup isn't just a little shop he can bulldoze and throw away. Tell him that by doing so he is sabotaging creativity and artistic progression.

I PROTEST you, Frank Canker. I PROTEST anyone who believes that words aren't a vital part of existing.

Open your eyes and take a good long look.
And while you're at it . . . KISS MY BOOK!

*   *   *

"You wrote this?"

Jacob looked up from the sheets of paper and stared at me. He didn't so much as move from his place on the stool. He didn't blink.

"Yeah," I replied, my voice quiet. "I did. I don't know if it's any good or—"

"Are you kidding me?" he asked, cutting in. "This is great! It's amazing. It's powerful."

It felt good to hear him say that. It felt good to have someone read *my* writing and comment on it. Inwardly, I was smiling. But I knew that the expression on my face was anything but happy.

It was two o'clock. The day had been unusual, to say the least. As word spread about Frank Canker's plans to close the Curious Cup, customers came streaming in from all over town. I swear, all 724 residents must have passed through the doors. Everyone was outraged. Aunt Fin and I kept fielding questions about the why and the how of the matter, and we couldn't seem to convince people that it was happening.

Lynn Bodders threatened to throw a hair dryer into Frank Canker's bathtub when he wasn't looking. Old Mr. Fuller tapped his cane angrily against the counter as he shook his head in disgust. One member of the Reading Moms Club broke down in tears as she bought the last romance on the display table.

"So, what are we going to do now?" Jacob asked.

"What's that supposed to mean?"

He held the pages up. "You wrote this. It's a letter of protest. The point is that we have a serious issue on our hands and we have to figure out a way to deal with it."

"There's no way to deal with it," I said. "Except to cry."

"Bullshit." He shook his head. "That's a crazy attitude to take. You think half the books we've read and loved would have made it into our hands if the writers had had that attitude? If they had just given up and conformed to society?"

"I get what you're saying, Jacob. I just don't see how we can fight this. Canker owns this space and he wants us out. Legally, there's no way to stop him."

He shot out of the stool, clearly riled up. "I can't believe you! That's why protests started—to rail against injustice. That's what *you* just wrote about!"

"I know." I sighed. "I believe what I wrote, and I believe what you're saying. But who are we going to approach with this? The town itself has no power."

"*We* have the power."

"How?"

He started pacing the floor. "Look at what's happened," he said. "You got just about everyone in this town to see how important books are. They came here. They bought the books you set up on the table. They're *still* buying them. It was a huge step for the people of this town because they never do anything. Look at what's happened to our boring nights down at the lake. Everything's changed."

"But that was different," I snapped. "We're talking

about a whole new thing here. I wrote that piece because I felt like I needed to, and because I want people to read it and understand what they're losing. Maybe they'll all hate Frank Canker more, but what happens after that? He doesn't care what people think of him. He's still going to close this shop."

Jacob threw up his hands in exasperation. "But don't you see, Georgie? The people here have already taken a big step by going a little book-crazy. The spark is there. Who's to say that with a little prodding, they won't get completely pissed off and force Canker to change his mind?"

I looked down. I wanted to trust in what he was saying, and I did, to a certain extent. But I was afraid. Afraid to try and fail. Afraid to trust in my own words.

Jacob stood there, defiant, angry. "You've made people see the power of words in one way," he said. "But what about *this* kind of power?" He held the sheets of paper up and shook them. "What about words against unfairness, injustice? What about that? For Christ's sake, Georgie, entire books have been written about this subject alone. Do you get what I'm saying? Words as weapons."

"Words instead of war," I said, correcting him. "Weapons don't solve anything."

"Fine. Agreed. Words instead of war. We'll call it a *campaign* instead of an all-out attack against the Cankers." He smiled and ran a hand through his Mohawk.

I leaned against the counter. I glanced at the display table. Saving the Curious Cup—saving the gathering space that gave books a home—was worth everything to me. "So what's the plan?" I asked him. "You're going to organize a rally?"

"Can I take this?" He held up the sheets of paper again.

"Yeah, I guess. But what are you going to do with it?"

"Just trust me. Okay?"

I couldn't say no to those bright blue eyes. I walked around the counter and sat down on the stool next to him. "It just blows my mind that we're facing the closing of this shop so soon after getting everyone excited about books. Sometimes I think back on the night of the reading and can't believe it actually happened—that it was a success, that so many people were into it."

"They still are into it. This isn't the end, Georgie. You'll see. We'll launch one hell of a campaign to save this place." The expression on his face suddenly softened. "I'm sorry I got so worked up. It's just that . . . well . . . it's important to me. The shop. The book club and reading nights we've been planning. And you."

"What about me?"

"You're important to me. I don't like to see you so upset."

I slipped my hand into his.

"I feel like I know you so well," he said, "but then I realize there's so much more to learn about you. Like this letter you just wrote. I mean, I had always assumed that you liked writing because you love reading so much, but I didn't know you were so good at it."

Okay. It was time to get totally uncomfortable. And I did. I scratched my head. I swiveled halfway around on the stool. And I said, "It was just the passion of the moment. Sometimes it all flows out when you're angry or worked up."

"No, it's more than that. There are parts of this that are lyrical. That's not churning sudden emotion out onto the page; it's talent, Georgie." He intertwined his fingers with mine. "What else have you written? I bet you've got a whole pile of good stuff you're hiding."

I stood up. I walked over to the cash register and pretended to look for something. My muscles felt as solid as stone.

"Do you?" he asked. "I swear I won't tell. But I'd like to read it."

"I don't write," I mumbled. "This was just a quick thing, what I wrote this morning. But there's nothing else."

"Yes, there is. You're just not telling me. But that's cool. I like that you're keeping me in suspense."

"I'm not keeping you in suspense, Jacob," I said, an edge suddenly in my voice. I looked up at him. "If I had any other writing to show you, I would. But I don't write."

"Well, I think you should." He stood up. He held out the pages. "This is great stuff. Honestly, it is."

That word: *honestly.*

That smile: so genuine.

Something trembled deep in my heart; it was a faint stab and a brutal blow. It was one of those proverbial flashes designed to startle us completely awake.

That was when I realized it. Right there. At that moment. As I was fiddling with the handle of the drawer beneath the cash register. The feeling flooded me like water from a ruptured dam.

Ruby, what are you doing?

My own voice. It fought through the cobwebs and the shadows, echoing in my mind with the force of a gunshot.

Ruby, look at yourself. Ruby!

I couldn't go on with it.

The lie.

The deception.

The fake name and the fake past.

Ruby!

I felt a surge of guilt so strong I trembled.

Maybe it was a mini-breakdown, a little short circuit of the mind. I don't know. And I don't know *why*. But the realization left me staring at Jacob and wishing it all could have been different. Wishing I'd told him the truth earlier.

Before building a life that I liked.

"Georgie? You okay?" His hand on my arm.

No, I'm not. My name is Ruby. Ruby Crane. You might have heard of me. . . .

"Hey, babe?"

I finally looked up at him. I felt tears swimming in my eyes. "I'm okay," I said quietly. "It's just that . . . it's . . ."

"It's what?"

It's that you don't know me at all. It's that I lied to you. It's that I've been lying all along.

I took a deep breath. Now or never. "Jacob, I'm not—"

And, of course, the back door swung open and Aunt Fin walked out onto the main floor. She was reading through a bunch of papers, oblivious to me and Jacob.

I couldn't help laughing. Inwardly, at least.

"Oh, hi, Jacob," she said wearily.

"Hey, Finny," he replied. "Don't worry. Everything will be okay. Just you watch."

She gave him an appreciative smile.

Jacob touched my arm. "I've got to get going. I'll call you later." He waved the sheets of paper—my writing—in the air and smiled broadly. "Kiss my book," he said. Then he turned and went out the front door.

The strangeness of what had just happened left me spent. I'd been about to do it. About to spill the truth to Jacob. *I'm Ruby Crane. Have you heard of me?* I imagined it was what standing on the ledge of a high building felt like—wondering if that strong hand would pull you to safety or if a sudden gust of wind would send you spiraling to the ground.

The hand had saved me. But maybe it hadn't been such a good thing.

"Honey, could you put on a pot of coffee?" Aunt Fin asked, still distracted with her paperwork.

I turned around and began filling a pot with water. By the time it was brewing, Aunt Fin had returned to the back room. I was alone again in the shop. Just me, my nerves, and the hissing coffeepot.

Ruby, what are you doing?

I was trembling again. Rabbit, Jacob. All the people in town. Was it even possible, at that point, to hope that they would forgive me, that they would understand what I'd been through?

I leaned my arms on the countertop and took a deep breath. I knew I wanted out of the lie. I just wasn't sure how to go about getting out.

Ruby . . .

"Yeah," I answered. "I hear you."

Little by little, the mangled feelings inside me dissipated. Several minutes slipped by. The coffeepot emitted its final hiss and I let the aroma of Aunt Fin's magical caffeine blend fill my nostrils.

You're okay, I assured myself. *Everything will work out just fine. You'll see.*

At the precise moment I started feeling better, the front door opened.

And Samantha Golding walked in.

The Last Chapter of My Second Life

Yes, you read that correctly.

Samantha Golding walked into the shop.

Samantha.

Golding.

Celebrity journalist, Hollywood personality, all-around golden girl. And, though it probably wasn't on her résumé, the bitch who had ruined my life. Remember her?

A more classic example of a surreal moment you just won't find.

It took about three seconds for me to register that it was really happening. And when that cold, hard fact hit me, I went completely numb. My muscles froze. My bones felt like cement. I was hit by vertigo so hard I had to grab on to the edges of the counter for support.

Samantha Golding hadn't come to Whispering Oaks in an official capacity. I knew that from the way she was dressed: denim shorts, a Yankees shirt, and white sneakers. Her blond hair was pulled back in a ponytail and she wasn't wearing a trace of makeup. She had no microphone. There wasn't a cameraman looming in the background.

She took two steps into the shop and immediately swept her eyes across the sales floor, smiling when she saw the curios and the dream catchers and the odd works of art. When she looked at me—a fleeting glance—her lips curled again in a perfunctory smile. And that was all.

She was nothing more than a potential customer. A tourist, actually.

I couldn't begin to comprehend the odd, sick, and unjust twist of fate that had brought her there—to my very doorstep. Of all the small towns nestled in the foothills of the Adirondacks. Dozens of exits on the thruway and a million chances to end up in another place.

But there she was, standing not five feet away from me.

She walked to the book display and gave it a fast onceover. Then she meandered into the aisles, where she studied the crystals, the love-spell kits, the gargoyles, and the Gothic candleholders.

I was still rooted to my spot. I couldn't move. Blood roared in my ears like a runaway freight train, and my heart was in the last throes of life. I didn't know what to do. It would have been easy to turn and walk quietly into the back room and tell Aunt Fin to get her ass out there. Yes, it would have been easy to hide until Samantha Golding left. She hadn't recognized me, after all. But my body literally shut down.

Quick lesson: you don't know how you're going to react to a traumatic situation until it happens, so throw out those instructional guides that promise to teach you the rules of calm, cool, and collected behavior.

"Excuse me," Samantha Golding called from one of the aisles. "Can you tell me how much this dream catcher is? There's no price on it."

"Twenty dollars," I replied automatically.

"Great, thanks."

Well, I'd spoken. That was a good sign. Catatonic people generally don't remember prices. Gulping as many deep breaths as I could, I pried my fingers from the edges of the countertop and took one small step to the left. The coffeepot was emitting thin trails of delicious steam. Didn't Aunt Fin catch the aroma?

The front door opened again, startling me.

A tall, good-looking man with salt-and-pepper hair and tan skin came into the shop. Definitely not a Whispering Oaks resident. He offered me yet another perfunctory smile, then spotted Samantha Golding and went to her.

"Honey," she said, "they have the most darling merchandise here. Look at the dream catchers. And look at these crystal picture frames. They're absolutely amazing."

"I told you these small towns are big on crafts," the man said stupidly.

"Oh, and that coffee smells divine," Samantha gushed. "Excuse me, miss?"

I tensed all over again. "Yes?" I said, keeping my voice monotone.

"May I have two cups of whatever is brewing?" She laughed. "I don't think I've ever smelled coffee that strong."

Can I pour it over your head? I fumbled for two paper cups.

And then Samantha Golding strode toward the counter.

She dropped three dream catchers and a crystal picture frame beside the register as her lover boy wandered in the background.

I stood at the coffeepot, trying to pour some of the magical blend into the cups without spilling it. My hands were shaking. My heart was still booming.

"Is this all handmade merchandise?" she asked.

I managed to fill the cups without spilling anything. I was standing with my profile to her. Did I still look like the Ruby Crane she knew? "Most of the merchandise is handmade," I replied.

"That's what I thought. It's too well made to be mass-produced."

I saw her peripherally, as if she were a shadow. She wasn't studying me. She wasn't getting impatient with my slow customer service. As carefully as possible, I placed the cups of coffee in front of her without turning my body all the way around. And without looking up.

"Sam?" the lover boy said. "Did you see these candles? They're beautiful. . . ."

Stay calm. You can do this. You're okay. Aunt Fin, where the hell are you?

I gave my head a little shake, hoping my sloppy split ends would fall forward and obscure my face. I rang up her items quickly and said, "Eighty-one dollars, even."

"Great." She smiled her Samantha Golding smile as she dug into her purse. She handed me five crisp twenty-dollar bills.

I reached out and took them. I hit the Cash button on the keyboard, and the register popped open. I didn't dare look up. But I could still see Samantha Golding clearly— and as I counted out her change and tore the receipt from the rolling tape, I saw her expression change suddenly and dramatically.

Oh, God.

The happy, dazed, I'm-on-vacation look vanished from her face. So did the relaxed stare. She lowered her head and leaned to one side.

I grabbed a plastic bag from beneath the register. Slow, even, robotic movements. No eye contact. No—

"Ruby Crane," she said.

It wasn't a question. It was a statement. A journalist's firm and confident declaration of truth.

My blood ran cold. Heat rushed into my face. I felt like a thermometer being passed from a meat locker to a brick oven.

I didn't respond. I fluffed open the bag and reached for her items.

She stuck out her hand and tapped my arm. "Ruby Crane," she said again. "It's you, isn't it?"

"I'm sorry," I muttered. "I don't know what you're talking about."

"Yes, you do."

And I froze. It felt as if all the air in the atmosphere—in the universe—had been zapped out.

The silence between us was monumental. As big as the sky over Montana. As wide as Lake Placid looks on a clear day.

Samantha Golding's predatory stare bored into me and didn't let go.

There was nothing to do. There was nowhere to run. At that unbelievable moment, all hell should have broken loose and every emotion I'd ever felt should have bubbled up to the surface, but none of that happened. I didn't slug her. I didn't tell her to get the hell out of the shop. I didn't feel like the world had come to an apocalyptic end. What I felt was the steely grip of reality sinking its fingers into my skin, ordering me to lift my eyes and face the moment bravely.

I placed the plastic bag on the counter; then I raised my head and finally met her stare.

She wasn't poised like I'd imagined a triumphant journalist would be. She was stunned, her expression almost dreamy. "Talk about the impossible," she said quietly.

I held her gaze. Tears didn't spring to my eyes, and the trembling in my hands stopped. I said, "What do you want, Samantha?" The cadence of my own voice was shocking.

"Well . . . I . . . my God. This is certainly a surprise." She swallowed. "Is this where you live now? Is this where you came . . . afterwards?"

I nodded.

"Sam?" The tall guy behind her sounded confused.

"Go wait in the car, John," she told him. "I'll be out in a minute." When he left the shop, she cleared her throat and set her eyes on me again.

"So, you've found me," I said. "I bet that makes you a really good journalist."

Her lips parted a little. Shock? Maybe. "I didn't come here looking for you, Ruby, if that's what you think," she replied. "This really is a coincidence. The most amazing coincidence I've ever encountered, but a coincidence nonetheless."

I didn't say anything. I was too stunned to move.

"For your information, young lady, my boyfriend happens to be a native of Derryville, the town just east of this one," she continued. "We were driving through Whispering Oaks on our way up to Montreal."

"So, what now? Are you going to make me front-page news again?" I asked the question flatly and firmly, but there was a tremor in my voice.

Samantha Golding regarded me with what seemed to be a mix of interest and disapproval. "You never answered my question," she said.

"What?"

She leaned in a little closer to me. "You never answered my question. Why did you plagiarize someone else's work, Ruby?"

Total slap. Those words hurt much more than any physical attack. "It took me a lot to get here," I told her. "I'm trying to think about the future, not the past."

She shook her head. "You'll never have a future if you don't face your past, Ruby. I know you aren't living in this little town honestly. Sometimes the headlines don't make it up to places like these. But no matter where you go after this, you'll still have to answer that question."

I crossed my arms over my chest. The heat returned in a bright, fiery wave. "I don't have to answer your questions," I snapped. "My life is none of your business."

"But what you did is *everyone's* business," she snapped back. "If I picked up these items without paying for them and just walked out of this shop, wouldn't you stop me and ask me why I'd done it? Why I'd *thought* I could get away with it?"

The tears finally came—a glassy sheen that blurred my vision. "You had no right to embarrass me like that," I said, seething. "It was a cruel thing to do. It was—"

"And *you* had no right to steal someone's work—someone else's words," she interjected. "I guess you haven't thought about what you did in the time you've been hiding out, Ruby. Because if you *had* thought about it, you'd know by now that plagiarism has nothing to do with writing; it has nothing to do with art or creativity. And whether or not you've gone through the trouble of trying to rebuild your life, you still owe everyone an explanation. You still owe *yourself* an explanation." She took the plastic bag from the counter and grabbed the two cups of coffee. Then she turned and started for the door.

"Samantha!" I called out. I heard the desperation in my voice.

She faced me.

"Please don't put me through that again," I whispered. "Please don't make me front-page news a second time."

Her eyes took on that familiar predatory gaze. "One day, Ruby, you'll thank me," she said. And then she opened the door and disappeared into the bright sunlight of the afternoon.

I closed my eyes and let the tears spill over. I don't know how many minutes passed before I moved again— five? ten?—but when I did, it was only to get a tissue and a glass of water.

It had happened. Samantha Golding had found me, and now she would expose me once again to the world. I knew it. There wasn't a doubt in my mind that Georgie O'Dell had just died.

But despite the fear and anxiety coursing through my blood, I didn't feel as though the world had come to an abrupt end. It sounds strange, right? You would think I'd tear my hair out and race for the nearest bus station. But instead, I felt a vast stillness—a resignation. Like what a soldier probably feels before heading into battle.

This is where it ends, Ruby.

I wiped the tears from my eyes and took a long glance around the shop. Inevitably, my eyes found the display tables, and the sight of what I had helped create honestly warmed me, if only slightly.

The back door opened. Aunt Fin came out rubbing her

temples. "Oh, good," she sighed. "I need that coffee. These phone calls with lawyers can last forever, and . . . hey, there. You okay?" She touched my arm. "You look like you've been crying."

"I have."

"Why? Is everything okay? Georgie?"

I gave Aunt Fin a weary smile. "You can call me Ruby," I said. I took off my apron, laid it down neatly on the counter, and then walked outside, toward home.

* * *

That inexplicable moment when I'd felt the need to tell Jacob the truth. That inexplicable moment when Samantha Golding stepped into the shop. Were the incidents related? Were they a supernatural force's way of trying to warn me that the end was near?

Initially, I wanted to believe that. But during the long hours of the night, I came to realize that those two completely jarring events had nothing in common. One had merely complemented the other. Coincidentally, as it turns out.

My desire to tell Jacob everything was natural. The thought of losing him because of the truth was too much to bear. I guess I had been thinking about it without really thinking about it for a while. A subconscious little equation waiting to be added up. I had held on to the crazy hope that I would never have to face the past, that somehow my life as Georgie O'Dell would simply operate in a straight line and bypass the detours that pop up around the most unexpected corners.

Like Frank Canker's announcing the closure of the Curious Cup.

Like Samantha Golding's finding me in the invisible town of Whispering Oaks.

My desire to tell Jacob the truth was a step toward facing the past. Yeah, it was about my fear of maybe losing him, but on a bigger scale, it was about my wanting to stop the lies. Maybe that was why I'd felt the strange sense of courage and acceptance in the wake of Samantha Golding's impromptu small-town shopping spree. Watching her leave, fully aware that she was going to do her job as a journalist and expose me a second time, I'd known that I would be able to handle whatever was coming my way.

Because I was ready.

Because there was no escaping it.

And because I understood, in those fragile and fundamental moments, that you can't run away from the storm if you're the one who created it in the first place.

I didn't sleep that night. I sat in my bedroom and watched the sky go from black to red to blue, all the while thinking about the one vital question that held my life in the balance.

Why did you do it, Ruby? Why did you plagiarize someone else's work?

Over and over: that huge question.

By the time the sun rose, I had answered it in my heart. Now all I had to do was explain it to the world.

The First Chapter of My (New) Old Life

Like any good journalist would, Samantha Golding had recognized a hot story and gone with it. The next morning came the first report of teen literary sensation Ruby Crane's "new life" in a small town in upstate New York; it was a brief one-minute mention on CNN, and as the anchorwoman delivered the details, the television screen flashed to the clip of that night back in June when I'd been yanked out of the American Literature Club and hauled into a waiting limousine. The same quick story aired on two other major networks. Then there were the articles in the *New York Times* and the *Boston Globe*, which Aunt Fin spotted online.

"Maybe no one up here will catch it," she said hopefully. "Most of the people in town who work in the factories are already on their way to work by dawn. It's possible they missed it."

"I don't think it's possible," I told her with certainty. "The name of the town is being mentioned everywhere, and how could that not become local news?"

We were sitting in the living room, still in our pajamas. Aunt Fin was drinking coffee and I sipped my glass of orange juice. Waffle and Pancake were still asleep on nearby pillows.

Aunt Fin's face was strained. In addition to the shop's closing, she had the stress of an imminent media storm possibly pulling her into its eye. "How do you feel?" she asked me somberly.

"Pretty bad," I said.

"Are you scared?"

I'd never thought that would be an interesting question, but it was. Half of me was feeling calm and courageous, and half of me was absolutely petrified. This time, however, what scared me most wasn't the embarrassment; it was the possibility that I might lose people who genuinely cared for me. Who trusted me. Who liked me for who I was on the inside. I had never made those kinds of friends. *Real* ones, that is.

"I feel like I'm going to try my best to get through this," I said. And that was all.

"You don't . . . you aren't going to disappear, are you, Ruby?" Aunt Fin sounded nervous. "I'm not going to wake up tomorrow morning and find that you've boarded a bus to . . . wherever, right? Please promise me you won't do that. Please. I don't think I could handle that."

"I'm not going anywhere," I promised her. *I'm staying here and I'm facing the damn music. It's been long enough and I can't go on living a lie.*

So I told myself. And so I tried to believe.

When the phone rang, Aunt Fin snatched it up. I expected her to slam the receiver down on the voice of a reporter, but her eyes widened and she said, "Oh, Anne! You what? It's where? Oh, no!"

I already knew: Mom and Dad had caught wind of the news. I waved my hand in the air, indicating that I didn't want to talk right then. I just couldn't.

"I promise you," Aunt Fin was telling Mom, "I'll make sure she calls home in just a little while. Yes. Yes. Okay. No. I promise. Yes. Okay. Talk soon. Bye."

We sat in front of the computer and the television as the story spread like a virus. *A plagiarist's tale,* one reporter began, looking into the camera with a wry smile, *is an interesting tale. Sixteen-year-old novelist Ruby Crane literally vanished from the radar following charges that she plagiarized . . .*

. . . now apparently living in the small town of Whispering Oaks, New York, another reporter continued. *The sleepy town is said to have fewer than eight hundred residents. . . .*

. . . why she resorted to plagiarism in the first place, and what life in a small town is like for someone who . . .

. . . her story has brought the subject of plagiarism into

the spotlight as never before, and people are apparently still wondering what Ruby . . .

. . . or if she will speak to reporters this time around from her new home . . .

"Oh my Lord," Aunt Fin whispered, flicking through channels with her trusty remote control. "This is unbelievable! It's everywhere! In a matter of minutes, it's gone from . . . Oh! Ruby!" She stared at me, wide-eyed and frightened. "How . . . What are you going to do?"

"I've been through this before, Aunt Fin," I told her. I hugged my knees to my chest and closed my eyes.

"Yes, you have. But last time you ran away from it. Now there's no place to run."

"There never *was* a place to run to, Aunt Fin. I know that now." I threw a glance out the bedroom window and into the backyard. "Maybe I knew it all along."

Suddenly, the doorbell rang.

"Who could that be?" Aunt Fin wailed, her face panic-stricken.

My heart did a little jump. Maybe it was Jacob, or Rabbit. Maybe they had come together. Maybe they would give me the chance to explain everything to them.

We both raced down the stairs.

Aunt Fin tiptoed to the door and peered out the keyhole. Then she gasped and spun around to face me. "*Reporters*," she whispered, cupping a hand over her mouth.

That didn't surprise me. It didn't scare me either. I stood there, staring past Aunt Fin at the front door, fully aware what lay beyond it.

"You're not going to talk to them, are you?" she asked me quietly. Worriedly.

"Not just yet," I replied. I needed to talk to the important people first.

Jacob. Rabbit. What's going through your heads right now? Will you forgive me? Will you even listen to me?

Aunt Fin waved me away from the door. The bell rang a second time, then a third. When the reporter, a young guy in a business suit, and his accompanying news van finally left, she turned the knob quietly and popped her head outside. "It's safe again," she said. She reached down, scooped up the day's copy of the *Whispering Oaks Gazette*, and then shut the door and slid the dead bolt into place.

"I'm sorry," I said.

"What?"

"I'm sorry that I'm dragging you into this," I told her. "I never meant for any of this to happen, Aunt Fin. Really, I didn't."

"Of course you didn't! I know that, Ruby! And you don't have to apologize."

"Yes, I do. I've interrupted your life. I've interrupted the lives of everyone in this town, and I hate myself for it." I dropped onto the couch and covered my face with my hands.

"You've interrupted our lives in a good way," Aunt Fin said. She threw the copy of the *Gazette* onto the coffee table, where it fell open right before me. When I saw the front page, I gasped.

There was a picture of the Curious Cup, the words

KISS MY BOOK! stamped in big block letters across the bottom half and across a smaller, grainier picture of Frank Canker.

I shot out of my chair. I flipped to the next page and saw the open letter I'd written the day before—printed for the world to see.

Kiss My Book.

Jacob, I thought. *Jacob.*

He had showed my writing to his parents, who had liked it enough to print it in the *Gazette.*

Kiss My Book by Georgie O'Dell.

I dropped the paper and started crying again. Jacob. He hadn't called yet. Maybe he never would.

"Ruby," Aunt Fin said. She had the newspaper spread open in her hands. "When did you write this? It's beautiful. It really is. And . . ."

"What?" I sniffled, glancing at her.

She was still reading. "It says here that there's going to be a rally today—a peaceful gathering to show support for the Curious Cup, for Finny and Georgie O'Dell. A protest against Frank Canker's plans to close us down. *Ha!*" She stomped her foot. "I can't believe it! An actual protest— here, in Whispering Oaks!"

Trust me, Jacob had said. *We have the power.*

Words instead of war.

The doorbell rang again. We both jumped. But it was just another reporter from a local television stations.

Nobody important.

*　　*　　*

254

It went on like that for most of the morning and afternoon. Aunt Fin and I stayed in the house as her front lawn got trampled by not only reporters, it turned out, but curious people too—Lynn Bodders and Lisa Marie Keating and even Mr. Watson en route to the general store. From the shady upstairs window, I watched as they stared at the house, muttering to each other, shrugging, and shaking their heads.

Neither Jacob nor Rabbit came by. They didn't call either. By then, I knew they wouldn't.

They had seen the television reports and the papers and felt shocked and betrayed. They were probably staring at the images of my face and then coming to the slow and painful realization that nothing was what it seemed. That they had been living the lie with me. That they were, in effect, part of the story.

I couldn't blame them for hating me. But I desperately wanted them to forgive me. More than anything else, I wanted them to know I had never meant to hurt them. And that my life—wherever it ended up—wouldn't be the same without them.

Jacob, Rabbit: I love you. I swear I do. I didn't know who I was until I met you.

It was noon when I picked up the phone in the kitchen and dialed Rabbit's house. Two rings, three . . . the answering machine came on, followed by the customary beep. I didn't leave a message. I hung up and then punched in the numbers to Jacob's house. Three rings . . . four . . . five. Same deal.

I couldn't imagine either one of them not being home.

Damn you, caller ID.

But it didn't matter anyway.

I knew what I had to do.

Slowly, still moving in that horrible nightmare world, I showered and got dressed. I slipped into jeans and a nice blue shirt. I put on makeup, following the instructions of my former publicist.

I might not have looked particularly attractive, but I certainly looked presentable.

I walked out of the bedroom and down the stairs. Then I opened the front door and stepped outside. . . .

All the while, I was remembering that chaotic span of days the year before when I'd been writing *The Heart Stealer*.

Sitting at my desk, feeling completely insecure about what I was writing, about my ability to tell the story I wanted to tell. Feeling uninspired and fed up.

And fearing that my ideas weren't good enough for publication.

Fearing that I would never live up to other people's expectations.

Fearing that maybe I didn't know enough about the true craft of writing to create a good book.

Pacing the floor like a prisoner in solitary confinement until my eyes caught the books piled in one corner of my room and the idea—the scheme—hit me.

Thinking *It's just a few words. It's just to get me through the next bend in the road. It's no big deal.* Not thinking about the consequences or the sheer selfishness of it.

Deciding that no one would ever notice my little literary infraction.

I remembered the exact moment.

The moment I'd picked up that copy of Adella Morgan's novel *My Broken Soul,* turned to the passages I knew and loved and had read a hundred times, and walked over to my desk and sat down.

And copied.

Robbed.

Shamelessly and heartlessly. Stupidly. I plagiarized Adella Morgan's work, believing in my arrogance that most people were generally very dumb and would never catch it. And not realizing until it was too late the irony of the whole situation: that in plagiarizing *My Broken Soul,* I had, in fact, broken my own soul.

The rally was in full swing when I got there. An impressive crowd had gathered in front of the town hall, all the people holding copies of the *Gazette* as they raised their hands in the air and chanted, "Kiss my book! Kiss my book!"

So many voices, but one voice collectively.

There were Lynn Bodders and Lisa Marie Keating and all the members of the Reading Moms Club. There were MaryAnn Conner, Kimmy Peterman, Jason Sydney, and just about everyone else from the Lake Redson crew. And there was Rabbit holding up a small picket sign that read KISS MY BOOK!

At first, I watched from a distance, hiding behind a streetlight and hoping no one would see me. Two news vans were parked in the lot behind town hall. A female reporter was talking in front of a rolling camera. And there, rallying the crowd with a megaphone, was Jacob, standing on the hood of his father's car, one arm raised in protest. His voice boomed through the air as he said, "We have our rights in this town. We're taking a stand today for ourselves, for each other, and for the books that have brought us together in the past few weeks—for the books that will continue to bring us together!" He turned the megaphone toward the front of town hall, where Frank Canker was undoubtedly sitting in his corner office, scowling. "What do we say to anyone who disagrees with us?"

The response was instant and earsplitting: "KISS MY BOOK!"

My heart flooded with every emotion known to man—happiness, fear, regret, frustration. But most of all, it flooded with determination. And with peace. Because I knew it would all be over soon.

I stepped out from behind the streetlight and made my way up the sidewalk. I walked along the fringes of the crowd, passing people one by one. I heard the shouts and the cries quiet with each step I took. As people recognized me, they fell silent. By the time I reached Jacob—by the time I climbed up onto the hood of the car and met his stare—the protesters had gone completely quiet.

I felt every eye on me, but I kept my own eyes trained on Jacob.

He stared back at me, and the hurt was clearly visible on his face. The shock and sorrow.

I nodded toward the megaphone. "Can I have that, please?"

He hesitated for a second, then handed it over.

I turned and faced the crowd. A sea of familiar faces, a sea of unreadable expressions. To my left, a news camera was rolling. I cleared my throat and brought the megaphone to my lips.

"I'm sorry to be interrupting you," I began, my voice echoing across Main Street. "I wanted to be a part of this rally today, but as you all know by now . . . well, I'm not who you all think I am. Or thought I was. You've all seen the local news reports. You all know that my name is Ruby Crane and that a few months ago, I was accused of plagiarism."

Silence. I scanned the crowd and saw Aunt Fin take her place at the back. Her eyes were soft and watery.

"Plagiarism is a serious offense," I continued. "In a nutshell, it's the act of stealing, of robbing someone else's creativity and of losing your own integrity. It's a common habit in high school and college, but no matter how small the plagiarism is, it's still just that—*plagiarism.*

"And I am guilty of plagiarism."

I paused so that I could hear the words boom up to the sky. Saying them made me dizzy. But as that breath left my body, so did the weight of the lie.

There was no sound from the audience.

I took another deep breath. "Last year, I did something

stupid and very arrogant, and I owe a lot of people an apology. I'm sorry—to the people who trusted me, to the readers who bought copies of *The Heart Stealer,* and to Adella Morgan. There is no excuse for what I did. I made a mistake, and I've learned from that mistake. I was scared; I was insecure. I didn't know who I was."

My eyes found Aunt Fin. She was smiling.

"This morning, I could have very easily decided to pick up and run off again. But I didn't. I won't do that. Not again. I won't do it because Whispering Oaks is important to me. *You* are all important to me. Many of you are my friends and I'm sorry for deceiving you. I ask for your forgiveness but understand if you don't feel like giving it. But I do want you all to know one thing: Georgie O'Dell might be a fake name, but she's a real person. She's Ruby Crane—a reader, a booklover, a writer. She's the person who believes in what you're all doing here today. She believes in the power of books to change lives and to enlighten the world. She believes that words can fix any problem, and that poetry lives inside every one of us. And it was *Georgie* who taught *Ruby* to stand behind her own words and believe in them."

I was crying. And it was the best cry I had ever had, because it was honest.

"I hope that you'll all continue to fight to keep the Curious Cup open," I said. "And I hope that no matter where you are or what you do, no matter how difficult life might get, you all remember that sometimes it's absolutely okay to run away, but *only* in a book."

I jumped down from the hood of the car and looked at Jacob. I held the megaphone out to him.

He didn't say anything, and I didn't expect him to. He reached out and took the megaphone from me.

I walked back the way I had come: around the fringes of the crowd and along Main Street. People were standing outside their various stores and shops, their eyes following me.

When I made it to Aunt Fin's house, I closed the front door and climbed the stairs to my room. My head was still buzzing. My hands were trembling just a little bit. But the tears on my face had dried and I didn't feel the need to sit down and collect myself.

I felt, in fact, like the girl I had been once upon a time.

I went into the bathroom and studied my reflection in the mirror. Ruby Crane, at last.

The Body and
the Book

A light rain fell as dusk blanketed Whispering Oaks. I was
sitting in the back room of the Curious Cup for once, letting Aunt Fin work the floor. And that, we had both agreed,
was best. I wasn't sure what everyone in town thought
about me, or if they thought anything about me at all.

Aunt Fin had told me that the protest had continued
long after I'd left. The crowd chanted and shouted for Frank
Canker to listen up. He never did come out of his office, but
he was reportedly spotted leaving the building through a
side door several hours later. He hadn't contacted Aunt Fin,
so she went on believing that the shop would close, just
as he'd promised. Nonetheless, she felt invigorated by the

action of her neighbors and friends, and she swore that she would find a new location for the Curious Cup.

"And I hope, Ruby, that you'll still be here," she'd said, fixing a pot of coffee.

I hadn't been able to answer her. I didn't know where I was going or even where I'd end up. I knew only that I had done the right thing. That I felt better struggling through the truth than I had living with a lie.

A new shipment of books had arrived. Five huge boxes were stacked one on top of another. They looked like a cardboard skyscraper. I had been trying to figure out how to pick up the top box for nearly twenty minutes because the damn thing was too heavy to lift. In fact, the floorboards around the boxes felt strangely weak. I was eager to see which new books Aunt Fin had ordered. I found the invoice buried on her desk and smiled as I read the titles. Whether or not I'd be there to sell them and discuss them, I was happy.

For the next hour, I busied myself with filing and cleaning up, stepping carefully around the tower of boxes. I listened to the staccato voices coming from the front of the Cup and was relieved that Aunt Fin's customers were still treating her with the love she deserved.

A knock sounded at the door.

"Aunt Fin, just come in!" I called from the bathroom, where I was Windexing the mirror.

The door opened with a slow creak. There were no footsteps.

I dropped the paper towels bunched in my hand and went out to see what was going on.

I saw Jacob standing beside the desk.

He was dressed in black jeans and a bright red shirt. His right hand was in his pocket. His left held a folder.

I honestly hadn't expected to see him. Not so soon, at least. And maybe not ever again. But the sight of him there made my heart beat ten times faster than normal.

"Hi," I said.

He waved.

"Is . . . um . . . is everything okay?" I asked him.

He shrugged.

"I heard the crowd went pretty wild today."

He frowned.

I was fidgeting and glancing around the room, trying not to look uncomfortable. I wasn't used to Jacob being silent. I finally let out a sigh and crossed my arms over my chest. "Say something," I whispered.

He looked at the floor and then at the tower of boxes. And then he said, "I don't know what to say."

Okay. Fair enough. So I said, "Thank you for printing what I wrote. It meant a lot to me."

"I was right," he snapped.

"About what?"

"About you being a writer. I knew it. Why didn't you just tell me?"

"I wanted to," I said. "Every time we were together. I swear, Jacob, I wanted to tell you. I should have told you sooner, but . . . well . . . you already know the story."

"Yeah, I do. I spent a lot of this morning in the library, going through back issues of the *New York Times*. It was quite a wild ride for you."

"Well, I'm ready to face it now," I told him. "And that's all that matters. For me, at least." I looked down at my hands and pretended to pick at a hangnail. "How about for you?"

His eyebrows knitted together. "For me? I don't understand."

"I mean, whether or not you can accept the real me. Whether or not you still like me."

"Of course I still like you," he replied right away. "But it's different. I feel like you should've trusted me enough to tell me about everything. Unless . . ."

"Unless what?"

"Unless maybe you never thought I was important enough," he said quietly. "Unless you thought we were just a summer fling and that you'd eventually leave Whispering Oaks and file me away in the past like everything else."

Oh, that hurt. Major arrow to the heart. But I knew where he was coming from, why that could have made sense to him. "Nothing could be further from the truth," I said. "That night when I first met you, down at the lake . . . that was when I started to let go of my secret. I had never intended to tell anybody that I even liked books, but you brought that out in me, from the very first day I arrived in Whispering Oaks. . . . You're the reason I was able to do what I did today."

His eyes got bright. "Me? Why?"

"Because I don't want to lose you." I got choked up. "Because I wanted you to know that what you gave me is way more important than any scandal. Those reporters could come banging at the door for the rest of my life now, and I just wouldn't care. You helped me find myself again. You helped me see that . . . love is just as powerful as words and books. And you made me remember the power of words, and what I can do with them. I mean, *really* do with them."

He smiled. "That's why there are sonnets."

That was when I remembered—*the sonnet*. I turned and grabbed the copy of Shakespeare's collected works he had given me the afternoon we'd first kissed. I flipped it open to sonnet 18 and held it out to him.

"What is it?" Jacob asked, confused.

"I didn't realize it until this morning," I explained, "but this sonnet . . . it's not about how beautiful a woman is; it's about the beauty of words. About how physical beauty fades in reality but words forever preserve it. It's about the *power of words*." I held back my tears as I stared up at him. "Of all the sonnets, you chose this one."

He laced his fingers around the book and studied the page. Then he smiled. "Yeah," he said quietly. "I did. And I see what you're saying now. That's amazing. Maybe it was subconscious. Maybe I knew all along—deep down inside—that you had the power of words inside you."

"Well, you know what?"

"What?"

"I would have chosen the same sonnet to give to you." I took a step toward him. Then another and another, until I was standing close enough to feel his breath against my face.

"You changed me too, ya know," he said.

"I did?"

"Yeah. Until you came along, I thought this kind of thing only existed in fiction. But now I know it's real. The great poets had to get it from real life."

My whole body was singing. "So I guess we're saying the same thing, right?"

He blushed and looked up. He gave a little nod.

"Well, I'll say it first, since I'm getting used to telling the truth." I wrapped my arms around his neck. "I love you, Jacob."

"I love you too, *Ruby.*"

And then he kissed me.

And then the door opened with a whoosh.

This time, we didn't pull away from each other. Our bodies stayed in position until we both had to come up for air.

"Oh, puh-lease! Does anybody read anything but romance novels around here?" Rabbit screamed.

I peeked over Jacob's shoulder, slowly wriggling myself out of his embrace. I hadn't spoken to Rabbit since the second wave of stories about me had surfaced that morning. I had seen her in the crowd, felt her piercing stare. Now I looked at her and prepared myself for whatever she wanted to say to me.

And she said, "You look better now than you did in those author photos."

Well, that was a shocker. I gulped over the lump in my throat. "So then . . . you forgive me, Rabbit?"

She stuffed her hands into the pockets of her shorts and peered at me over the rims of her glasses. Her expression was unreadable. "So long as you promise to stay," she said.

"As long as you promise to karate chop Frank Canker the next time you see him," I replied.

"Ha! Don't you wish!" She laughed. "I could take him out with two punches."

"One punch, probably," Jacob said.

And I knew it then and there: I'd be staying.

We fell silent, glancing around the room. The Curious Cup had never felt so warm.

Rabbit walked up to the tower of boxes and slapped her hands against them. "You gonna open these babies up, or what?"

"Here," Jacob said, "I'll get it." He moved around to the back of the tower and hoisted himself up on two crates. The top box seemed to be packed with lead from the trouble he was having with it. He sighed and grunted and shifted his weight as he tried to pull it down.

"Careful," Rabbit warned.

That was when I heard the floorboards give way—a screeching, earsplitting crack that sent us tumbling forward and into each other like a bunch of drunken sailors. The collapse ended with a thunderous boom as the whole tower of books went crashing through the floor and into the space beneath.

"Oh my God!" Rabbit shrieked, grabbing my arm to steady herself.

"Jacob?" I screamed.

"Ruby?" he screamed back.

When the dust and dirt and wood particles settled, we found ourselves standing over a big dark hole that wasn't a hole at all.

It was a cellar.

A *hidden* cellar.

The musty odor spiraling upward was the smell of countless years of decay from being sealed shut.

"Ugh!" Rabbit cupped a hand over her nose. "What a stench!"

"That's, like, two-hundred-year-old mold," I said, coughing.

"Be careful," Jacob said.

But I wasn't careful. I got on my knees and, balancing myself on the edge of the jagged floorboards, peered down. The light from the back room illuminated the scarred walls and the dirt floor. "Oh my God," I heard myself gasp.

"What is it?" Jacob's hand clutched my shoulder.

"I'm not sure," I answered. "I can't really see that much."

Slowly, holding my breath, I lowered myself into the cellar until my feet touched the rutted ground. It couldn't have been more than five feet deep. "Get me the flashlight in the bathroom," I said. I pinched my nostrils as the musty odor intensified and the dust made my eyes tear.

Rabbit lowered the flashlight into my hands. Then she and Jacob climbed down beside me.

I flicked on the flashlight and swept it across the darkness. The little cellar was about the size of the back room. The damp dirt floors crunched like gravel beneath our feet.

"What is this place?" Rabbit asked.

The beam of light bounced as I tripped over something. Jacob caught me and held me up.

"What the hell?" I said. I steadied the flashlight, aiming it at the floor.

That was when Rabbit screamed.

And Jacob said, "Holy God."

I was too shocked to move, but I knew I was staring at the skeletal remains of Mattie Dembrook . . . and I was also staring at a thick, priceless hardcover book still clutched in one of her bony hands.

EPILOGUE

My Own Words

It took the county historians four days to verify the find. One of the biggest stories ever to hit the northern regions of upstate New York, it drew reporters from all over the United States and several from Great Britain. The residents of Whispering Oaks were none too pleased to see their quiet streets turned into a media circus. But they were glad to finally lay Mattie Dembrook to rest and thrilled to have discovered a literary treasure in their own backyard.

The volume of Shakespeare's collected works was, in fact, real, a rare first edition published in 1623. It was the Whitfield family heirloom that Eamon had given to

Mattie. It had suffered minimal damage over the course of the past three centuries, and though most of its pages were yellowed and slightly scarred, it was entirely legible. Book conservators from the famed Morgan Library & Museum in Manhattan tended to the book lovingly, wearing masks and thick latex gloves and setting up shop for themselves in a technologically equipped van parked just outside the Curious Cup.

And as for the Curious Cup . . . well . . . it remains open for business. Following the discovery, county officials named the site a historic landmark, thereby blocking Frank Canker's plans to build on the property. Aunt Fin had to move all her merchandise out of the back room to make way for the excavation of the cellar, but it's been well worth the inconvenience. On any given day, people visit the shop from as far away as Niagara Falls and Montreal; they're allowed brief glimpses of the centuries-old cellar, and more often than not, they drop a couple of bucks for coffee and muffins while they discuss history and haunted America. The supernatural twist in the tale didn't escape Aunt Fin in the slightest: twice a week, she holds "spirit communication sessions" in the shop. In keeping with the book theme, she expends her psychic energy only in contacting literary luminaries. To date, she says she has hosted Nathaniel Hawthorne, Charlotte Brontë, Henry James, and Walt Whitman. She hopes to snag Jane Austen next. If you're in the area, please stop in; you never know which famous writer might pop out of the ether.

Upon full verification, the Shakespearean volume was

returned to the Whitfield family—or, more specifically, to Eamon Roger Whitfield IV, the clan's current patriarch and the great-great-great-nephew of the first Eamon Whitfield, who had died in the woods. In an astonishing gesture of charity, Mr. Whitfield "purchased" the book from the town of Whispering Oaks to the tune of several million dollars. The money is going toward erecting a cultural arts center on Main Street that will be used by all the towns in the county.

On a sunny morning in early September, Mattie Dembrook was given a proper burial. Everyone gathered at the town hall and made the long walk through the woods to the shores of Lake Redson. There, on a grassy knoll surrounded by lilies, she was buried. The spot is marked with a headstone, and the inscription on it is a quote from *Twelfth Night*:

> JOURNEYS END IN LOVERS MEETING,
> EVERY WISE MAN'S SON DOTH KNOW.

Even now, no one really knows the full story of Mattie Dembrook's life and death. An examination of her remains revealed that she likely died of natural causes. But those of us who have experience with the legend know that she died of a broken heart.

Jacob did end up researching the legend, and he uncovered a most interesting fact. Back in the 1800s, a small paved footpath ran from the Deer Heart Hotel on Lake Redson straight to what is now Star River Road, the current location of the Curious Cup. The path is visible on old maps of the area; interestingly enough, however, it was completely abandoned in 1904 and lost to the woods—to trees, grass, bushes, and more than a century of green growth. It's impossible even to trace the path today.

Which makes me think a lot about the night Jacob and I got lost in the woods and stumbled through the darkness only to find ourselves at the back of the Curious Cup. We'd been led there . . . somehow. Maybe it was Mattie. Maybe it was Eamon. Maybe it was the two of them—long-lost lovers yearning to be reunited on the other side.

According to the historians and excavators, Mattie fled the Deer Heart Hotel shortly after being told of Eamon's death. She took the footpath through the woods, perhaps thinking she could save him. But on the morning of August 26, the weather was still dangerous. A second mammoth storm—recorded in only a handful of newspapers—rose over the mountains, probably forcing Mattie to take refuge in the structure that is now the Curious Cup. Seeing the green sky, hearing the lashing winds, Mattie probably broke into the cellar and waited there. But when the storm got bigger, she likely found herself trapped in a watery grave. Maybe she tripped and fell. Maybe she panicked and suffered some sort of attack. But the historians and the excavators believe that the cellar had been Mattie's resting place for more than a century. When the floors were sealed, her remains could have easily gone unnoticed, given the darkness and the small circumference of the space.

I guess you could say I've become something of an expert on Mattie Dembrook and Eamon Whitfield. A few local television stations wanted to interview me about everything—the scandal, the time I spent in Whispering

Oaks, my involvement in the discovery of the body and the book—but I decided to steer clear of the media for a while. People don't really recognize me anymore. If they do, it's with a confused look, as if they're still deciding what to make of me.

I never heard from anyone at Frasier High School again. In fact, my parents are the only reminders of my old life in Manhattan. Mom calls me once a day. Dad gets on the phone sometimes too. We don't talk about plagiarism, but we *do* talk about books. Lately, Mom has been asking me if I have any plans to try my hand at another novel, one that won't get me into any trouble. I haven't really answered that question yet, because I'm not sure where my writing will take me. The only positive sign is that both my editor and my literary agent replied to an e-mail I sent them.

Whispering Oaks made room for one more resident, and that's me. I'm now a junior at the local high school and president of the recently formed Literature Society. Jacob and Rabbit are its other two founding members. It boasts a membership of twenty-eight students, and we meet once a week to discuss our English assignments and critique each other's writing. It's been the best therapy for me.

Now when Jacob and I walk down by Lake Redson, it's simply to enjoy the scenery. The other teenagers in town have abandoned it as a hangout. There aren't any bonfires. Beer cans don't litter the grass anymore. It's a place for reflection and writing.

Or simply a place to curl up with a good book.

ACKNOWLEDGMENTS

My thanks to:

Michael Bourret and the amazing team at DGLM

Beverly Horowitz and the amazing team at Delacorte Press

and,

for exemplifying the meaning of true literary excellence,

Krista Marino, Editor Extraordinaire

A lover of books, words, and libraries, Jamie Michaels was born and raised in New York City and can often be spotted reading in Central Park, on the subway, or pretty much anywhere.